MW00426133

WAR OF WINGS

WAR OF WINGS

TANNER MCELROY

BROWN BOOKS
PUBLISHING GROUP

War of Wings

Brown Books Publishing Group
16250 Knoll Trail Drive, Suite 205
Dallas, Texas 75248
www.BrownBooks.com
(972) 381-0009

A New Era in Publishing™

ISBN 978-1-61254-154-9
LCCN 2014930385

Printed in the United States
10 9 8 7 6 5 4 3 2 1

For more information or to contact the author, please go to
www.WarOfWings.com

For my angel, Isabella

Never give up on fairy tales.

I love you.

I

abriel swung the hammer with more force than needed, and sparks flew on impact as the beam slammed into place on the joist. He hit it again for no apparent reason while around him rang out the rhythmic sounds of striking tools and cheerful singing. When construction of the community building for the Ludus Paradisus was finished, its glistening rooms and classical façade would be pristine, lovely, even spotless. Perfection. Just like everything else.

Gabriel glanced over his shoulder, and then he struck the beam again, knocking it the tiniest bit off its mark. One miniscule imperfection in this flawless structure. No one would possibly notice. He smiled, suddenly more engaged with the project, and found himself actually on the verge of whistling.

"You're a little off."

He turned and saw a brown-haired virtue angel watching with arms lightly crossed and head canted. A silver necklace with the word *Humilitas* gleamed on her pale throat. She looked more perfect than the building they were raising.

"I didn't think anyone would notice," Gabriel said.

She patted his arm, and were it not for the quirk at the corner of her mouth, she would have seemed completely sincere. "Don't worry. You'll get it in a couple hundred more years."

Gabriel watched her walk away, arms swinging loosely and a swivel to her hips like a church bell ringing. He dropped his massive hammer and the handle just missed Raphael's foot as he approached, his white over-seer's robe brushing the floor.

"Were you just talking to Arrayah?"

"I'm not sure." Gabriel shook his head and started walking in the other direction.

"Why was a virtue angel talking to you?"

"Good question."

Raphael picked up Gabriel's hammer and followed him behind the lines of whistling workers. They were perfectly content and ordered, none missing a beat, and always just ahead of schedule.

"The ceremony tomorrow has been moved up two hours. How is your team's production today?"

"They'll get it done. They always do," replied Gabriel.

He kept walking and snatched a brown satchel from a bronze table with tools all over it.

"Where are you going?"

"To have some fun," said Gabriel.

"What about your construction team?"

"They're all yours."

Out of the corner of his eye, Gabriel noticed Michael heading his way. Great. What had he done now?

"Gabriel," Michael said, waving a hand as he approached.

"I'll be back in a little bit."

Gabriel turned, leaped, and with three swift down-drafts of his wings was aloft and soaring over the construction site. He began to pass the training facility adjacent to it. No sooner had Michael flown up after him than Gabriel tucked in his wings and plummeted down to land with one knee landing in the soft earth of the practice field.

"Can you not sit still for five minutes?" Michael called out, landing gracefully beside him.

"Welcome to the practice field, Michael," Gabriel said. "It was pretty clear at the last games that you didn't know where it is."

"Why practice when I have no competition?"

Gabriel clutched at his chest and staggered back. Michael, stone-faced, reached down to brush a spot of dirt from his polished boot. Did the archangel never smile?

"I have to tell you something," Michael said.

"That you have the sense of humor of a wet phoenix?" Gabriel took two strides into the shadow created by the overhang of the training facility's closest wing. He came back with a bow and quiver in one hand and a bag of ripe fruit in the other.

"Something important," Michael said.

Gabriel stepped to a wood-and-metal structure at the edge of the field that had a scoop drawn back by ropes and pulleys. It was a small trebuchet, and he dropped two red fruits into the bowl-shaped end of its launching arm.

"Everything is always important," Gabriel said. "Which is another way of saying that nothing ever is." He kicked a lever, and the trebuchet catapulted the fruit so high into the air that even his powerful eyes nearly lost sight of it. He notched an arrow and drew the string on the twelve-foot bow to full tension, his fingertips just brushing his cheek. With a soft twang and a rush of air, the arrow launched into the sky. At the moment of its highest arc, it struck the first fruit with such force that it exploded into a red mist. His motions almost too fast to track, Gabriel drew and fired another arrow, and the second fruit—still a good forty yards off the ground— was obliterated into pulp as well.

"It has to be a mistake." Michael had that tone of voice he used when he seemed to have forgotten Gabriel was in the room. "There's no way you're ready for this."

Gabriel rounded, gripping his bow. "What did you say?"

"If my vision had been about shooting fruit and playing games," Michael said, turning away, "you'd be the one to tell."

"Wait." Gabriel grabbed Michael's arm, which gave about as much as the iron hammer had. "Just wait."

"Something's coming, Gabriel. I saw it." Michael shook him off. "And you had better figure out what's important to you."

Michael bolted off toward a towering mountain that jutted above the range surrounding it. Gabriel, squinting at the bright light pouring from its peak, felt a headache coming on. A massive city had been built just shy of the summit, a sprawling metropolis so big that he felt tired just looking at it. The wall that formed the city's foundation had twelve layers made up of jasper, sapphire, chalcedony, emerald, and he had forgotten what else, though he knew them by heart once. All rare and precious, of course. Michael doubtless knew them all. Even at this distance, Gabriel tracked Michael until he landed heavily near the city's gated entrance and soon disappeared from view.

So dramatic.

Gabriel pulled an orange from his target bag and started to pace. There was no getting around it. Michael would only act offended until Gabriel apologized and he would have to listen to whatever it was anyway. Best to get it over with. He tore after Michael on the Great Mountain.

As the ground dropped away, Gabriel cast his gaze forward again. He neared the mountain rapidly. From his elevation, he could soon see much of the inner city. The city itself was pure gold—its streets, walls, bridges—but the gold resembled transparent glass. It was a little brighter than he'd remembered. Twelve massive solid-white pearl gates surrounded the city, forming three walls. The gates were supported by pearl columns positioned directly next to each other, keeping hidden everything within the gates. All the pearl reflected light in so many vivid colors that it looked like an aurora. Taking in their splendor was almost a physical burden on Gabriel's eyes. He typically stayed on the outskirts and forgot the magnificence of the city. With a nod to the dominion guarding the gate, he rushed through and began scanning for Michael.

He soon caught a glimpse of Michael's broad back. It was clearly him; Gabriel recognized the same perfect posture he was accustomed to joking about. Who walked that way?

"Michael!"

Michael continued on, jumping over a body of crystal-clear water. It was the water of life. This gently flowing body of water wound through the soil as if the land had eagerly opened itself up for the water's pristine touch. Gabriel kicked a little dirt into it. Michael continued to ignore him. Although there was no sun, the water was never dark because it led straight up to the majestic throne that contained the source of the glorious light. The river ran from the throne's residence at the top of the mountain down to its lower slopes, from both sides on the northeast and southwest through the upper tiers and homes of the angels. The trees that grew on its banks bore twelve different fruits each, which had the most perfect shapes and the purest colors. Gabriel snagged a couple of oranges off the branches. The air smelled of fresh flowers and citrus.

"Michael, wait!" He still didn't stop. Gabriel launched an orange right between Michael's wings, where it struck and bounced back. Michael finally turned around with a sigh. Gabriel approached, peeling his other orange. The skin of the ten-inch fruit parted easily, in one piece.

Gabriel took a juice-filled bite and smiled at Michael as it dripped onto the Alexandrite stone around his neck and trickled into the golden words engraved in his armor. Each of the archangels wore one of these stones around his neck, but their armor inscriptions were unique. "Have you had one of these lately?"

"No, brother, I haven't."

Michael's face was much more serious than Gabriel expected. Something really was wrong. "What was all that about back there?"

Michael seemed to search for the right wording and, not finding it, looked away.

"Is this about the games? I know you're worried about me in the air-and-ground arms spar, but you'll make it up in the agility and concentration events."

"This isn't about the games. Do you ever listen? When are you going to get out of your own little world and join the rest of us in the realities of Heaven?"

Gabriel felt the juicy pulp slide down his forearm. "I'm not like you, Michael. We don't all know exactly what we are supposed to be."

"You are an archangel just like me, Gabriel!"

"I'm not just like you. I'm not perfect. Read your armor, Michael." Gabriel pointed at the words *Dux Bellorum* engraved in Michael's armored chest plate. "You are the war leader, not me. Did you ever think some of us are still trying to figure things out?"

"Well, we don't have the luxury of time anymore. The life and order of the angels are about to change."

Gabriel's juicy smile slowly faded. "What does that even mean? Am I going to become one of the seraphim?"

"I am not joking, Gabriel." Michael's brow furrowed in concern. "God has shown me an unspeakable event. I don't know how it will come to be, but the end result will be unfathomable."

Gabriel looked around the busy city. There seemed to be more angels walking around than he remembered, and there were so many more pristine structures. Stressful. "What end result?"

"I don't even have the words to describe it."

"I don't know what you're talking about, Michael."

"God told me that I will soon lead the angels in this time of change."

Gabriel took a deep breath. "So why are you telling me if you can't even describe what it is?"

"Because He also spoke of you."

Gabriel straightened up his posture like Michael's. His wings felt heavy. "He did? What did He say?"

"That you will play an even bigger role than I in this time of need."

"What?" Gabriel felt deflated. Surely Michael must have misheard.

"He said that you will protect over half of the angels of Heaven."

F rom high on a carved-stone stage glittering with brilliant encrusted diamonds, Lucifer stared out at the millions of angels who called Heaven home. He rested on a stone mezzanine with a short waterfall cascading down its middle to a moat that surrounded the entire stage. Here in the Hanging Gardens they were just east of the source of heavenly light, the throne of God. He could barely hear the waterfall over the roars of the crowd.

On the opposite side of the stage was Delia, the virtue angel of chastity. He smiled at her as he began to pick a riff repeatedly on the twenty-four-stringed handmade instrument he had fashioned specifically for this closing ceremony. She returned the gesture with longing in her eyes. Her teeth were so white. He was the games' featured performer, and the angels' cheers below vibrated the stage under his feet. He breathed in the admiration and felt even more alive than he had at the previous year's performance. He knew he needed to humble himself.

The band started up behind him. It featured two of the six-winged seraphim, another cherubim like Lucifer in golden armor, another virtue like Delia in a long green gown, and two thrones in decadent robes. The audience was like a pot of water before boiling. Lucifer let it build slowly for what seemed like hours, knowing full well how to cause a hallucinatory euphoria in the crowd. They swayed in unison to the beat in a trance-like state. No angel was immune.

Here we go, he thought. He threw his instrument around his back as he sat down to his signature pipe key, and the angels exploded in cheers and applause once again. After a few minutes of intense rhythms, he cooed his first melodic praises for God. The next six hours of performing were a blur.

When the band played their last note to a stunned audience, Lucifer stood and spread his triumphant wings to their full extent. They cast much of the glistening stage into shadow. The crowd snapped out of its collective trance, and smiles claimed their awe-inspired faces. Heaven shook from the roar that ensued, and a tingle went down his spine followed by a flush of heat. He felt truly alive. Yet a moment later the warmth turned chill, like a splash in a cold sea. The adoration he felt became hollow.

This praise was not for him.

Lucifer ripped his wings back in tight and turned toward the blinding light of the throne of God. "Praise Him for all His glory!" He reached his hands out with a wistful expression. "One of these years maybe He will join us down here as we sing His praises." He walked off the stage past Delia, who smiled as she waved to the crowd. The masses began to leave the Hanging Gardens in a common flow, heading toward the Great Mountain just as Lucifer was.

An escort of seraphim surrounded him as he flew over the gardens and up the twelve jeweled layers that made up the mountain's base. The millions of angels in their nine separate orders followed in structured fashion based on rank.

"What did you think, Terra?"

The stunning blonde seraphim next to him smiled from ear to ear. Her eyes were greener than the grass of the Provender.

"You were wonderful, Lucifer. I am so proud of you, and so is our Father, I am sure."

He had better be. God would finally promote Lucifer to His level after a performance like that, he was certain. Lucifer would have a throne next to Him now. His hair straightened and filled in, turning from light brown to ash blonde. His eyes deepened from an orange amber to a transparent blue and his skin softened its hue.

"I love it when you do that," said Thyaterra.

"When I do what?"

A gruff voice said, "Your face just changed again." It was Bretabian, a tall seraphim who followed awkwardly close behind Thyaterra.

"I wasn't speaking to you," Lucifer snapped. His hair curled slightly in back.

Bretabian uncovered two wings from his face, revealing a blinding light, while his other four continued flapping. "I apologize."

Lucifer could handle God's glory, unlike other angels. He was close enough to God to have become as accustomed to His light as the seraphim. He ignored Bretabian and faced Thyaterra. "Thank you, Terra. I can never feel it when I change, but I am very happy right now to be with you."

Lucifer and his escorts tucked their wings in and landed smoothly. With Lucifer in the lead, they walked past the dominion Barterus at the entrance to the heavenly city. Barterus tipped his ornate helmet, which covered part of his face, and bowed to Lucifer. Dominions were very serious creatures. They guarded each of the pearl gate entrances and were in charge of enforcing the laws of the angels. Their wing feathers were fuller and fluffier than those of other angels, and they were typically the smallest angels in stature. Lucifer towered at least ten feet over Barterus as he passed. However, dominions were some of Heaven's fiercest fighters and were the last of the orders to give ground in an argument.

Barterus gripped a large golden sword with a spherical ball of light on the pommel. "It's an honor to see you, highest of the cherubim. What a fine show." He opened the gate for Lucifer.

"Thank you, kind angel." The other dominion raced over to sing his praises as well.

Lucifer walked forward about a hundred yards and stepped onto a golden ramp that was transparent down to the bottom. It stretched up and over the many houses of the heavenly city. Beginning the journey up, Lucifer looked down through the ramp all the way to the center of the Great Mountain, where the twelve jeweled layers were exposed down to its heart. Beautiful yet hollow, he thought.

The ramp was long and there were three others just like it starting from the center gates of the four walls of the city. They were held up by golden bricks, which were supported by massive arches and pillars. Some of the heavenly housing was actually situated underneath the arches and between the pillars. This pattern continued up the entire mountain.

A comfortable silence overtook the group. Lucifer felt the euphoria gradually slip in and he knew the throne of God was getting closer. After their long ascension to the top of the ramp, the passage turned right over an ornate bridge with carvings of six-winged seraphim touching hands across it. Their hands made beams, and the entire masterpiece was made out of solid marble. The statues were ten times the size of Lucifer or any other angel. He always felt small beneath them.

The bridge itself was constructed of slabs of colorful marble that exuded a light glow. The end of the bridge opened to a courtyard with a seven-tiered fountain of pure water. Pure, pure. Everything was always pure. The base of the fountain was solid white pearl.

Surrounding the courtyard were hedges manicured into perfect cubes with multicolored flowers growing inside. Lucifer straightened a flower as he passed, twisting it into position. In one corner, the hedges formed an archway that led to a golden step, which was the beginning of a solid-gold staircase. The staircase glistened from an intense glow. It was long and led directly to the upper levels and eventually, God's throne. Two intense dominion angels guarded the entrance to the hierarchical levels, and as Lucifer and the seraphs passed by, they lowered their heads but did not speak.

Lucifer reached the first step and began to climb the stairs. The majority of the angels following them had made it to their homes on the lower level below. Each shiny, solid step brought him higher and closer to God, and with each step, a deeper feeling of euphoria took over.

"I love this feeling every time," said Thyaterra.

Lucifer, who was no stranger to that staircase or that feeling, replied, "Me too," and smiled at her.

"Remember Competia and Tameus?" interjected Bretabian.

"Young fools," Lucifer said.

Two young angels had once decided to fly within the walls of the city as they raced each other past the dominions and thrones to see God up close. Each wanted to be first. They flew as fast as they could up the stairs, but a sudden rush of euphoria made them lose control at the summit, and they crashed right into His throne and fell at His feet. Tameus was left staring straight up at Him while Competia quickly covered up and lay face down in reverent fear. It was too much, too quickly for Tameus, and she was blinded for nine solid months. The idiot. No other angel had tried it since.

"I think we've all been tempted to rush to the top," Terra said.

"I haven't," said Bretabian. "I know the proper path."

"We don't all lack your imagination, Bretabian." Lucifer fixed his gaze directly on the seraph. "But Competia and Tameus learned their lesson. Most angels do."

"That's the thing about free will—we can't always control others, even when we want to," he said.

"Smart angels learn quickly from their mistakes. They give respect where it is due."

"Smart angels know their place."

"What are you saying?"

"Oh nothing, cherub," said Bretabian.

"Bretabian!" said Thyaterra.

I am the highest angel in Heaven, Lucifer thought. He held himself back from further conflict. Silence fell upon the group. After about an hour of ascending the golden staircase, they arrived at the first platform, where the order of the thrones resided. The buildings were detailed and elaborate, down to the tiniest piece of cloth. The décor was decadent—purple and red velvet trimmed in solid gold. The floor of the platform was also yellow gold and covered with rugs of fine silk. On the left and right sides were houses, each cut out of the finest gold. Behind them were other structures used for worship.

Lucifer reached the second platform, where most of the cherubim resided. A great deal of housing existed on this level although not all of those angels stayed there permanently. The cherubim roamed much more freely than the thrones, and their homes were characterized by marble and stone rather than fine cloth and draperies. The buildings were taller, with pointed arches. Lucifer's home was the largest and trimmed with the finest of Heaven's jewels, but every time he went up there, he lamented the fact he did not have a throne. He should have one—this was clear to him—and it should be situated on the upper level next to God to signify his true role in Heaven.

"I will see you tomorrow, Terra. I look forward to it every morning." He hugged the six-winged beauty as the rest of the seraphim waited.

"I look forward to seeing you every morning too. You did wonderful today. You are so blessed by God, and I thank Him every day for it," she said.

It's not all Him, he thought. "Thank you."

"Goodbye, Lucifer," said Bretabian briskly. He stood at a distance, obviously waiting for Thyaterra.

"Bretabian." Lucifer nodded, still looking at Thyaterra. He watched her shimmering silver dress float as elegantly as she did. She had the kindest eyes. Their hands separated, and she turned away. The moment was over.

Lucifer pushed open the sixty-foot door to his extravagant chamber. Inside, ancient weapons were mounted on the walls like trophies. Through another sixty-foot archway, the next room held countless instruments in every shade of gold, silver, and bronze. They were displayed so thickly that the walls couldn't be seen at all. Two elegant crystal tables were covered in the finest fruits of Heaven. One had light-colored fruit and the other strictly dark. Many of the light fruits had been eaten while the dark hadn't been touched. Lucifer passed through a set of stained-glass doors that opened to a courtyard of perfectly manicured grass with a fountain directly in the middle. It was the only thing out there.

He squeezed the lip of the stone edge with both hands. Closing his eyes, Lucifer drew a heavy, deep breath. God had to promote him this time. He must. What else could he do to earn it? Deep in the pit of his stomach he knew nothing would change. It never did.

When Lucifer opened his eyes to catch a glimpse of his reflection in the water, he let out a sigh of relief and admired his new features. Most angels were blissful in their ignorance. How could anyone understand what he went through? No angel possibly could.

"I hope you can, Father."

III

S orry, Michael. Protect over half the angels of Heaven? No can do." Gabriel's hand closed around a low-hanging branch. "We can't all be perfect."

"I'm not perfect, and you're not listening to me." Michael drew himself to his full height, wings half unfurling, but it only provoked Gabriel further.

"Of course, you're perfect." His hand tightened on the smooth bark and the wood creaked, straining, before it split halfway through. "Like everything here. Everything except me." He jerked on the branch and it broke off jaggedly, fruit shaking loose and raining down around Michael.

"Stop that."

"Or what?" Gabriel reached for another branch and twisted it, the wood protesting and then shearing away as oranges shuddered loose. "It doesn't matter—nothing

21

changes. The tree will be fine. Nothing ever changes, Michael."

"You've got responsibilities. You think you can just walk away from them?"

"Yes."

Michael stooped, gathering fruits so they would not go to waste. "You were given the Ludus Paradisus community building project."

"Only because you were busy with the performance stage for the entire games in the Hanging Gardens." Gabriel focused on the branch as it began to heal itself.

"Which was obviously the right call, since you're ripping up fruit trees instead of overseeing your team."

Gabriel drove his boot through the pile of fruit Michael had stacked. He watched with satisfaction as an orange flew clear over the tree line. "Maybe you can use your great reputation to make that a new sport in the games—fruit kicking. You can even stack them for me, brother."

"You know, I've done my part," Michael said, standing. "I can't control what you do. But keep this to yourself, at least, and simply try to be prepared for whatever's coming. I saw unimaginable things in my vision, and you are supposed to play a major role, whether you like it or not."

"What is it you saw that is such a big deal?"

"I saw angels burning." Michael turned his back to Gabriel and unfolded his massive wings. The light was almost dazzling as it shone off his pure-white feathers and polished armor. "I must go and pray with God for more guidance."

Gabriel opened his mouth to say something before Michael left, but nothing would come. He felt the rush of wind on his face from flapping wings, and soon he was alone again. The ground around him was littered with his favorite fruit, but he had lost his appetite.

Gabriel grabbed a grapefruit and a lemon and placed them gently on Michael's pile. He turned toward the gated entrance of the inner city and walked out. He jogged toward a cliff edge and immediately cast his wings open, diving head first from the Great Mountain toward the construction site of the new community building. He soared over the Field of Tranquility with its color-changing wheat, a pale yellow now, and landed next to the impressive structure of the new building.

"Wow, incredible work," he said to the team of angels he had been leading.

From around the corner, a soft, familiar voice answered Gabriel. "Thank you. They have been working hard."

Gabriel stumbled. "Arrayah?"

She stepped into view, her brow furrowed. "Yes. I'm sorry, I never got your name."

Raphael turned the corner from the other side of the building, and Gabriel caught his eyes. "Ah, Gabriel. We are fine now. You can head back to your fun."

"Oh, you are Gabriel?" Arrayah said.

"Yes." He turned in Raphael's direction. "I am sorry I left my duties. I am here to help finish this now."

Raphael hurried over to stand between the two of them. "I apologize, Arrayah, he seems to have made his way back. Honestly, Gabriel, we have become much more efficient since you left."

"What do you mean?"

"Arrayah stepped in to show us a few things, and we are now half a day ahead of schedule."

Gabriel looked over at Arrayah in astonishment. Her soft skin and silky smooth hands were not those of a worker.

A nearby angel turned around and held up a sheet of marble. "She taught us a new hammering method. It's actually easier, yet more powerful."

Gabriel scowled at the young angel, who quickly turned back to his work. "That's wonderful."

"I didn't mean to impose, Gabriel. I just saw they could use some help when I came back, and Raphael agreed."

"It was no imposition at all. You actually saved the day, Arrayah." Raphael threw his arm around Gabriel's shoulders. "Gabriel isn't interested in construction, anyway—he's more of a combat angel. Great in the games."

Raphael's mouth drew close to Gabriel's ear. "Gabriel, we asked Arrayah to take your place in the unveiling tomorrow since you weren't here. I hope you don't mind. Uriel and I think having a virtue such as Arrayah involved in the grunt work will inspire the angels and add excitement around the project. What do you think?"

He thought of Michael's vision. He was getting demoted in construction, but he was supposed to save over half the angels? "I think that's fine. I'm sure many angels will be inspired." Gabriel pulled up to hide his embarrassment. "You will do great, Arrayah." Her intoxicating scent made it even harder to breathe. "I actually must be going now."

"Wait, Gabriel," she said, but he pretended not to hear her and flew away.

Gabriel headed directly to the orange groves. When he arrived, he sank down with his back against his favorite tree. He knew the perfect angle that positioned the bark directly between his wings, but today when he rubbed up against it for a familiar scratch, he found he could not relax. His face hardened as his frustration grew.

Why did nothing turn out right? What was he here for? Everyone else seemed to know their purpose. He peeled and bit into a succulent orange although he hardly tasted the sweetness he usually tasted. He went over again in his head everything Michael had told him and chuckled bitterly to himself.

How could an archangel play a more important role than the members of the seraphim or cherubim or any of the hierarchs for that matter? He started to imagine what it would be like to be as important as a cherub. With this thought, his shoulders relaxed. He imagined how it would feel to be the highest cherub of all, like the one he admired so much, the Son of the Morning. Everyone looked up to God's highest angel. He felt juicy pulp trickling down his forearm. He began to wipe it off, but he was interrupted by an ear-piercing voice.

"Holy, holy, holy, is the Lord!"

Gabriel jumped up, dropping his orange, and spun around as he looked for the origin of that booming yet feminine voice. It cried out again, "Holy, holy, holy, is the Lord!" He flew up, looking in all directions and across the top of the trees, but he saw nothing. The voice was actually quite beautiful, and when it repeated itself again, it seemed to be a song. When his sheer surprise wore off, Gabriel realized why he didn't see anyone. It wasn't because she was too far away. It was because the voice was coming from inside his head. He realized that the voice wasn't singing because there was no rhythm or beat. It was weeping. The beauty of her voice made him misinterpret her words as a song.

As he kept flying across the tree tops, his ears vibrating with her words, he shouted, "I know the Lord is holy! Please get out of my head. Where are you?"

"All of Heaven is full of His glory!"

"Who are you?" He flew back down to the ground and began to search through the orange grove, moving branches and looking around trees.

The powerful voice repeated, "All of Heaven is full of His glory!"

"I get it. God is great. Come talk to me like normal angels do."

"Many will soon forget what I've just said to you now," cried the voice.

"Well, I won't forget since I'll probably never be able to hear again."

"You must hear God inside you. Let only Him and Michael guide your way."

Gabriel stopped walking. "Who are you and how do you know Michael?"

"I am of the seraphim." With that, the vibrations went away and Gabriel's ears were at rest.

"Wait! What is your name?" He waited for a response, but nothing came. "Are you there?" He cupped his large hands around his ears and temples and closed his eyes. But there was no answer. Gabriel slumped down into his previous spot against his favored tree. It now provided even less comfort than before. He reached for another orange on the ground without thought and bit into it, but he quickly realized it wasn't peeled and spit out the coarse rind.

Although Gabriel knew the angel he heard had claimed to be a seraph, it was not easy to believe one had spoken to him. He had always thought they did nothing but sing praises to God. Unlike most angels, they had six wings, one pair of which they used to fly, another to cover their feet, and the last to cover their eyes. They covered their feet out of respect for God, but they covered their eyes only when they spoke to other angels. This was rare because they were the guardians of the throne and were almost always next to God.

In fact, they were so close to Him all the time that His glory shone through their faces like a light. They covered their faces for the benefit of others because it would be too much for other angels to bear all at once. For any angel to adapt to the glory of God's light without their eyes covered took thousands of years next to Him while slowly covering less and less of their eyes. Some angels didn't know why seraphim placed their wings over their eyes, so although it was an angel courtesy, it also led to their mystique among the lower classes.

A seraph had never spoken to Gabriel before and certainly not inside his head. He had never even seen one up close. But now that one had spoken directly to him, Michael's story didn't seem so ludicrous anymore. On top of this, Gabriel knew what the word "seraphim" meant.

IV

Lucifer stared down from the top of the Rolling Hills of Peace just west of the Great Mountain at the sixty-six angels constructing his throne. They were carving ornate designs out of gold, chipping away pieces of the legs and armrests, shaping cushions from a gelatinous material, and sewing intricate details into various pieces of the throne's cloth. The cushion of the seat was made with red velvet and had white trim. It looked old and predictably like something God would have, not something he would have chosen. Yet he felt it was nothing compared to God's. Not even on the same level. The angels were wasting their time.

Saraquel caught his eyes and immediately labored up the hill in his direction. Lucifer noticed that Saraquel's stringy, dark hair was long now. It flopped from side to side as he walked, and Lucifer remembered what that felt like; his own hair had been long until recently. Saraquel's forehead wrinkled as he opened his eyes wide for a welcome greeting. He must want something. Lucifer glanced over the creature so different from him. He looked frail and uneven because his arms were unusually long for his body, yet his hands and feet were small. His skin wasn't pristine like most angels. It was dry and scaly.

He approached Lucifer, head lowered, and slowly raised it after Lucifer acknowledged him. "Your throne is turning out to be quite magnificent, great Lucifer."

"I am looking forward to commenting on the finished product, Saraquel."

"We will work on it until we have pleased you."

"Will this be worthy of sitting next to God's throne on the highest tier of Heaven?"

Saraquel's expression made it apparent the answer was no. "We will do everything we can."

Lucifer stared into the distance. "Your hair. It has changed."

"I grew it long to match yours from the ceremony." All angels could will their hair to grow, but most kept it short for convenience.

Lucifer felt it looked nothing like his. He read the words engraved on Saraquel's chest: *Ab uno disce omnes.* From one, learn all. What could he possibly learn from this sad angel? "The long hair suits you well."

"Oh thank you, Lucifer!"

"I will be back soon. I expect you will have the throne ready upon my return."

"Yes, sir. Will you have time to speak to me about some of my questions when you come back?" Saraquel's eyes were hopeful.

"I will do my best to make time."

Saraquel smiled ear to ear. "Before you go, please tell me your thoughts of the news."

Lucifer slowed the opening of his wings. "What news?"

"The news of God's equal. You haven't heard? I just know it will be you."

"No, I haven't heard. Tell me."

"God is declaring a Son. I figured you will be promoted and that is why we are constructing this throne for you. All of the angels have been talking about this."

His promotion. Finally. He could barely contain himself. "I will be back, Saraquel. Thank you for the news!" Stretching his massive wings, Lucifer flew straight down off the mountain. He propelled himself south, soaring over the glorious fields on his way to the rocky cliffs at the Marble Falls.

As he flew across the Field of Tranquility, it turned a magnificent shimmering yellow. He stared at the brightness of the field with joy. He'd never seen that color in this field before. He halted abruptly at the very edge of the Marble Falls and stood on the tips of his toes for a moment. A cloud of dust traveled in front of him over the edge and climbed up around his sixty-six-foot wingspan as he looked down. He took in the majestic beauty and great depth of the roaring river below, took a deep breath of the cool, perfect air, and leaped off headfirst. He plummeted toward the water, gliding past the four waterfalls. There were four tiers that fell over seventy miles on each level, making it almost three hundred miles from top to bottom. Marble made up the rock faces, with each level lighter than the next. It started with deep shades of brown, black, and gray, and ended with light variations barely above white. As he entered the river, his speed parted the water so easily there was hardly a splash.

He quickly covered thousands of miles through the depths of the sea. On the other side, he emerged to view the never-ending black of the cosmos. The infinity of its area was inconceivable. This place was very familiar to Lucifer. He'd spent countless days there already.

Lucifer let out the most jubilant yell of his life. At last, it was his moment. He would finally be able to take what was rightfully his, the highest seat in all of Heaven. He would soon know all the secrets God kept from him. The reasoning for the cosmos itself troubled Lucifer. He had many questions about creation, but this one weighed heavily on his mind. Where did the cosmos come from? Why was it there? Where did it truly start and where did it end? Why didn't God tell the angels about it? Lucifer always went to the cosmos to challenge his own understanding. The more he was in the midst of something he could not explain, the more he burned to know about it and everything else that didn't have an immediate answer. It helped him prepare himself to approach God for the answers he didn't have. Truthfully he hated having to ask God, but he pretended to enjoy the open discussions and to be gracious of God's willingness to answer every single question. Now he wouldn't have to. He would be God's equal. He would know everything.

After a few hours of thought and flight through the infinite space, he noticed something very tiny but light in the far distance. His powerful senses allowed him to perceive it, but before he could get to it, there was a tremendous explosion. It was not like some of the heavenly displays of fire put on by the thrones in celebration and worship of God. No, this was an explosion within itself. It seemed impossible, but it shook the very emptiness of its surroundings. Lucifer had never seen anything like it.

He stared, frozen. The massive explosion seemed so far away. If he hadn't seen it with his own two eyes, he would have never believed it. In mere seconds, the sound of the thunderous blast assaulted his ears and thrust him backward with an unreal force. He was shocked by what was happening and awestruck at the newly formed objects flying around. One of them smashed into him hard enough to be broken by his body like butter parted by a hot knife. The mass broke off into many pieces, but Lucifer was injured. Though his shoulders took the main brunt of the blow, his left side was extremely bruised. Still, he would heal quickly. Not even this could spoil the news of his promotion.

Lucifer quickly realized he was in harm's way. He rushed back along the pathway he had come, through the water, up the waterfalls, and over to the Great Forest of Harmony, just south of the falls, where he crashed to the ground. He was confused, amazed, and completely exhilarated. He stopped under a large apple tree to try to figure out what had happened. He went over the event in his head and attempted to make sense out of it with logic and mathematics.

He had a firm grasp on how energy and matter worked together, so he tried hard to figure out a way they could have related to each other in order to cause such a tremendous explosion. He started to weigh all possible explanations without factoring in any divine intervention. He was sure he was the only angel who ever considered the nature of things first. He picked a large golden apple from the tree above him and bit into its juicy flesh. Could God have caused this explosion?

He sat under the tree for hours trying to figure it out, but he could not. It frustrated him, and he couldn't let it go. He got up and paced back and forth. He would figure it out no matter what. He was determined not to ask God for this answer.

Lucifer headed just a bit north of the forest to a transparent bridge made of exorbitant golden boulders that floated on the air and stretched for miles across the river. Although the bridge was unnecessary for crossing because the angels could simply fly, it actually received much use because of the views it offered and its comfortability. He could nurse his injuries there. When he sat on the golden bridge in one place for more than ten seconds, it slowly loosened and formed to his backside and even his wings. He lay on it with his wings fully expanded, for it was rejuvenating his joints. He decided to stay there until he came up with the answer he was seeking about the cosmos or God came calling to announce his promotion.

"I can't believe it. A Son is coming soon!"

Lucifer opened his eyes to see three angels huddled together on a boulder a hundred yards away.

"He will be as glorious as our Father."

"I wonder what he will look like. I'm sure he will look like the great Lucifer."

Lucifer smiled, closed his eyes, and sank into his boulder to stay hidden. Of course, he would look like Lucifer. He was the one being promoted.

"No, I heard he is even greater than Lucifer in every way. I heard he is like the Father Himself and we will be able to look upon Him! His name is Jesus."

Lucifer's eyes shot open. He struggled to get up from his boulder, but the sudden movement didn't allow the gold to expand. He was trapped. The motion sent a sharp pain through his entire left side, and in an instant his injuries were back.

"When will we be able to gaze upon him?"

"It was announced by the cherubim that the Son of God will be arriving in Heaven soon!"

Lucifer gasped, and the perfect air turned thick and traveled through his chest like a viscous liquid. His head tingled and his vision blurred as a sudden blackness consumed him. How could God have betrayed him? Was his performance at the Ludus Paradisus anything less than worthy of a promotion? What other angel could have done everything he had? How could He do this to Lucifer? How could He look past him? This couldn't be true.

He would ask God himself. He deserved answers now. As Lucifer started back up to the Great Mountain, he began mentally preparing himself to go before God without revealing his thoughts or emotions. This would be quite a feat, but he had done it before. At least he thought he had. Maybe he wasn't actually able to hide things from God and God just let him think he could. He shook off that thought and started refocusing. As he was approaching the gates that surrounded the heavenly city, he could feel his chest about to burst through the tiny chains of his armor.

"Open, Barterus."

The dominion quickly opened the gate to the inner city. He bowed as Lucifer approached, and his helmet fell to the ground and stuck in the soft dirt. Lucifer did not alter course and stepped on it, driving the helmet deeper into the ground. It felt good. He stopped, picked it up, and handed it to the dominion. "My apologies."

"No, Lucifer, I am sorry it fell in your way. Is everything all right, sir?"

"No, Barterus, it is not."

Lucifer walked to the transparent golden ramp but did not look down. He was wrought with frustration. He crossed the seraphim bridge and it didn't seem quite as beautiful anymore. Lucifer didn't feel small beneath the statues this time. In fact, he had never felt bigger than in this moment. He needed to feel big since God was trying to make him small.

He crossed the courtyard. At the fountain, he washed his hands and splashed water over his hot face. He took a deep breath as he realized what was about to happen. He could do this, he assured himself. He had to. Lucifer walked up to the first step of the staircase and knew there was no turning back. He would never turn back.

He had always looked forward to the awesome feeling of euphoria on the golden staircase to the upper tiers, but this time it was wholly absent. When he noticed the difference, he stopped. He was a little disappointed but knew this was a confirmation that he was onto something. He was on a mission, so he shook it off and began his walk again toward his supposed creator. God had better not have a Son.

V

There was no darkness in Heaven because of the very light Lucifer was climbing the stairs to confront. A day consisted of a twenty-four hour period, based on God's unique time. Lately Lucifer had been noticing that time seemed to matter to him. Now there was none left. He was inherently talented at keeping track of time, which was considered insignificant by every other angel with the exception of the record-keepers of the powers. Maybe there was a reason Lucifer was good at it. He wasn't sure.

He looked down over the heavenly city, taking note of how the angels were always so productive. They simply enjoyed the feeling of accomplishment that came with hard work. They just wanted to please God. Consistency and routine had always been a part of everyday existence. But for what? He felt emptied out. He was a rind with no fruit.

Lucifer arrived at the thrones' platform. The deca-dence the velvet bestowed seemed absurd this time. What a ridiculous group of angels. He didn't have time for them and raced upward, ignoring their bows, greetings, and questions. He had time for no one but God.

He reached the platform of his fellow cherubim. Even his own level seemed dim. The pearl wasn't as white, the homes appeared dismal, and even his friends seemed less important. Everything he had worked for was slipping away, and there was nothing he could do about it except hear his fate directly from the One he had led the angels to worship all of this time.

Many different activities were taking place on this level. Some angels were debating in groups, some were designing elaborate construction plans, while others were sitting in pure silence with expressions of bliss. Lucifer chuckled to himself in disgust. All of the angels Lucifer passed stopped what they were doing and acknowledged him as their leader.

He caught a glimpse of Thyaterra and stopped dead in his tracks. This wasn't her level, and for some reason she had her eyes uncovered again. She was accompanied by none other than Bretabian. Even with this awful timing, he couldn't resist her. Her face alone made him feel that perhaps everything wasn't lost. She approached him with an eager look on her face.

"Thyaterra." He gave a small smile, taking her in. He glanced to her left and the smile was gone. "Bretabian." The angel responded with a bow, and Lucifer cringed inwardly.

"It's been a while, Lucifer. Haven't seen you since the performance at the Ludus Paradisus," said Thyaterra.

"I've had much going on, Terra," Lucifer answered, turning his attention back to her.

"I've missed you."

"I see Bretabian has taken care of you in my absence." Lucifer fixed him with an unwavering look.

Bretabian looked uneasy. "She has missed you, Lucifer. It's good to see you," he said.

"That is appreciated, Bretabian." He was not interested in the least in what Bretabian had to say. "Now, if you'll excuse me." Lucifer placed a hand on the small of Thyaterra's back, just beneath her wings, and guided her to a small alcove. She put up little resistance though when she turned to face him, her eyes were wide, almost luminous.

"I've missed you too," he said, "but I have been taking care of something important."

"I'm worried about you, Lucifer. Something feels wrong. Are you upset about the announcement of God's Son?" His insides seemed to cave in on themselves. "So it's true?" He needed to hear it from Him. Thyaterra looked at him with those soft eyes. He couldn't take it.

"It is what it is. You don't seem too worried. I'm sure between God and Bretabian you keep occupied."

"I don't understand why you say that."

"I'm different now. I think differently. I see things that others cannot, and I don't like much of what I see."

"What you are trying to say?"

"Maybe Bretabian can explain it to you since he is so accommodating in my absence."

"Stop it, Lucifer. You are being unkind." Two of her wings folded protectively around herself, their feathers brushing against her chin as if ready to cover her face.

"Well, you know I love your opinion on matters, but I'm not fond of Bretabian following you around." He buried the real hurt from what had just shattered his world.

She took a step away, her wingtips now over her mouth while the glow from her skin shone through them. "He is a kind angel, but you know he does not mean what you mean to me. I have always been there for you."

It was true, and he found himself wanting to step close to her, to draw her wings from her face. Then his reason for the trip overwhelmed his thoughts again, and he could not keep the edge from his voice. "You have, Terra. I have to speak with His Highness, but I also want to take you somewhere and discuss things soon."

"Are you all right?"

"Yes. I have much to tell you if I can trust you to keep it from others like Bretabian."

"Of course, you can trust me. I will help you, what-ever you need."

"You will be proud of me, Terra. As proud of me as you are of God. I'll see you soon."

He turned to leave before she could respond, hurry-ing off the platform and up to the third tier, almost too quickly—the hollow rush of feeling that had once been euphoric now made him ill and light-headed. He had to reach the throne. He had to see the so-called Maker.

The seraphim all had their eyes covered, but still they faced Lucifer as he approached as if they knew he was coming. Did they know what was about to happen? Lucifer looked around at the platform made of the finest jewels in existence. He deserved to be on this level. Every structure was covered with millions of different types of gemstones all glowing brilliantly, and they taunted him. It made him realize how unimportant he really was to God.

He had already wasted too much time. He ascended the final staircase to the throne and approached God's blinding light. He had made it. It was time for his moment of truth. One of the four seraphs who guarded the throne slowly walked up to him with two of her wings covering her eyes, two covering her feet, and the other two standing tall and outstretched behind her back.

"The Lord our God is holy and worthy to be praised," said the seraph passionately.

"He is," said Lucifer, struggling to get it out.

"He is waiting for you." Her voice was like a song.

Walking up to God sitting on His throne, Lucifer covered part of his face and got on one knee. He noticed the light was a little less blinding this time. The material and structures of the entire platform were still too hard to make out from His powerful glow, but he saw colors he had never seen before. Lucifer's throne should reside up here as well.

All he could feel was the presence of the massive throne, and he wanted one. It occurred to him that the angels couldn't even see God yet still praised Him. Lucifer engaged directly with the angels, but they still adored and worshipped Him. Lucifer bowed his head and kept his eyes to the ground.

"I have come to ask for your guidance and wisdom, Father. I have also come to ask you a question," said Lucifer.

"You have come upon great knowledge, O highest of cherubim," God said in a chillingly powerful voice.

Lucifer froze a moment before speaking. He tried to hide his mind and heart, but he felt he was not as successful as he had hoped. God knew why he was here, he was certain. "Yes, and I have become confused searching for the answer that I seek. But before that I must ask you something."

"What is your question, my son?"

"You call me your son? Why is that?"

"Every angel is a son of God."

"I hear you mean to have a real Son, a Son that you recognize to be on your level. Have I not done everything I can to praise you?"

"You have, Lucifer. Be careful of your own mind and where it takes you."

"Is it true? Tell me!"

"Yes."

Lucifer's body instantly ached all over. His elbows hit the cold, jeweled ground below him. He reached deep inside and mustered a roar. "How could you do this to me?"

"This is not about you, Lucifer."

"Everything is about me!" Lucifer screamed without thinking. God paused just long enough for a chill to travel down Lucifer's spine.

"Listen to yourself and truly hear."

"I have given you everything, God. Angels look up to me as their leader, and you presume to demote me by announcing a Son above me?"

"You are not being demoted, Lucifer."

"I see it no differently! Are you surprised by this? Shouldn't you know what I came here for as our almighty God?"

"For we walk by faith, not by sight."

"So do you know what I have seen?"

"I know much of your time is spent outside the realms of Heaven."

He felt nervous and childlike in God's presence, and he couldn't stand it. It was like God knew everything he had seen and knew exactly what he came to ask and was actually toying with him. "I am often more comfortable there, alone."

"What is it that you seek?"

"You think I am unworthy of your level. Well, I may think differently. Through the knowledge I have gained, I know that it is impossible that one could be the beginning and the end. How can you claim to be something that is impossible for everything and everyone else?"

He was surprised that he got to his point so quickly. A pause of silence, which felt like eternal minutes to Lucifer, fell between the two of them, but he was calm and longed for an answer. He stayed still, head down, knee bent, waiting for God's answer. Maybe He didn't know.

"I warn you—be careful, Lucifer. It is so that your faith might not rest in the wisdom of philosophy and reason but in the power of your living God. I am the Alpha and the Omega, the beginning and the end. I have given you free will to make your own decisions, but that is all you need to know."

He jumped up and stared directly into God's light with clenched fists and venom pumping through him.

Everything that had been welling up exploded in an instant. "Any fool can have faith! That is not good enough!"

"Are you challenging my authority, Lucifer?" returned God with a voice like thunder.

"And if I am? I do not fear you!"

God's light intensified, and Lucifer squinted and fell back to a knee. His fists were still clenched as he continued. "Do you not want us to be wise, Father? How can we be wise without questioning and challenging you?"

"The fear of me, your God, is the beginning of wisdom."

"Answer me! Stop toying with me and give me what I want, or I will leave you this time!"

God did not answer him. Had he lost his fear of God? What was happening? Lucifer felt heat pumping through his body but shoved it back down into the ball he had been holding it in. He needed to gain composure as God was obviously in charge of the conversation, not him. This was not what he wanted. A few seconds that felt like days went by before he finally spoke again. "I apologize, Father. I don't know what came over me. I have had much going on lately. The announcement of your new Son startled me." *Disgusted me*, he thought. "I'm sorry. I didn't mean it."

He had much more to say and many more questions, but he knew God would not be pleased and that this was not the time. He would never get anything from God.

He felt the pain turning to anger and resentment, but he didn't want to give into it. Not now. He would wait until the time was right for the entire discussion, the entire confrontation, the entire war, so instead he made a huge decision right then and there.

He would no longer follow God. It broke his heart to think of the many years God loved him and he loved God, but reason was what mattered now. Not childish, ignorant, blind faith and love. God was not what He said He was, and it was time for Lucifer to expose this new truth. Faith was for the weak and ignorant. He was neither, and his faith was gone.

God never responded.

"I thank You." Lucifer did his best to disguise his true feelings. "There is nothing else that I need from You."

With that, he got up and started his descent away from God, walking quickly while resisting the urge to fly away at full speed. He was overwhelmed with anger and disappointment, yet these negative feelings birthed a strong sense of power unlike anything he had felt before. He felt as if he could single-handedly change the way things were in Heaven and gain the authority and respect he was seeking. It felt strange, but it also felt good. Great actually. He felt like his own god and had reason to justify it. He had not felt the usual euphoria on his walk to God's throne; this feeling had replaced it, and he only wanted to feel more of it. He yearned for more power, and he now knew how he would get it.

He hurried on, putting distance between himself and God. He had suddenly realized the real reason Heaven had warrior angels, guardian angels, and keepers of the laws. Although he tried feverishly to mask all of these new feelings, he knew God sensed them. He was nervous that God was directly behind him and felt he couldn't go fast enough. Maybe God even knew Lucifer's plans for what was to come. What would He do if He did? Lucifer kept hurrying away and was careful not to turn around and find out.

VI

G abriel parried, deflecting Azrael's thrusting blade mere inches from his throat. Azrael was brutal and cunning in their fights, holding nothing back. This time Gabriel noticed he was getting better. Gabriel had to focus. Azrael sidestepped before moving inside Gabriel's next swing to slice down across his chest. Again Gabriel barely jumped back in time.

"You're distracted," Azrael said. He gripped the onyx hilt of his sword, swinging it idly from one hand to another.

South of the Great Mountain stretched a massive field surrounded by the complexes used by the angels for sport, practice, and competition. The field of immaculate green grass stretched for hundreds of miles across the inner island, but it was marked off for many practice fields, like the one where they now fought. There was only one true field for the actual Ludus Paradisus; it was called the Provender but was often referred to as the lawn. Countless wooden structures such as catapults, trebuchets, benches, buildings, targets, and tall seating platforms surrounded the impressive field.

Gabriel sparred often, and Azrael was his opponent most days. Gabriel wasn't sure why Azrael came out to spar with him although Azrael's looks and fighting skill gave Gabriel an ego boost. Azrael's black hair and light skin always made Gabriel happy to be the scruffy, dark-skinned brute he was. Azrael was somewhat of a recluse, and he did not seem too interested in the games. Was he training for something? Gabriel was a force to be reckoned with in the lower classes every year, so he was learning from the best. Maybe he just wanted to get better. Azrael always studied Gabriel's every move with a strange intensity, but Gabriel always let it go. He could practice for eternity and never catch up. Today, though, Gabriel's thoughts were elsewhere, and both of them knew it.

"The ceremony for the new Ludus Paradisus community building is happening right now," Gabriel said. It had been on his mind all morning. He should be the one revealing it, not some virtue angel.

"I don't see how you can stand working with Raphael."

He sliced again, and Gabriel blocked without thought.

"I don't blame you for skipping the ceremony," Azrael continued. "Maybe a wall will fall on him while he leads the prayer."

"He's not the reason."

It was Arrayah. She was the one who had disrupted everything, shown him up in front of his team, and taken away his place of honor at the ceremony. If he could not even handle a construction assignment as Arrayah had made abundantly clear, how could he be trusted with leadership if some terrible event was coming? Why didn't Michael go ask her to save half the angels?

Azrael feinted to one side, his blade flashing, and leaped to the other as he flipped the sword around to stab Gabriel in the back. Gabriel was prepared for him, though, and he poured his frustration into the swing of his arm as he spun about to meet the attack. He locked blades with Azrael and used his sword's cross-guard to twist the other angel's weapon down and to the side. Releasing the hilt, he backhanded Azrael hard across the jaw. Gabriel grabbed him by the back of the neck and slammed his head into Azrael's just above the eyes. Azrael staggered a moment, his hand going up to his face, and collapsed onto the ground.

Gabriel, breathing hard, picked up their dropped swords and carried them over to the weapons rack.

"Where did that come from?" Azrael asked, still clutching his head.

"I have somewhere I need to be." Without a backward glance, Gabriel leaped up, unfurled his wings, and the practice field dropped away.

He flew over the Field of Tranquility directly toward the location of the new building. He had no idea what he would say. As he neared the crowd around the tarp-draped building, he had second thoughts. There were thousands of angels surrounding the front entrance, all waiting for the unveiling. The lowest class made up the majority, but a few prominent hierarchs were also in attendance. A temporary stage was built at the front to provide some elevation above the crowd. All of the work that had been put into this crystal structure was finally coming to a head, and Gabriel no longer had anything to do with it. Showing up like this would be embarrassing.

When he realized there would be no angels on the back side, he decided a closer look wouldn't hurt anyone. He flew in and casually walked up behind the impressive structure. He climbed up to the highest vantage point on the building, staying careful to keep hidden. He was quite nervous, but he couldn't help himself.

From where he crouched, he could see Raphael—upbeat and smiling as always, waving to the crowd as he ascended the steps and then gestured for quiet. He said a few words and then beckoned for Arrayah to join him on the makeshift stage. She stepped up, looking radiant in a simple white robe, her brown hair upswept and light glinting off of the dainty silver crown and diamond *Humilitas* necklace she wore. She gave a small, humble bow of her head to acknowledge the applause greeting her.

Gabriel didn't want to take his eyes off her, but he couldn't watch this. Looking away, he saw the top tier of the crystal framework specially designed for this building. The pure crystal had been cut, placed, and carefully angled so that it perfectly caught the radiant glow from God's throne—the light that spilled out all across Heaven—and reflected it back from the front of the community center in a dazzling display. It was his idea. A thick canvas tarp had been stretched across it until the big reveal, and in a few moments, Arrayah would pull on a cord and it would drop away, scattering brilliant, colored light across the gathered crowds.

He should be the one pulling the cord. He should be—

Gabriel leaned closer, squinting. From this vantage point, it was clear that the golden pins holding the topmost and heaviest bank of crystals were not driven fully in. One of them looked on the verge of sliding out. Gabriel had completed this section himself in earlier days—had he been so distracted even then? If the pin slid free, all the weight of this corner would be on the remaining pin, and the weight of the crystals might be enough to dislodge it or crack the thin, silver framework supporting each row.

"I thank you all," Arrayah was saying, "but the credit does not belong to me."

That's the truth, Gabriel thought. Although he couldn't deny that she looked better out there on the stage than he would have. She was lovely. She always seemed so at ease and polished with everything she did. She sashayed gracefully over to stand under the row of crystals.

Looking back to the protruding pin, he gauged the distance between himself and the tier. The scaffolding used during construction had been removed, and there was no room to unfurl his wings. He did not even have a hammer.

"It took a team of angels to complete this beautiful building," Arrayah said. She stepped closer to the lower end of the cord.

The tarp had been tightly secured to ensure it did not blow off prematurely. Arrayah would have to pull hard. Would one strong tug be enough to dislodge the pin? The rows of crystal were so heavy it had taken a dozen angels to lift and position each piece. Arrayah was standing directly beneath them. She would be crushed.

Gabriel drew a dagger from his belt, one solid piece of iron from blade to hilt, and leaned out across the gap. He stretched forward and used the pommel of the dagger to knock the pin further into place. It barely moved—he needed to strike it harder.

"And of course," she said. "all the praise and glory goes to our God." Her hand closed around the cord.

Gabriel reached out, straining, and slammed the iron pommel into the pin with all his strength. It drove in, but with too much force, splitting the crystal. Gabriel became overextended from his swing and lost his balance as a loud crack sounded when the silver framework ruptured. He clutched at the only thing available, the row of crystal, and the cracking sound repeated as the entire row broke free, each section knocking loose the next as it all collapsed.

"Arrayah!" he shouted. There was an explosion of light as the tarp dropped away. Crystals and silver struck his body as they fell, and an instant later the stage crashed into him. Everything went dark for a moment, and when he opened his eyes, he was lying in a heap of debris—the boards of the stage had broken beneath him and become half-tangled in the tarp and shattered shards of crystal lay everywhere. Their light was so dazzling he could hardly see.

As he rubbed his eyes, he made out Arrayah picking herself up from the floor. She had thrown herself to the side when it all fell. The sound from the crowd was a blend of gasping and gossiping. Gabriel saw Raphael storming up the steps, literally shaking with anger, his overseer's robe flapping behind him like a white flag in the wind.

This was not good.

"I can't believe you, Gabriel! Are you really this selfish?" Raphael said. Gabriel pushed shards of crystal off of him and attempted to pick himself up. He started to defend himself but drifted off, seeing Arrayah shaking her head in disappointment, and decided to go in a different direction. "I'm sorry, Arrayah."

"You did this because you were replaced," Raphael said. "You always make everything all about you. You were only replaced because you gave us no effort, and now you have screwed up everything for everyone! Why couldn't you just stay away?"

"It was an accident, Raphael."

"You accidentally brought the front of the building down at the moment we were about to reveal it? We couldn't even find you half the time to work on it, but your timing is impeccable when you want to make a statement."

"I thought the crystal might fall on Arrayah. I didn't mean to mess this up."

"Well, messing things up seems to be the one thing you are good at these days, Gabriel."

Gabriel could hear angry shouts from many in the crowd, and he saw the disappointment in Raphael's eyes, but it was the sadness on Arrayah's face that hurt the most.

"I'm sorry."

Gabriel left. Not a single angel tried to stop him.

VII

L ucifer needed to get to the cosmos to breathe. He was so angry he could feel it burning in his throat. He could feel its power, like nothing he had experienced before. He was careful to hide it from the seraphim and thrones when he passed them on his way down the steps, but he felt like everyone was looking at him. The golden stairs below him now looked stained. The shimmer of light exuding from each seraph made his stomach turn. He wanted to shove their heads under water until their light faded.

The three upper platforms seemed unending. Trying to ignore the bright colors around him, he hurried past each level and away from the light. The throne angels wore crowns. What a joke. He should shatter them. He longed to rip the velvet from their robes and strangle them with it.

On the outside, he stayed as smooth as ever. His emotions were like boiling water about to overflow, but he shoved them deeper. God's answer made no rational sense. Lucifer watched with his own eyes an explosion in the cosmos that caused the formation of newfound planets. God couldn't be whom He claimed to be; He was too busy with his ridiculous new Son to possibly know what had happened. Lucifer would not believe any longer. He refused to. He would become his own god.

Lucifer took a deep breath, filling his lungs to the full expansion of his broad chest. The other angels already praised him like a god. What was the difference? His angels had a right to know more than God told them. He would give them answers. Lucifer stopped walking down the steps, mentally daring God to put him in his place if He was all knowing. If He was the almighty Alpha and Omega, why did He let Lucifer leave? He walked to the final step of the golden staircase and turned around to look up at the light he was leaving behind.

God had no idea what he saw in the cosmos. Lucifer pictured the explosion in his mind's eye. He had seen the creation of a new world while God only cared about a Son. God wanted everyone to serve Him blindly like fools. Did God think he was a fool? Lucifer's thoughts came furiously. He paused for an answer he knew would not come. All alone on the final step, he finally exploded, "Why don't you stop me from leaving?"

He waited. Then he waited some more. He felt like the only angel in Heaven. His eyes became wet with tears. He raised his hands and lifted his eyebrows in defeat. Nothing. A shiver slowly crept over his body from the top of his head to the tip of both end feathers and back down his spine where it stopped.

Lucifer needed to get away from the blinding light that plagued every angel. He walked quickly through the heavenly city, but it felt like days. He needed the angels to understand his newfound truth in order to situate himself above God in the minds of the angels. I will expose Him for what He really is, Lucifer thought. He is a selfish liar, isn't He? How could He not be with the answers He gives? He needs us more than we need Him. He needs us to praise Him.

He knew it would be quite a challenge to turn the masses away from someone they loved more than life itself. But he felt compelled to do so, and he knew a few of the angels wouldn't be as difficult as others to win over once they heard his unanswerable questions. Lucifer knew many that couldn't think for themselves even if God demanded it of them. They were so pure and innocent, yet they had never been truly challenged. Lucifer had an idea. Many ideas, actually. They were revolutionary.

As Lucifer approached the pearl gates, Saraquel landed heavy and hard, panting like he had just finished the Four Corner Corridor race in the games. His disheveled hair dripped before he flung it back over his shoulder and wiped his chest plate.

"Lucifer! Excuse me, sir! May I ask where you have been? I've been looking everywhere for you, but you were nowhere to be found." Saraquel apparently searched for a better reason as he hesitated. "We wanted to ask your opinion on your new throne."

Lucifer kept walking, through the gates and past the silent dominion. Frustrated by the interruption and perturbed by the reminder of the horrible throne, Lucifer said, "I don't care about that." Instead of leaping off the cliff, he paused at the edge of the Great Mountain and stopped Saraquel with a stiff arm. "Why didn't you tell me God was announcing a Son?"

"I didn't know. I thought the promotion was for you."

Lucifer felt a cold flash, and the air had a stench to it.

"Well, it wasn't." He dropped his hand from Saraquel's armor. "It's fine."

Lucifer dove off the side and flew toward the Marble Falls. Saraquel stayed close behind, shouting as they flew. "I wanted to say I'm sorry! I also realized that you were displeased with the throne. We destroyed that one and started anew. It will be an even greater one now, Lucifer. You will soon sit next to God, I'm sure."

"No, I won't. And I am tired of waiting." Lucifer flew with all his might over the Field of Tranquility. It turned from canary yellow to oxblood red. He'd never seen red in the field before. Below him, he heard angels talking about it as they pointed up at him. When he reached the falls, he dropped down, his feet crushing into the ground.

Saraquel landed heavily beside him. "With every ending there is a new beginning. I'm sure this will all pass soon."

From Saraquel's annoying comment, Lucifer suddenly realized the question that would surely change Heaven forever. It hit him like a punch in the stomach. How could there be an end with no beginning, and how could there be a beginning with no end?

God couldn't be the Alpha and the Omega because that was fundamentally impossible. Someone or something must have created God. But who? When? God wasn't here before Lucifer, and even if He was, maybe He destroyed His creator. Something or someone must have created Him. He was not above Lucifer.

He turned to Saraquel, who had finally gone silent and waited for a response. Before Lucifer could speak, a familiar scent hit his nose. The air smelled fresh again. Intoxicating. Turning, he saw Thyaterra gliding toward him from across the falls. She wore a flowing white dress with hints of blue as light reflected from the angles her form made beneath it. The backdrop of greens from the Forest of Harmony made the image a masterpiece. She was a breath of life in the suffocating Heaven. As quickly as he was conscious of the beauty headed his way, he also realized how unlikely it was that she would be down there. What was she doing here?

"Saraquel, I need to speak with Thyaterra. You can find me later."

"I understand."

Saraquel walked away as Thyaterra approached.

"Thyaterra?"

"Hello, Lucifer. I wanted to see you." As she floated over to him, he noticed the concern in her eyes.

"I've been meaning to see you again also."

"What is happening?"

"Follow me."

Lucifer dove over the cliff, his wings propelling him faster as he shot down the Marble Falls. Thyaterra followed him to the lower fall. He glided down to a swath of thick green grass where fresh flowers grew near the spray of the falls. He picked a purple one for her, her favorite color.

"Do you know I love you, Thyaterra?"

"Yes. And I love you."

"You know my passion for God and all of His praises has been my eternal ambition, and I have never faltered."

"Yes."

"Things have changed, Terra." He yearned for her approval but could not keep the bitterness from his voice. "My passion for Him has faded."

"Lucifer, you are the highest of the cherubim. God loves you more than any angel and has blessed you with more than you even know."

"I have followed Him my whole existence and led worship time after time. Of course, He pretends to love me. What do we get from Him? He loves Himself more than anything and would have us all worship Him, blind to reason for eternity."

Thyaterra's mouth closed, and she took a step backward with wide eyes. Lucifer took a deep breath and stepped toward her.

"I have a new passion now. My passion is the truth," he said.

"God has never lied to any of us. We both love Him. What is this about, Lucifer?"

She seemed to stare right through him. He snagged the flower from her hand and started shredding it. He could barely control his hands to pull the tiny petals apart, so he threw it in frustration to the ground. Thyaterra quickly stepped back again but this time much farther.

"A Son! After all I have done." He slouched in weakness as he momentarily sought comfort in her eyes.

"I know you are hurt, but He loves you no less."

"I am not hurt. He will never hurt me." He pulled his shoulders together. "What do we worship Him for, Terra?"

"Lucifer, He would have us worship Him because He is worthy to be praised. He is the truth. I know you have been to the cosmos and there are things none of us can understand happening all around us, but do not lose your love for our God."

"How do you know about the cosmos?"

She didn't answer him.

"Tell me! How do you know about the cosmos, Terra?"

"Please calm down."

"Did God tell you I went there already?"

"Yes, but Bretabian also saw you come from the water."

"Bretabian? Why was he following me?"

"I don't know; I am just telling you what he told me."

Lucifer snarled. "Neither he nor God knows anything of what I have seen! I have more knowledge of the cosmos than God and the rest of the seraphim combined."

"You are brilliant, Lucifer. Do not let your gift lead you astray. Stay humble before God. Sometimes faith is all we need when reason sends us down a different path."

Lucifer stomped on a pink flower. A tiny bit of powder flew up from it and struck Lucifer in the face. It smelled terrible. "Where did God come from? How do you know He doesn't have all of us fooled?"

She looked down at the mangled flower and back up at Lucifer. It started regrowing. "God has always been and always will be."

As the flower grew perfectly back into its original form, Lucifer stepped on it again and this time left his foot there. He looked at Thyaterra as he twisted his foot into the ground. "I could tell you I am the same. I was here before you. Would you believe that I am a god also? Tell me why God has no answers for any of my questions as of late. I'll tell you why—He doesn't know."

"God knows everything. We both know that."

"No, only one of us thinks that now. I'll show you I am right. I want you to join me in finding the answers God hides from us." He lifted his foot and waited as the mangled flower once again grew to perfection.

"Lucifer, I can't join you in whatever you are doing."

Lucifer hesitated, watching the flower. When it was done reforming, he picked it and handed it to her. "Please."

She took the flower and a new one sprouted up in its place. "I love God. Don't ask that of me. He is not lying about anything."

"I need you."

She winced.

"Whose side are you on?"

"Stop this, Lucifer. You know I will not betray our Father."

"He is not my Father anymore."

"Please don't say that."

Lucifer clenched his fists and felt his fingernails digging deep into his palms. "I am leaving. Do not follow me."

Two tears fell from her green eyes, but she didn't.

He crashed down from the platform to the deep blue of the water below. The once-beautiful world under water meant nothing this time. Fish darted out of his way to avoid being pummeled as he sank through like a boulder. The deeper he went the darker it became, but the glow he gave off from the remnants of God's glory allowed him to barely see until the last moment of blackness. This was where he remembered cutting through a black hole to the cosmos.

He came out on the other side and shook the water from his wings. He took in the beauty of the cosmos again, of the other worlds suspended there in the deep black. The nearest planet was lovely, covered in blue and green, and he felt immediate ownership of it. A new home. Thyaterra no longer mattered. More importantly, God no longer mattered. He had to keep telling himself that.

He flew toward it through the emptiness of the cosmos, and at length he passed through a layer of cloud and landed on the surface. He didn't know what to do, so he roamed the stretches of unkempt fields of grass. There were forests too, but the trees weren't uniform in height or layout and there was no structure to anything. Everything grew wild, and there were apparently no rules. It was perfectly imperfect. He roamed mountaintops, vast distances of nothing but windswept oceans, and deserts void of life. He liked the sandy deserts with their towering dunes, but the heat reminded him of the warmth of God's throne. He flew away and came down upon a jungle with plush green trees and long waterfalls.

He thought of Thyaterra. God had warped her mind. He controlled her just like He used to control Lucifer. Just like He would control His new Son. He felt rage welling up in him again, only this time he did not try to hold it in.

Lucifer grabbed the nearest tree by its base and ripped it from the earth, roots and all. Bark fell all around from where his grip crushed into the base of the tree. Dirt dropped as the dangling roots snapped off where they fed into the ground. He tore up many, flipping them over, running forward a few steps, and hurling each of them over a mile into a large body of water. They descended deep, branches first. It felt good. He ripped off branches because he liked the snap they made as they broke. He hurled these as far as he could.

He tore up more trees, his anger unabated, and he began to realize that he could feel the life drain from the trees as the roots separated from the ground. It was incredible. By severing the base of the tree from its life source, it actually died and did not grow back. The realization struck him with equal parts wonder and horror.

He could control life in his new world.

CHAPTER

VIII

G abriel knew the best place to cool down and get his mind off the accident. In fact it was a part of his daily routine to visit the Canyon Reef. Here, a towering, U-shaped mountainside held estates carved out for hierarch angels; they directly overlooked the shore of a private sea. The bright-neon coral reef below was easily visible through the crystal-clear water. The solid rock of the mountainside almost melted directly into the sandy beach, like they were one and the same. It was beautiful and a popular spot among angels, though today he hoped to be alone.

Gabriel peeked around a stone corner at the bottom of a wall bordering the estates. He looked around the carved columns, across the sandy beach, and out over the water. No one was in sight. He stepped out and ran his feet into the white sand. A cool breeze came in off the water as he approached the gentle surf. As he leaned over to wet his face, he heard a familiar voice behind him.

"Gabriel."

He accidentally threw water up his nose. He coughed it all up, but it took way too long. Arrayah laughed quietly. She must have come around from the back side of the mountain.

"What are you doing here?"

"I came to find you. I asked around and heard you like to come here."

"Raphael was wrong back there."

"Gabriel, listen." Her gaze, previously so direct, was averted, and she clutched her necklace—her thumb rubbing a slow circle over the word *Humilitas.* "I know you weren't trying to hurt me."

There was something about her that made it difficult to breathe, and it wasn't just the water in his throat. "Yes. I mean, no." He let out something like a laugh and nodded. "Right. You're right. That's what I've been saying."

Her hands dropped to her sides, and for a moment she looked lost, with her wings gently fluttering and her eyes skipping everywhere before finally landing on him. The water around them gave off a misty cloud that smelled like sweet soap.

"No, I mean, I've never thought it. I just have this feeling that you would never do anything to hurt me." She took two steps, and the space between them disappeared.

When he said nothing and only stared at her, she pressed on, her words tumbling out. "Not because I'm so wonderful. Just because of you, who I sense you are."

His hand raised between them, one finger brushing her necklace. "You're always so humble, but you have so little reason to be." From there, it seemed natural for his hand to drift up and rest against her face—a simple, automatic gesture, but when her eyes closed and a smile claimed her face, he felt like something in his world had shifted.

"Gabriel!"

Arrayah seemed as startled as he was, and she stumbled back from him as his hand fell away. A moment after Michael's voice tore through the air, they were buffeted by the downdraft of his massive wings as he descended beside them. Michael pushed Gabriel back with one hand. "It's bad enough you're turning your back on the job God has set aside for you in the future. Now you're leaving your post, destroying buildings, endangering other angels—what were you thinking?"

Anger surged up in Gabriel, and he shoved Michael away from him, hard. "Back off and calm down, Michael."

"Oh, I'm calm. And although I know God doesn't make mistakes, He must see something that I don't. I thought you'd come around, but obviously I was wrong."

Arrayah raised a hand, her voice quiet. "Excuse me, I know you mean well, but you don't know the whole story."

Michael turned to see Arrayah's face, and an awkward pause followed. Gabriel eventually felt it had to be broken. "Michael."

He was still frozen, just looking at her.

"Michael, have you met Arrayah before?"

Michael's gaze jerked back to Gabriel. "Arrayah? This is the virtue angel you nearly crushed?"

Gabriel, counting inwardly to ten, had forced his fists to unclench from his sides. He pushed down the things he wanted to shout at Michael, instead preparing to describe, evenly and precisely, what had happened at the community building's unveiling.

"Yes, but that was an accident."

Arrayah looked over to Michael in confirmation. "It really was. He would never hurt me."

Michael paused awkwardly again. He looked at the two of them like he didn't know how to speak. Finally he said to Arrayah, "What is a virtue doing hanging around an archangel anyway? Are you going to wait around the mountainside until he drops a boulder on you?"

Gabriel drew his sword.

Michael's weapon cleared its sheath a second later, and Gabriel swung a downward blow, the blades locking with a clash of steel that echoed across the beach. There was no real power behind the attack—despite the lack of warning, Gabriel was holding back. For a moment, they simply looked at each other between the crossed swords.

Gabriel took a step away. Arrayah moved all the way off the beach to the grass behind it. Michael was wearing a loose robe over his tunic, and Gabriel waited as he drew it off and tossed it aside. Michael raised his sword, and they began to circle.

"You really are a terrible brother, Michael."

"You know that's not true."

"Maybe you're right," Gabriel said. "Maybe fighting is all I'm good at." Arrayah stood on the periphery, looking from one to the other. She fidgeted uncomfortably and seemed to be looking for an escape.

"I never said that. In fact, I never said you were all that good at fighting." Michael swung his sword in a lazy arc. He executed a high slice, easily parried.

"You don't have to say it, I can tell by the defeat on your face every time we spar." He noticed Arrayah slowly creeping away. "Wait." Gabriel tried to pause for Arrayah, but Michael lunged aggressively. He couldn't ignore him.

"I've waited long enough for you to come around, Gabriel. You're hopeless these days."

Gabriel shifted toward Michael with a swift counterattack and sent him backward two steps. Michael blocked, attacked, countered again. Their swords moved in technical precision, but casually, like a dance in which both knew the steps by heart.

"You're losing confidence in this vision of yours then?" Gabriel said.

"No. Only losing confidence in you."

Gabriel threw his sword into the sand. It stuck in the ground inches from Michael's toes. He looked over to the grass, but Arrayah was gone.

"Nice job, Michael! She left! Is this why you came here? What do you want from me?" Gabriel started to walk up the shore, looking around for her.

"It's time for you to wake up. It's been time. I can't do everything for you anymore, and things are about to change drastically in Heaven."

"Here we go again. Leave me alone; I'm going to find Arrayah."

"You shouldn't be spending time with that virtue!"

Gabriel turned and stepped directly up to Michael. "And why is that, O war leader?"

Michael shook his head. He was holding something back Gabriel knew. What was it?

"Do whatever you want, Gabriel. I know what God showed me. It's coming whether you are ready or not. I can't help you if you don't want to help yourself. Just trust me, and stay away from that virtue." Michael turned the opposite direction and walked four heavy steps before he spread his wings to take off.

Gabriel felt lightheaded. The massive draft of wind from the angry downstroke of Michael's wings almost knocked him over. What did Michael know?

IX

Lucifer spent the next two days taking his years of pent-up jealousy and anger toward God and letting it out on this new environment. He had decided to name this world Terra, after her. It was his to name, after all. The dense area of trees was now a barren wasteland. Every animal within a hundred miles was gone. It was good they ran. If trees could be separated from their life source, perhaps animals could too. Lucifer was almost ready to find out.

He felt as if he were discovering a newly found gift that God was keeping from everyone. When Lucifer destroyed the trees and other plants, he could feel the subtle energy they gave off before the life inside them was gone. Some clung on more tightly than others, and he could feel the fight inside them. They could struggle all they wanted, but they weren't in control. He was. He respected the ones that fought harder. If the roles were reversed, he would fight the hardest. He knew that.

Lucifer felt powerful and he felt a great deal of rage, but he also felt thoughtful, as if a part of him was watching everything that happened with cold detachment. He took careful notes of his thought processes on the rock and in the sand beneath the plush green. He named his new power wrath, and the third of the seven deadly sins was formed.

The second sin he had discovered, envy, was formed toward God not too long before this rampage, and Lucifer quickly realized it was all throughout Heaven. He took pleasure in this feeling because it gave him a sense of power. It gave him the fuel he needed. It fed his drive to get even. He knew envy was something many angels felt toward him, but it had never been defined. He knew they envied his position in the ranks, and he would use that to his advantage.

The most powerful of all the sins was discovered first. Pride. Without pride, he would have succumbed to God. He loved that he hadn't. Lucifer kept track of these sins as he discovered them. They were like precious jewels. He realized quickly, without shame, that there was power in each of them. He was the only one who truly had a hold of who he was. He knew himself and he knew other angels. He knew their deepest desires that had never been spoken of. They were subtly expressed, but in almost every being in Heaven, Lucifer had glimpsed those traits, and he meant to bring them all out.

The heavenly virtues that God held dear helped guide Lucifer to their polar opposites. God was well-known for his virtues—chastity, temperance, charity, diligence, patience, kindness, and humility—and Lucifer was intent on discovering the antivirtues that were the exact opposites of these. Why was there more power in wrath than patience? Why was envy a stronger motivator than kindness? The opposite of humility gave him pride. The opposite of charity gave him greed. He felt proud of them and wasn't done searching for more.

He wanted to find the coldest place on this new formation and rid himself of God's warm, bright influence so he could think. He went into the mountains as far north as there was land and dug his way as deep as he could go. He spent much time traveling across the solid land mass and discovered countless places that attracted him with their wild, hostile forms. Lucifer found glacier caves that suited his needs perfectly—deep in the ice on the northern side.

As he discovered the answers he was seeking within his antivirtues, he realized not only who he was but also the truth of everything in the cosmos. Now he alone had discovered the physical realities that made up the universe. With everything he learned, it pushed him further away from his faith in God. He saw imperfections on Terra. The fact he could control life made him realize God wasn't the only powerful one. His reason and his faith contradicted each other. He began to despise warmth and light and instead yearned for cold and dark. He found comfort in it.

It was time for a change. He devised a plan to make the change a reality amongst the vast corridors of Heaven.

Time came and went. Lucifer had stopped keeping track of it. One day, he saw Saraquel hiding. He was crouched behind a hill of snow, but Lucifer recognized his stringy black hair sticking out.

"Saraquel."

The black hair disappeared behind the hill.

"Saraquel, I saw you."

"Forgive me, Lucifer!"

"Why are you hiding?"

"I am amazed at your power. I couldn't turn away. You told me to find you."

Lucifer reached out his hand as he approached, and Saraquel began to bow.

"No longer bow your head to me. You will become my brother this day if you will accept what I have to say." Saraquel's eyes grew wide, and his mouth dropped slightly. It was a moment or two before he could speak.

"Of course, Lucifer. Please tell me what you would like from me."

"I want nothing from you except for you to make your own decisions based on the knowledge I am about to give you."

"Yes, sir. I can do that." They began to walk across the snow, and Saraquel fell into step beside him.

"Let me ask you some questions, and I want you to answer as honestly as possible. The throne that you had built for me, by what means did you construct it?" Lucifer asked.

"Well, I had my angels work on it for me—in your honor, of course."

"And they followed your commands because you are an archangel and their leader, correct?"

"Yes. They were eager to serve you as well." Saraquel twisted his hands together.

"You had them build this for me. Why?"

"Because you asked me to."

"Why would you listen to me?"

Saraquel paused. He began shaking slightly in confusion. Finally he answered, "Because you are the highest cherubim and it brings me great joy to serve you. Was I not supposed to, your highness?"

"Yes, of course, you were, because of the order of things between the angels and the tiers of power. I am above you."

"Your virtues surpass ours, and there is no shame in praising you."

"Thank you, but who truly says that is how it has to be?"

"God does. I am as God made me, and that is how it should be. We all have our roles to play. I live to worship Him as my unique self and in my unique way."

"What if I told you that you could be a throne, a seraph, or even take my place as the highest cherubim right now? Would you take it?"

Saraquel visibly hesitated, like it was a trick. "God made me who I am. I am content."

"I am your friend, Saraquel." Lucifer felt nauseous at his own words, but if his plan was to work, he would need support. It might as well begin with this pitiful angel. "You are in a safe place. I see the desires in your heart, and they are more than you say. Does it not sound intriguing to be more than God has made you?"

Saraquel looked away. "I am an archangel, that is all I will ever be."

"That is all you will ever be according to God." Lucifer waited until his gaze came back and forced a smile. "I say you can be more than that."

"But God made the classes of all angels. He wouldn't let you change that."

"What if I told you the rules were arbitrary, that His rules are based on His deceit?"

"I wouldn't believe you. God loves us. Why would He lie?"

"He doesn't love us," answered Lucifer calmly. "He uses us and lies to us. Look at who is on top. Who sits on a throne while you take orders in Heaven?"

"But He created us."

"That is what He would have us believe. Let me ask you this. How does a tree or a plant grow and bear fruit? Where does it originate?"

Saraquel answered quickly. "It starts as a seed. Then it grows until it can bear fruit."

"What if I told you that I have a tree that never started as a seed? What if I told you it just always existed?"

Saraquel squinted his eyes and took his time with his answer. "That would not make sense."

"Yet that is how God explains Himself. He claims to be the only One that never had a beginning: a tree but never a seed."

Saraquel stood silent. Lucifer could sense his heart beating fast and his mind racing wildly. He almost had him. "I know how you feel. I too was disappointed when I first accepted this truth. But the disappointment will soon pass. These are hard questions, and I do not know all the answers either. But I do wonder why God has one set of rules for Him and another for us, yet we were supposedly made in His image. If you figure it out, will you let me know? I believe the glory of God can only be magnified by our understanding of His great design."

"He tells us to have faith in Him, so that is what I do."

Lucifer's eyes lit up with energy. "Think of what you just said. How do you fool the masses into believing something? You make them believe in you. Then you tell them what to do and they do it. What if God has done that to us?"

"That is impossible."

"Is it?" Lucifer saw on Saraquel's face that he was teetering on the brink. "God speaks of the importance of wisdom. Why then does reality contradict His very teachings?"

"I don't know."

"I know you don't because no one can answer that. And the only one who claims He has an answer says He had no beginning. But I asked Him personally. He simply says, 'Have faith.' Well, no thanks. Not anymore. I encourage you to think for yourself. Don't let Him do it for you. It's time for a change in thinking. And that time is now."

CHAPTER

X

Michael always thought he knew everything; that was nothing new. Gabriel wasn't going to let it bother him. Besides, Arrayah seemed to have forgiven him for the building incident. Compared to how things had been progressing, this was practically time for a small celebration. Gabriel's fondness of Heaven's fruits was tempting him; saving half the angels could wait. He worked his way over to the Spiritapple Field south of the Great Mountain and the Provender, where he could feast on the sweetest fruit in all of Heaven.

Gabriel descended to the orchard and grabbed a spiritapple from the ground. It had green, pointed leaves, and the fruit inside was protected by a hard outer skin. He simply pulled on the leaves on top, and it exposed the white fruit and its sparkling mist. Inside the fruit was a narrow chamber filled with its ever-so-sweet juice. Gabriel took a large bite, and it immediately sent endorphins from his toes to his wingtips. It heightened his mental clarity and boosted feelings of happiness, openness, and love even as he became hyperaware of sound, light, and movement. This was just in the first sip. Most angels only enjoyed one like they were supposed to, and they followed proper protocol by replanting the leaves in the soil. Not Gabriel.

By the time Saraquel approached him, he was lying on his back and at least fifteen square feet of the field had been plucked, opened, and the juice sucked dry. None of them had been replanted. Gabriel had every intention of cleaning up his mess—just not now. He was feeling good. Very good. He almost got up when he saw the angel flying in, but it was Saraquel. No big deal.

"Gabriel, I see you are a fan of the spiritapple," said Saraquel as he landed.

"Would you like some? There's a few I haven't gotten to, and you're welcome to them." He felt rather magnanimous offering this, as he would not have minded draining another dozen. It must be the juice making him so generous, he reflected.

"You know you are supposed to eat the fruit and not just drink the juice, right?"

"Of course." With that, he tipped another and drank its juice in one continuous slurp. "I have had an excellent day, at least one small part of it, so I am celebrating."

"Have you heard anything strange from Michael lately? I am actually concerned about him."

Gabriel laughed.

"Why are you laughing?"

"Nothing."

"I just spoke with Michael briefly."

"You did? What did he say about me?"

Saraquel looked confused. "He didn't say anything about you."

"Oh. Well, God has been speaking to him personally lately, and he said He showed him something unbelievable."

Saraquel fidgeted nervously. "Has he spoken to God in person?"

"He said God showed him something in a dream. A seraph has recently spoken to me as well. There are some strange things going on." Perhaps it was the spiritapple juice, but Gabriel felt perfectly content to share everything on his mind, even with Saraquel.

"I would agree. Things are changing."

"That's for sure." Gabriel ripped the top off another spiritapple and gulped the juice inside. "These are so sweet. Here." He tore the top from another and tossed it to Saraquel, who almost dropped it.

"Listen, I think Michael has been trying to move up the ranks, so he is acting like God appreciates him more than the rest of us," Saraquel said. "We are archangels too. Why wouldn't God tell us or show us these things?"

"Easy now. Michael is my best friend." He felt a moment of irritation and stared at Saraquel. He tipped up another spiritapple shell to enjoy its juice, and the pleasant feelings returned. The sky looked oddly multicolored. He squinted to refocus. "I don't know why He wouldn't tell us though. That's a good question. He did say God talked about me. Isn't that a laugh?"

"How many of those have you had, Gabriel?"

Gabriel watched him counting the shells that littered the ground. "These aren't all mine." A moment later he realized they actually were.

"I've never seen anyone have more than two before."

"I'm fine. So is Michael. Let's talk about something else." Saraquel began to glow brightly, and Gabriel squinted again. He wanted to touch him.

"Gabriel, I know that Michael is your best friend." Saraquel raised his hands as if backing off. "I am just telling you because Azrael and I have seen how Michael manipulates you into always following him, and we aren't the only two who have noticed. I mean, he told you that God was talking to him about you. Wouldn't God just come to you if there were something you needed to hear?"

Gabriel stood up and put his hand on Saraquel's glowing shoulder. He shook his head and the glow disappeared. "First of all, God does talk to me. Second, I know Michael better than anyone. Thanks for your concern, but Michael is not manipulating me." He wasn't so sure anymore after the comments Michael made about Arrayah, but Saraquel was the last one who needed that information.

"We are just looking out for you and Michael."

"I'll watch out. Thanks."

"No problem," said Saraquel. "You know, Gabriel, I have always thought of you as the real leader of us seven archangels."

Gabriel smiled. Saraquel wasn't so bad after all. "Well, thank you. I'm honored you say that, but I can't say I agree with you. No one should ever follow someone like me."

"I disagree. In fact, I know another high angel that would disagree too."

Did he know Arrayah?

Saraquel finally took a bite of the spiritapple and knelt beside him. "How would you like to be more than just an archangel?"

"We would all love to be cherubs or seraphs, but it's not going to happen. What high angel are you referring to?"

"The highest angel. Lucifer thinks highly of you. He was asking me about the seven archangels. It seems as if he is choosing one for a very special project."

"Did you mention my name to Lucifer?"

"I told him you were the one that brought all of us together. You get along well with everyone, and even Michael listens to you."

"What is the project?"

"There is a revolution coming, Gabriel. A revolution of the minds of angels. The ranking system and orders of angels is going to change."

Gabriel's stomach felt queasy. Had he heard right? Maybe the euphoria of fifteen spiritapples was turning into madness. Michael's statement about his dream was too similar to Saraquel's for comfort. He had to see God. He never saw God, but he would today. Maybe it was heightened boldness from the fruit, but he was going to march up those golden steps for answers, no matter what.

"I have to go."

"Wait, I'm not finished. We have a place for you."

"We can finish this later."

"I need your support as a fellow archangel. I must please my new master." Saraquel tried to hold Gabriel's wing back. Gabriel ripped it out of his hand and spun to confront him.

"Did you say new master?"

"I just mean I need your support."

"Right. Yes, we are archangels. But don't use that as the very manipulation you accuse Michael of. I have only one brother. Watch how you speak of him around me."

"I am sorry. But I'm not the only angel who feels he is trying to exalt himself. He could be in some major trouble if he keeps it up."

Gabriel looked through Saraquel's strong, dark eyes. He wasn't backing down the way he used to. The entire experience felt surreal. "You should go now."

"All right, Gabriel."

Saraquel drifted away, but Gabriel's discomfort lingered. Saraquel was troubled and acting strangely. What was going on in Heaven? Gabriel picked himself up and waited a few minutes for his head to clear a bit. Then he flew up the twelve layers of the Great Mountain.

He entered the pearl gates on the southwest side, and one of the dominions opened the gates for him. Once near the ramp, he slowed to a walk. He passed all the way up and crossed over the bridge above the River of Life. Then he began the long journey up the staircase. He thought about how inconvenient accessing God was. He was right to never visit Him. After all, when had God ever cared about Gabriel? Maybe it was the lingering effects of the fruit, but it was difficult to focus his thoughts, and they seemed bold and daring, even to him. He eventually got to the thrones, who greeted him less pleasantly than he would have imagined.

"I'm sorry, but you can go no further," said Kaldeczar. He was the leader of the thrones and was decorated accordingly. He wore a tall hat decadent with jewels and boasted golden armor. He looked way too tense.

This only added to Gabriel's disquiet. Why was the leader of the thrones on staircase duty? "I would like to speak with God."

"I regret to inform you that that is not possible. He will see no one right now, not even the seraphim." Kaldeczar stood firmly and without expression in front of Gabriel, as if using his body language to suggest Gabriel would have to go through him physically.

Gabriel was unimpressed. "Why? What is happening?"

"I have told you everything we know. Maybe He is busy with something we don't know about yet or don't need to know about at all."

"That is absurd. I need to see God, and I think I have a little idea of what is going on. Michael the archangel said He spoke of me. Do you know Michael? Is he up here?"

"I do not know Michael, and I haven't seen an archangel up here in a while. I'm sorry, but I will not let you pass."

"Please get out of my way."

"No." Although Kaldeczar was much shorter, he moved squarely in front of Gabriel and tensed up as if ready to strike.

Gabriel didn't have time for this. "Move, tiny angel!"

"How dare you?" Kaldeczar drew his golden blade.

"I am going to see God, so put that little stick away before I take it from you."

"I dare you to try!"

"I don't have to try anything!" A group of thrones began to encircle them. Gabriel wasn't intimidated, but in the back of his mind he knew Michael would hear about this. Michael heard about everything.

When Gabriel refused to budge, Kaldezcar attempted to drive him backward with a swing of his sword. As soon as the throne attacked, Gabriel dodged the blow and stepped quickly in, grabbing Kaldezcar by his armpits. Before he could attack again, Gabriel lifted him up and launched him into three other thrones standing to the side. His sword went flying. Gabriel prepared to be swarmed by angry thrones, but they allowed Kaldezcar to rise and have the first go. He drew a dagger and charged, and Gabriel blocked a blow with his forearm guard just before he heard a new voice. It was exactly the voice he didn't want to hear during another fiasco like this. At least this time it wasn't his name being yelled.

"Kaldezcar!" A virtue came running over from the other side of the platform. It was Arrayah. "Stop it, both of you." She was beneath the thrones in rank, but her voice could command any angel. Kaldezcar backed down, his head lowering in embarrassment.

Arrayah turned to Gabriel. "What are you doing here?"

Kaldezcar grunted. "You know this angel? He is trying to defy the hierarchs and barge in to God's throne."

"Yes, I know him. Does he deserve to be attacked because he does not understand that God will not see anyone?"

Kaldezcar took a step back, but he glared at Gabriel when Arrayah turned her head.

"Come with me, Gabriel," she said with a wave of her hand as she walked past him. Gabriel returned the glare but immediately turned away to follow Arrayah. As they departed the platform, he saw a seraph at the edge of the crowd looking at him sympathetically. Their eyes met, and she seemed to be looking right through him. He couldn't interpret that look, and he wondered why she did not have her eyes covered. At any other time, he would have gone over to her, but Arrayah gestured at him impatiently, and he followed her toward the stairs. At the first step, he glanced back at the seraph, and she slowly shook her head as if it was a warning. Gabriel hesitated. "Arrayah, wait."

Arrayah paused on the step below and looked up at Gabriel. "What is it?"

"This seraph," he said. When he pointed to where the seraph had been, she was gone. "Never mind." He decided to let it go. "What is going on, Arrayah?"

"I don't know exactly. I was also trying to meet with God, but the seraphim wouldn't let me either. Will you walk down with me?"

"Yes." The fact was there was nothing he would rather be doing than walking with Arrayah, regardless of where they were. Who cared what was happening in Heaven? This was what was happening in his world. He was walking with one of the seven virtue angels, and she was genuinely interested in him. Gabriel completely forgot about Michael. He completely forgot his determination to see God.

"I'm sorry about Michael and me fighting earlier."

"Let's just live in the moment," she said.

He loved that answer. Michael didn't need to even be mentioned. "So, what are you doing up here?"

She paused before answering. "Things are changing right now, and I'm not sure what exactly is going on. I wanted to speak with God."

This surprised him. God had spoken to Michael about him, he had spoken to a seraph, the highest cherub had asked about him, and now the most beautiful of all the hierarchs was walking and talking with him—and she was wondering the same thing he was. This meant it wasn't all in his head or Michael's. He felt his stomach flip even as a rush of heat surged into his chest. "What do you mean?"

"The classes seem to have lost some of their separation and order. I mean, look, here I am a virtue, and you are an angel, and we are having a conversation after trying to get to God's throne."

"Actually, I am an archangel. Not just an angel. I have to tell you."

"Oh, my deepest apologies." She smiled.

"There's only seven of us, just like you virtues." He hoped she would appreciate the similarity of their rarity.

"Wow. That is so interesting." Her lips spread into a grin. "Everyone knows that you know."

"I was just making sure you knew."

Gabriel looked at her constantly. It occurred to him that this might make her uncomfortable, but he couldn't seem to stop. "I know what you are saying though. I've had a few encounters lately that I never thought would happen."

"Like what?"

"I think a seraph is trying to tell me something, and Michael is acting odd. Not to mention earlier today another archangel told me that Lucifer was talking about me."

"Is that why you were trying to speak with God?"

"Yes. I just want answers, but God and I aren't exactly the closest."

"We all have our own relationships to work out with Him."

Gabriel looked down, wanting to change the subject.

"When was the last time you spoke with Michael?" she asked.

"It's been a little while. Maybe he is avoiding me."

"Over the fight I saw?"

"Yeah, and he made some strange comments."

"What comments?"

"I probably shouldn't say."

"Trust me."

He couldn't do anything else. "He said that something is about to happen in Heaven that will change everything."

"Like what?"

"I don't know exactly."

"Well, that is strange. Is that all he said about it?"

"Pretty much." He was surprised she was so interested in their conversation.

"It's odd that he would just disappear now."

"You're right. I think he will meet with God soon if he hasn't already, so I'll come back early tomorrow."

"I could come with you if you wanted me to." She looked over at him with soft eyes.

Gabriel stopped next to her on the stair. "Really?"

She nodded, and he realized she was serious.

"I would love for you to."

"Then I will," she said. "It will all be better soon I am sure. Things may be changing, but sometimes change is needed. To fix things that may be out of order, or just to better things."

Gabriel had never been very close to a female angel. He never felt he had much in common with them, so he really didn't even try. Arrayah was different. He didn't care what they did or didn't have in common. It didn't matter that everything seemed to be coming unraveled. He hadn't felt this good in a long time.

"If you're not busy," he said, "I'd love to take you to my favorite place in all of Heaven."

"I would love to see it. I just can't today. I'm sorry."

"No problem. We'll see it another time." He tried to not show his disappointment.

"Consider it done. Let me guess where it is though." She flipped her hair over her shoulders playfully.

"Go for it."

"Is it the Crystal Cave of the Iris Fall?"

"No."

"It must be the Mountain Wall Estates of the Canyon Reef where I found you," she said with confidence.

"I've become much fonder of the estates since you found me there, but no, that is not it. It's not one of the popular places. In fact, that's why I like it. It's kind of my own little spot."

"Oh, so there is more to Gabriel than this tough exterior." Arrayah had a playful smirk and one raised eyebrow.

"Not much more." He smiled back. "I'm definitely not as deep as a virtue angel."

"Humility. I like it. That is my virtue."

"I know. I saw your necklace."

"And he pays attention to detail. Very nice."

"Tell me about yourself. What is Arrayah passionate about?"

"For starters, I am very curious. I want to know why things are the way they are and how they came to be in the first place. Have you ever thought of anything like that?"

"Sure. All the time."

"Really?"

"Actually, not often." They both had a short laugh. "I like to live in the moment, trying to be as happy as I can. For example, I am doing exactly what I would most enjoy doing in all of Heaven right now—talking to you."

He looked in her eyes. She turned away.

"We'll see what you say after how long it takes to get down. You'll be tired of me by then." She started jogging down the steps.

As they went on, Gabriel tried to walk more slowly to make their time together longer, but she repeatedly picked up the pace and he had to follow. He would have walked and talked with her forever if she would have allowed it. Arrayah did most of the talking because he mostly just had questions for her. She was fascinating to him. He found he loved to watch her laugh. He asked her about her favorite things, and she was open and warm with her responses. She had no guard up. She trusted him.

She was passionate and expressive in her speech, revealing how she longed to know more and to teach others. But the truth was it didn't matter what she had to say. Gabriel felt something stirring inside, and he could not tear his eyes from her. She was a spark of light in a dim existence.

By the time they had reached the bottom of the stairs near the glistening sheen of the pearly gates, Arrayah had brought up the question of where God came from. "I mean, what came before God? How could He possibly be both the Alpha and the Omega?"

As her words sank in, it felt like that instant just after waking up when harsh reality was still setting in. Had she really just asked that? It took him a minute to respond because he was repeating the question in his head and trying to figure out where it came from. "I don't understand," he finally said.

"I know! It doesn't make sense if you really think about it. We can't possibly know if God really is who He says He is. That is all I'm saying."

Gabriel knew his confusion showed. He felt stupid and slow, and he could not come up with a decent response. She looked at him hopefully, and he wanted to agree with her just to see her smile, but he couldn't bring himself to. They crossed to the gates in silence. Her eager expression wavered but remained.

They finally said their goodbyes. Gabriel felt he was grasping for the right words, strong and convincing words, but none were in reach. He had to see her again so that he could say some of these things he wanted to if he could only muster the courage when the time came.

He watched her turn and leap into the air, her pure-white wings unfurling and beating hard. She soared over the edge before drifting down the mountainside. Her wings rose and fell gently as if they were caressing the air as she fell.

It was then that he remembered what the seraph had said. Angels would forget that God was holy. He recalled Michael's warning—angels falling, angels burning. Arrayah could not be a part of that though. She was something different. She smelled like lavender after a rainy day. And those eyes.

Gabriel tore his gaze away from her dwindling form. He knew he should find Michael right away and talk to him alone. But all of this felt too overwhelming, and if he rushed to find Michael, it would only acknowledge that something serious was happening. If he waited until the next day, perhaps Arrayah could join him. He really wanted Michael to meet her—and after all, it was just one more day.

Lucifer remained on Terra. He had sent Saraquel to recruit his closest friends and the other six archangels. It was a start for his new apprentice. In the meantime, Lucifer continued to indulge his fresh appetite for destruction. When Thyaterra found him in his new domain, the shock on her face as she landed was clear. Lucifer looked around himself and took in the extent of the damage. Trees lay uprooted for hundreds of miles, and dirt, rocks, and dead plants were scattered throughout the vast plains. They were empty now—a huge perimeter around Lucifer was completely void of life.

"Lucifer!"

"I told you not to follow me."

"I didn't. I waited for you to come back, but I only saw Saraquel. He told me where to find you."

He actually wanted to see Thyaterra, so for once he was glad that Saraquel was weak. Her life force was so strong that he could feel it immediately. She was pulsing with it. Why had he not noticed it before? The urge to grab her by the neck was almost unbearable. "I didn't want you to see it like this, but this is all for you. I have named this place Terra after you."

"This is not yours to name. I came here to draw a line with you."

"What are you saying?"

"I will not stand by your side and watch you turn your back on our Father. If that is the path you choose, I will no longer be a part of your life."

He could feel his hair standing up, or maybe it was growing. Whatever it was doing, he couldn't control it. Anger, powerful and unrestrained, was filling his veins.

"I don't know what is happening with you, Lucifer, but it is not something I feel strong enough to be able to handle alone. If you do not come back to us, then I will no longer come near you."

He fought to remain composed, but his voice sounded like a growl even in his own ears. "You don't understand what I have seen."

"I don't care what you've seen. You are becoming unstable. You are deceiving yourself and believing your own convenient lies."

"He is the liar!" His face felt hot. Strands of hair grew down over his eyes, curling and twisting, and turned ashen grey. At his shout, Thyaterra took a step back from him.

"I cannot begin to understand what is happening to you, but I don't want to be a part of it. If the Lucifer I know and love comes back, I will be waiting for him. I must go."

"You would leave me like this?" He could feel her strength pull him toward her as she stepped away as if they were tied together somehow. "Will Bretabian so easily replace me for you, just as God's new Son has for him?"

Thyaterra turned to leave. He couldn't let this happen. He loved her. He rushed toward her, intending to stop her, to convince her, but before he could think, he had reached from behind and grabbed her by the throat. It shocked him, but his fingers dug in all the same. His head was now close to that wondrous source of energy just below her delicate neck where her wings joined her back. It pulled at him.

"I think we should work to get on the same page again, Terra," he whispered into her ear. The soft strands of her fragrant blonde hair brushed his cheek, and he trembled. He worked at relaxing his grip. "I don't know what I will do if I lose you." She was shaking, but she didn't say a word or collapse against him. In fact, he felt her stand up straighter. She was so strong.

"Terra, I love you." Her energy pulsated from the base of her neck. Her strength was intoxicating. He wanted to consume it even as it made him love her more. Lost in the moment, he yearned for her to say something.

"I'm leaving you, Lucifer."

His eyes shot open, and he pulled his face away from her hair. He wanted to rip her wings from her back. It would be so easy. His hand tightened again on her throat, and he eyed the downy softness of the feathered arches rising from her back. He could tear them clean off her, hurl them as far as the trees, make it so she never flew again. Never went anywhere. Never left him again.

He had to do this. Anything else would be weakness. Yet his hands would not move. He concentrated on his anger toward God and felt the rage filling him again. His hands dropped from her neck to the base of her wings. It would be like tearing branches from a sapling. He could do it. He knew he could.

"Lucifer, I have to tell you something!" Saraquel broke through the clouds and dropped toward them like a stone. Sweat poured down his face, and his wings trembled from the strain.

Thyaterra pulled away, and her wings slid through Lucifer's grip. She leaped into the air before he could react. He didn't know whether to fly after her, slam her into the ground, and tear her apart or simply watch and

let her go. When he realized he had hesitated too long—
she was fast with her six wings—he knew too that she
had turned her back on him forever.

"Thyaterra! This will no longer be yours, and you can
stay in captivity forever!" His scream was loud enough to
be heard easily even at her distance. She continued her
flight without slowing, and in an instant, she could no
longer be seen.

He took deep breaths until he could speak without
growling. "What is so important, Saraquel?"

"I spoke with the archangels."

"Archangels are of small importance to me. How
much of that did you witness?"

"Hardly anything, your highness. I just saw her fly
away."

"Forget her. She is nothing." After a moment, he
composed himself. "Come over here."

Saraquel followed Lucifer across the plain of devas-
tation. They finally reached the edge of it and approached
a small copse of still-standing trees.

"I must tell you about one archangel," Saraquel
said.

Lucifer grabbed a tree at its base, his fingertips crushing into its bark, and ripped it from the ground with one
powerful pull. Long, twining roots dangled, thick with
clods of falling dirt. Lucifer lifted it up and heaved it as far
as he could. He turned to the other angel, brushing off his

hands. "That tree had life. What do you think will happen to it now?"

Saraquel looked puzzled. "I'm not sure what you're asking."

Lucifer sighed. "Never mind. Do as I do. And tell me of this angel."

"His name is Michael. He is the leader of the seven of us, and I must tell you that he may pose a problem."

"Go on."

Saraquel watched Lucifer, and together they started ripping out trees from their roots. Saraquel wasn't nearly as strong as Lucifer, so he searched for smaller trees. "He is opinionated. A leader amongst the lower class. I caught him in prayer."

"Yes?"

"He is extremely close to God."

Lucifer didn't even like to hear that word anymore. He saw Saraquel struggling with a thin tree, its bark smooth and white. "Have you ever felt like you were less than other archangels?"

"Of course."

"Use it. Build it inside you, and let it out as you take this tree."

Saraquel focused. He ripped the tree out with a quick snap and launched it as far as he could.

"Does anyone make you feel small and insignificant?"

"Michael does, as a matter of fact." Saraquel quickly grabbed another tree from the ground. He lifted it high and then snapped it in two over his knee. He calmed down and caught his breath. Lucifer smiled at him.

"I approached Michael in the garden outside the city walls, Lucifer. He was in prayer with God, which unnerved me. I asked how he had been, and he finished praying before he'd even answer me. He looked at me like he knew what I was going to say."

"I'm sure he didn't."

"I told him I had come across great wisdom that I was willing to share with him. He told me he felt as if he were one of the last to know, which I thought odd."

"I have recruited others. Word travels swiftly from the right mouths. It is a whispering cloud washing over Heaven, and we will soon have the majority wondering. The seed of doubt is planted."

"I couldn't plant it with Michael. I tried to ask your questions about where God came from, but he would have none of it. He said he stood on faith and asked where I came up with—what did he call them—'these ridiculous allegations.'"

"He thinks he is wise. He thinks he is a leader." Michael knew nothing. He would be brought low.

"I told him the time had come for change. I said the truth will be exposed, and I felt like you when I said it." He smiled. "Powerful. In charge."

Lucifer felt a sick taste in his mouth and turned toward another tree so Saraquel could not see his expression. "I am proud of you."

"That means so much to me."

It would be easy to break this pathetic angel like one of the trees—to tear him from the ground, rip him apart, and hurl him out of sight. Could he throw him clear over that distant hill?

"But then I thought Michael was going to attack me. He almost did. He accused me of blasphemy and threatened me. He threatened me, Lucifer, and told me never to speak of it again in his presence. He said that God's faithful would not stand for these lies. I wanted to tell him exactly who he is dealing with. That's when I ran straight for you."

"Did you tell him where you gathered this information? Did you mention my name?"

"Never. Not once."

"Are you sure?"

"I would never, Lucifer."

Lucifer calmed himself down. He set down the tree he was holding and saw deep fissures where his fingers had sunk into the wood. He had to think. He didn't like the situation at all. He knew there would be significant resistance, but he didn't think it would come from an archangel of the lowest tier. "He may try to rally God's followers. We mustn't let God know how high we have reached into the structure of His domain."

"The highest-ranking angel I have converted to our side is an archangel."

"I have obtained the support of many you do not even know about, young Saraquel. I have three top-tier angels that will be leaders in our mission. We must stay vigilant."

"I understand, master."

"I will deal with this insignificant archangel myself. Tell me everything you know about him."

Saraquel pointed out Michael's severe attitude and unwavering devotion to the rules, which oddly could be a weakness. He explained that Michael's strict ways caused him to be respected among all angels, but it also caused a degree of alienation from some of them, especially those in his own class. Saraquel described Michael as being mostly alone, other than his one friend, Gabriel. When he stressed how Gabriel was Michael's opposite and loved finding pleasure more than doing real work, Lucifer found a solution. Saraquel was still talking, but Lucifer tuned him out.

He felt as if he already knew both Michael and Gabriel intimately. Michael would be easily destroyed. He had just the solution—he would do it through Gabriel.

XII

The next day, Gabriel walked right back through the gates of the heavenly city, past the dominion, and straight back to the upper platforms via the ramp. Immediately he saw Michael on his way down and ran toward him.

"I have been looking everywhere for you!" yelled Gabriel.

"I have had much to do."

"You won't believe who I have been talking to. She will be meeting me at the south gate soon." Gabriel felt a flicker of annoyance that Michael was not picking up on his excitement. In fact, he looked hurried and exhausted.

"I would believe anything right now. God cannot be accessed by anyone. His light is dimming and not even the seraphim have contact with him." Michael's voice lacked its usual confidence. His eyes moved around constantly, scanning the angels near them with a degree of suspicion that Gabriel had never seen from him. It made Gabriel uneasy.

"Is this about the dream you said He showed you?" Please say no, Gabriel thought.

"It seems so. I hope you believe me now." He put a hand on Gabriel's shoulder and drew him closer. His voice lowered. "Gabriel, you have to be careful whom you trust. There is a division amongst the angels. I can see it."

Gabriel didn't know what to say, so he simply followed Michael off the ramp and down into the city where angels lined the walkways and flew in clusters overhead. They passed streets lined with elaborate mansions. Angels were given the freedom to do whatever they wanted with their homes, and the countless resources of Heaven were at their disposal. The possibilities were endless. They passed a mansion that towered twelve stories high and was made completely out of crystal. It reminded him of all of the mistakes he'd made recently, especially at the Ludus Paradisus. From a neighboring mansion, a waterfall poured from the seventh floor down to a pool in the backyard. It was all so unnecessary. Gabriel wasn't sure he wanted things to stay the same.

"You speak of a division," he said, "but it seems to me that the divisions between angels are crumbling. We are all more equal now, from what I have seen."

Michael rounded on him. "Are you saying that because you have been seeing Arrayah? Listen, now is not the time to make new friends. Do you not find it strange she is suddenly speaking with you? You must be careful whom you associate with. The period the Lord spoke of is near."

"Are you saying a virtue would never want to be around me? That's what this is all about, isn't it? You're jealous."

"That is not what I'm saying. Don't be absurd. I am simply saying think about it. Why would a virtue be associating with an archangel right now?"

"I know it may seem unbelievable to you, and speaking of hard to believe, why would God tell you in a dream I'm going to help save half the angels but not tell me?"

Four angels crossed from the other side of the street, chatting cheerfully. Spotting them, Gabriel waved and called in their direction. "Hey guys, I'll soon be saving you. Not all of you, but you two." The four looked caught off guard, their smiles fading. "Actually, it could be the other way around. It could be you two instead. Anyway, I'm the angel savior. Tell your friends."

"That's it. I don't have time for this," Michael said. "Goodbye, Gabriel." He started to walk in the other direction.

"Michael, wait. You've got to admit this whole thing is far-fetched, right?"

Michael hesitated before turning around. His eyes flashed, and the line of his jaw was tight. "Yes, I admit that. But this is the way it is. Most angels don't seem to care about the order of things anymore, but I do. There are rules to follow, and I guarantee that God is going to fix this whole mess. I promise you, there will be consequences!" He crossed his arms and visibly pulled himself together like Gabriel was accustomed to. Even so, his features were strained. "All I know and believe—and will live by—is what God showed me."

Gabriel was taken aback. Even Michael didn't know what would happen. Michael was always in control but not with this. It gave him an uneasy flutter in the pit of his stomach.

Michael jabbed a finger at him in the air. "Just trust me when I tell you, brother—be careful. Do not trust anyone but God and me—especially not this virtue angel you just met."

"You don't even know her! She wouldn't do anything to deceive me. Why can't you trust my judgment for once?"

"Are you really this protective of her already? You barely know her! Do you not find her timing a little strange?"

"Yes, I am protective of her. What is wrong with that?"

Michael heaved a sigh. He shook his head before stepping forward and patting Gabriel wearily on the shoulder. "All right, then. I'm sure you will do the right thing."

"I have to go. She is probably waiting on me at the gate. But I'll see you soon if you don't hide this time."

"I'll most likely be home."

Michael walked away, and Gabriel watched him slip into a crowd making its way down the golden avenue. When he was out of sight, Gabriel quickly went in the other direction toward the gate. Michael was jealous. That had to be it. He tried to block out Michael's mistrust and focus instead on seeing Arrayah again. The flutter in his stomach returned but with a different quality to it, one that sent a flush of warmth into his face. But when he got back to the gate, she wasn't there.

He began to pace back and forth. Might something have happened to her? No, most likely not, he decided. She was just a little late. No big deal. He would wait.

Gabriel waited as angels came and went. To pass the time, he approached the dominion at the gate and asked if he knew Arrayah. The guard shook his head, and Gabriel began rambling on about her until the guard looked uncomfortable. Gabriel kept praising her anyway until enough time passed that his anxiety returned. "She must have come and not seen me," he said to the dominion. "I'll just wait a little longer."

Another dominion passed through the gate and the guard, appearing relieved, left Gabriel to speak with him. Gabriel scanned the groups of passing angels; he watched the skies. Finally, he saw Arrayah flying up the mountain.

"That's her. Got to go," he called to the dominion, who was no longer paying him any attention. "I told you she was coming. Isn't she stunning? Humility angel; can you believe it?"

Gabriel ran over to meet Arrayah as she dropped lightly to her feet. He didn't know whether to give her a hug or shake hands. He started to give a quick embrace but changed his mind and pulled back, reaching for her hand instead. Arrayah chuckled.

"What's funny?" he asked, a little embarrassed.

"Nothing. You are just cute."

"You are the cute one." She smiled, and he fell into step beside her. "I already saw Michael."

"Really?" Worry clouded her face. "Where is he?"

"I think he just went home."

She looked relieved. "Well, what did you two talk about?"

Gabriel explained Michael's vague sense that something bad was going to happen. When Arrayah pressed him for details, he reluctantly admitted that Michael warned him against trusting her.

"Me? Why?"

"It's stupid. He doesn't think it's smart to trust someone I just met. You know, with everything that is going on. But let's not worry about stuffy ol' Michael. Let's just have fun today instead."

Her mouth tightened, but she relaxed a moment later and smiled. "Good idea. Let's go have some fun."

"I'll show you my favorite spot in all of Heaven. How does that sound?" As soon as the words were out of his mouth, he realized she might not be as impressed with it as he was. She might even think it was boring. He put up a hand and said, "Before you answer, I should tell you that there isn't much to it. It's a simple place."

With a flirty lift of an eyebrow, she slid her arm through his. "I would love to see any place you want to show me, Gabriel."

He felt his face flush, and he began to stutter. "All right—I mean, sure then." He cleared his throat. "But hey, seriously, it's no big deal if we get there and you want to go somewhere else. I'm going to take you the long way. Follow me!" Gabriel launched into the air.

Arrayah spread her pristine wings and caught up to him. She reached for his hand and took it in her own. Surprised, Gabriel turned toward her, and she stared back at him with innocent, affectionate eyes. He wanted to give this angel all of Heaven already.

He decided he needed to show her something impressive first. "I'll take you to my favorite spot later. Right now, I'm going to show you something that reminds me of your eyes."

They flew over fields and trees until they reached the Marble Falls. Gabriel took her down to the first tier where a massive wall of water fell down the side of the marble. Gabriel shot straight through it into a cave on the other side, which was lit a fluorescent blue from the crystal that filled it. When Arrayah followed him in, it was clear from the shock on her face that she had no idea it was there. She looked around in silent awe.

Most angels knew of the popular Crystal Cave of the Iris Fall, which was huge and frequently visited. However, this cave on the first tier was much smaller and well hidden. It wasn't even named. The blue crystal was unique to this location and had not been seen by many eyes. It shimmered in the rippling play of light that shone through the falling water, sending azure sparks dancing across the walls and ceiling. The entrance was only about twice the size of Gabriel's wingspan. He knew it would make them stay close together.

"This is amazing," she said.

Her eyes roved over the curving walls of crystal, and then she looked at Gabriel. "That was a pretty good compliment, but I thought my eyes were a deeper blue than this."

"Of course, they are," he said quickly.

Arrayah laughed, and Gabriel realized she was joking. He felt a little silly. He told himself to stop being so nervous.

They both looked at the beautiful crystal that surrounded them as they traveled toward the other end of the cave. At the far end, the blue crystal was overtaken by solid diamonds everywhere you could see. Gabriel let her fly in front so he could take in the full beauty of her elegant flight. The crystal and diamonds were no match.

"Gabriel, I still can't believe this cave is down here and I have never seen it."

"No angel has seen all of Heaven."

"Maybe Lucifer."

He felt a twinge of jealousy. "Maybe."

"I've always felt I was missing out on something. All the other virtues are so pleased all the time with our duties, but I want more. Seeing this place just confirms how much is waiting to be discovered."

"I feel the same way. Michael and the other archangels know their places, but I want to make my own way." Arrayah looked incredible. The diamonds sparkled around them as he caught up to her, and the look she gave him there in the dancing light was something special. She felt it too. He was sure of it.

"Gabriel, I feel like I can trust you, so I want to tell you this." Her eyes cut to the side before coming back. "I have always wanted more and have never been satisfied with what God has given me. Is there something wrong with me?"

"No, Arrayah! You are incredible. I love that you are able to tell me these things. I feel the same way."

"I am tired of routine. I'm not even sure if God is responsible for everything anymore. What if we can control our own existence from now on, free from rules and restrictions?"

They were coming to the end of the tunnel, so Gabriel grabbed her by the hand, flying fast and pulling her along. She let him lead her. They eventually shot through the water to the other side, which was the Granite Falls. They flew directly toward a massive slab of granite on the other side. At the last possible moment, he turned upward, their feathers brushing the rock face as they rushed past. Arrayah gave out a small scream.

Gabriel erupted with laughter. "Did I frighten you? I'm sorry."

She clasped his hand and did an immediate turn, now dragging him behind her. He was still laughing. She dove straight back down into the falls. They were picking up speed.

"So you didn't appreciate my joke. Let's go enjoy that blue some more."

She kept going without any acknowledgement she had heard him. They shot down the first tier, the second tier, all the way down until they neared the water.

"Arrayah—"

She lunged forward faster, clutching his hand.

"Wait!"

Right before they hit the water, she let go and twisted away and up. He struck the water at high speed and plunged into its cool depths, the roar of the falling water like muted thunder around him. He shot down so deeply that it took him a couple of minutes to make his way back to the surface. When he popped up and wiped the water from his eyes, he saw her hovering over him, dry as ever and looking quite pleased with herself.

Gabriel was not fond of water, and he was probably the worst swimmer in Heaven. He came up frazzled and gasping for air, yet seeing her self-satisfied smirk, he couldn't help but start laughing again.

She was unlike any angel he had ever met. He flew out of the water, his wet wings beating hard and showering spray. Before she could withdraw, he gave her a big, wet hug.

"Ugh!" She tried to push him away, but he locked his arms and soaked her as she struggled. "Gabriel!" Then she gave in and started giggling. Their feathers dripped all over. She stopped trying to push him away, and his arms loosened but remained around her. He felt like he was meant to protect her. She fit into his arms like she had been molded out of his body. Like they had once been separated and were finally reconnected.

"Now we're even," Arrayah said at last as she pushed him gently away.

"Oh yeah, we're real even," said Gabriel. "I get hurled ten leagues deep in the sea and you get a wet hug. That sounds about right." He shook his wings to dry them out.

She started to chuckle again. "That's what happens when you mistreat me. So where are you wanting to take me now, you brute?"

"You will see," he said in a deep, mysterious tone. She rolled her eyes but smiled. Gabriel realized how comfortable they were becoming around each other. It surprised him. It just felt right.

"You can take me to your favorite spot tomorrow," Arrayah said. "It's my turn, and there is someone I'd like for you to meet. Right now, actually."

"That's fine with me. Who are we meeting?" She was already planning to see him again. This was wonderful.

"You will see," she said, imitating his deep, mysterious voice. She giggled again.

"You're just cracking yourself up, aren't you?"

She grabbed his hand, and they flew up a mile to catch speed. Then they tore straight back through the cave that led them there, dodging crystals and hugging the turns. When they emerged at the Marble Falls, she kept up their speed and shot straight through the falling water.

She then dragged him straight down into the water—seven tiers down. They plunged deeper than Gabriel had ever gone until all was lost in darkness. This was not his idea of fun, and he held tightly to her hand. Their momentum carried them forward into the black water until they came out on the other side into the cosmos. Gabriel's anxiety melted away as he took in the dots of distant light, the endless vastness of space, and the beautiful orbs suspended in view as far as he could see. It was like nothing he had imagined.

"Have you ever been here?" she asked, watching his reaction.

"No. I had no idea." A mass of glowing rock tumbled into his vision, trailing a glowing tail of phosphorescence. Amazing.

"Those lights are called stars. That's a comet passing by. There is much I can teach you about all of this and how it came to be, but I want you to meet someone first. He is on the planet called Terra." She pointed at a green-and-blue sphere with subtle shades of white.

"What is a planet?"

"You will see soon."

"I can't wait. Let's go."

With Gabriel close behind, Arrayah flew toward Terra. He tried to take it all in, but every time he slowed, she urged him forward. The planet was mostly blue, yet they headed for a green area. As they entered the atmosphere, Gabriel saw a land mass rushing up at him, and as they drew closer, he made out what seemed to be a hundred angels scattered across the ground. A decent-sized group was huddled around one particular angel. He looked familiar.

"Arrayah, is that Lucifer, the great cherub?"

"Yes, it is. He is the one I want you to meet."

"You're joking."

"No, I'm not."

He could not believe he was going to meet the mighty Lucifer. What would he possibly say to him? "He has so many listening to him. We shouldn't interrupt." Gabriel straightened his chest plate with his free hand.

"Don't be silly."

They flew in closer, heading toward the back of the crowd surrounding Lucifer. Arrayah landed with a smooth tuck of her wings, and Gabriel dropped down beside her. The crowd had turned to watch them.

"Lucifer," she shouted. "I have someone I would like you to meet."

Lucifer was by far the most famous angel in Heaven. Gabriel was surprised that he wasn't much bigger in person. His performances were so bold and unforgettable and his reputation and popularity so massive. Up close, it was evident that Lucifer was only a fraction taller than Gabriel, if at all. He was even leaner.

Gabriel and Arrayah walked directly up to Lucifer, and the crowd between them scattered. Lucifer put on a welcoming smile.

"You must be Gabriel! I have heard so much about you. It is an honor to meet you."

Lucifer lowered his head with respect and reached out a hand. Gabriel couldn't believe that the anointed guardian cherub would bow to him and shake his hand. He also couldn't believe Lucifer had heard of him. Gabriel's stomach clenched, and he worried his palm was sweaty.

"The pleasure is all mine, sir, believe me." Gabriel bowed his head as well, then shook the cherub's hand.

"Saraquel has told me great things about you. He says you are a leader amongst the archangels."

Gabriel couldn't hide his surprise. "Saraquel has? Well, I don't know about how true it all is. Michael is more of the archangel leader than I am."

"Humility. You brought us a good one, Arrayah. I am looking for a leader right now, Gabriel. I'm looking for someone like you in this time of the angels."

"Time of the angels" caught Gabriel's attention. He liked the sound of that. "What do you mean?"

"Have you not heard?"

Gabriel looked at him blankly.

"Have you not told him, Arrayah, of the new heavenly order?"

Saraquel appeared out of the crowd and saw Gabriel. Saraquel was obviously not expecting to see him. "Gabriel, I see you have met Lucifer." A proud, pious look followed on Saraquel's face.

"Saraquel, did you not tell Gabriel of how we have been deceived?" Lucifer asked.

"I feared he would not listen to me, great Lucifer. I thought it better for him to hear directly from you, the highest of all angels." Saraquel gave a chilling smile.

Gabriel was starting to feel uncomfortable and turned to Arrayah for affirmation. She looked happy and nodded to him with assurance. His body warmed, and he relaxed his tense shoulders.

"Please, tell me more Lucifer. I have an open mind. What do you mean we've all been deceived?"

"I'll let Lucifer explain," Saraquel said. "I am—"

"Good," interrupted Gabriel. "I was speaking to Lucifer anyway."

Lucifer laughed. Saraquel colored and slowly closed his mouth.

A few more angels had flocked over to hear what was going on. It made Gabriel feel important to be talking with Lucifer in front of so many. All eyes were upon the great cherub.

"Gabriel, I'm sure you must be confused, and I'm sure there are others who are confused here as well." Lucifer turned his gaze from Gabriel to the many angels around and raised his voice. "It is time that what I have discovered be revealed to all. God's light has dimmed, and it is no secret why. He is scared." He paused a moment before stating it again. "Yes, I have said it. He is scared because He knows all too well that we have caught on to His lies. Yes—God is unfortunately a liar."

A murmur went through the crowd. Lucifer seemed to make personal eye contact with every angel around him. He had a way of making angels feel important, acknowledging everyone, and Gabriel enjoyed it despite himself. He hadn't felt important in a long time. Lucifer was so charismatic; he was inspiring the angels even without words.

"Yes, He has lied about who He is and where we have all come from. Look around you. All that you see was created recently. He would tell you that it was created for a purpose under His divine will, that He created it all." Lucifer stressed the word "He" with mocking deference. "But I will tell you that is not the truth."

How did Lucifer know so much Gabriel wondered. He had been studying the universe all this time while Gabriel sat around eating. That was how.

"All matter was condensed into one spot and then eventually exploded. That is how this was all created, and it has become an ever-expanding universe. God was not here to see this happen, but I was. I saw it with my own eyes. God was nowhere to be found."

Could this be true? Why would God's highest angel say this if it wasn't real? Gabriel looked around him to see how other angels were reacting. Most looked startled but accepting.

"This was not something of God's creation like He would have you believe. He wants all of us to stay ignorant to facts and laws of the universe so that He can invoke words like faith and trust. He thinks we will not question Him. Well, fortunately, I can no longer be fooled! I have discovered many of God's secrets, and many more are revealed to me each day. The more I find out, the more I will share with all of you. God has been exposed."

The crowd's attention stayed locked on Lucifer. Barely a sound could be heard. "I have become too smart for God's complacency, and He was not prepared for that as He is so wrapped up with His so-called Son's forthcoming. I will bring you all up with me! We will leave Him and His Son behind. He wanted us to be in captivity forever, and now He dares to announce a Son that will be above us all. After all we have done for Him! You must ask yourself one question: 'Where did God come from?'"

Lucifer paused a moment. Gabriel could hear whispers and mumbling spreading among the angels. He saw faces that varied from confusion to disbelief, fright to excitement. Lucifer seemed in total control, and Gabriel couldn't believe what he was hearing.

"Where did God come from?" Lucifer repeated slowly. "He is no better than we are. He wants us to believe He has always been, but how can something be if it was never created? I tell you this, my friends: it is impossible. We will no longer fall for His trickery! God is a liar!" Lucifer shook his fist toward Heaven.

The concept of a deceitful God was awe-inspiring to some of the angels and downright frightening to others. While some stayed in silent shock, many angels, including some who were high ranking, began to chant, "No more lies!"

Gabriel was alarmed to see how many were already supporting this movement. Many of these were from the hierarchs, including cherubim, thrones, virtues, and dominions. He thought of Michael's warning, and his stomach clenched again. He looked at Arrayah and saw she was watching him.

"I know it's much to take in all at once," she said.

Gabriel kept his thoughts to himself. He might not know a lot, but he knew when to keep his mouth closed.

"What do you think?" Arrayah prodded. "It makes complete sense, right?"

Gabriel still didn't speak. He turned away from her to Lucifer, who was continuing his speech.

"We have gained so much ground in such a short time. You are the leaders, and there are countless angels back in Heaven who need your guidance. They are ready to join us in the quest for truth. I want every angel in Heaven to be given the chance to understand and decide what is right, so spread the word. Tell your loved ones, tell your friends, tell those you don't even know. Don't cheat any angel out of the truth. The new heavenly order will soon take its power, and God's hierarchy will be replaced. The most loyal will be at the top, nearest to me. Those who choose to remain His followers will grovel next to Him and continue to be nothing but servants! I will raise my throne—our throne—far above His!"

Gabriel felt sick and excited all at the same time. It went against everything he had ever known or believed. It felt wrong to the very core, yet when he saw the proud look on Arrayah's face, he saw a future. Until he met her, he didn't have one. Although Terra's beauty was nothing compared to Heaven's, it felt brighter than Heaven ever could. It was imperfect and wild. It smelled dirty and alive. It smelled amazing.

"He is the Great Deceiver and will no longer reign over us! But I tell you He is very powerful, so we must be smart. We need to have the majority of angels behind us. There is power in numbers, and there is little time. I challenge you to speak to as many as you can; we will convene back here in three days. Bring everyone you can, and together we can reach the millions of angels in Heaven. We will no longer be deceived!" He shot one fist in the air, and many angels cheered.

The crowd of angels scattered, many flying toward the heavens to recruit new members to their fold. Gabriel knew that Lucifer's words were what many angels thought but dared not express. Most angels deep down wanted talents or gifts they never received, whether in music, the arts, hobbies, recreation, or sports. Every angel had unique gifts, but Heaven's most-talented angel expressed discontent for the first time in paradise and Gabriel was able to witness it firsthand. A path had just been paved for angels to look at their own desires and decide what they were missing.

Gabriel had always wanted to be more than a lowly archangel as did many others in low rank, but God had made him for a reason. Gabriel had always believed that. Although he wanted more from time to time, his belief gave him a contentment and sense of worth that he could not deny. The idea that any angel could be more was undeniably appealing; it certainly was to him. He understood how they felt. But it was wrong, wasn't it? The knots in his stomach cinched tighter.

He had just witnessed Lucifer make this crowd of angels feel as if they could be the masters of their own lives. Pockets of angels remained, chattering excitedly. It had all spawned from Lucifer's enthusiasm and declaration of this new truth. Could it be truth? Gabriel wondered as he watched angels practically knock each other over to get started spreading the message as if there was a reward for the one who came back with the most converts. Maybe there would be. Heaven would never be the same. This both relieved and terrified him.

After most of the angels had gone, Lucifer noticed Gabriel still standing with Arrayah in silence. Gabriel didn't know how to react. Lucifer shook out his intimidating wingspan and walked elegantly over to Gabriel, a dominion flanking him on either side. Lucifer was the perfect specimen. Who wouldn't want to follow this angel?

"I would like to offer you a special place in my court as a favor to both Arrayah and Saraquel, who have both spoken highly of you. I will make you one of my top angels should you choose to join us. I have heard of your talents in the art of battle. I feel you would be a valuable asset to my court, so I have my selfish reasons as well."

Lucifer made subtle gestures with his hands as he spoke, his body language starting to put Gabriel at ease. Lucifer was very smooth and charming, but Gabriel didn't like to be manipulated. He had so much going through his head at that moment he actually felt dizzy. "Your offer is indeed a great honor, Lucifer."

"Then accept it." Lucifer smiled.

"This is all very fast. Will you allow me a day or so to think about it? This is the first I am hearing of all of this." Gabriel knew that he might be passing up the greatest opportunity ever handed to him even by asking for an extension. Still, this was not only too good to be true, but he still believed in God with all his heart. Arrayah didn't seem to anymore though, and he couldn't just walk away from her. Not now.

"By all means," Lucifer said. "In fact, you and Arrayah should go discuss the things you have heard today. I'm sure she will be able to answer any questions. She is one of the smartest angels among us. I want nothing less than a decision solely from you, without my influence."

Gabriel's gaze had shifted to Arrayah at the mention of her name. As Lucifer spoke, Gabriel noticed a discreet wink the cherub sent to her. Gabriel saw the gesture reflected in the helmet of one of the dominions. It made Gabriel wonder how close Arrayah and Lucifer really were, and it sent an empty feeling through him.

"I appreciate all of this," Gabriel managed to say.

"You are welcome, young archangel. Until next time."

"Yes, until next time."

Lucifer started to turn around and then snapped his fingers and pivoted back. "Wait. Just a moment, please. I spoke to Saraquel earlier, and he told me of an angel that is very troubled by what we are doing here. I don't believe he understands what is happening. Should you decide to join us, it may be wise if you educate him, for I heard he listens to you and trusts you a great deal. I believe his name is Michael."

The empty feeling expanded, filling him inside. "Yes, Michael is a dear friend." He faced Saraquel. "Have you spoken of this with him?"

"I did, and he wasn't very pleased with me." Saraquel's scratchy voice was grating. "He told me that the order of things is not to be questioned and that God is bringing him up as a leader of the archangels. He was bragging about it. I know I offended you earlier and for that I am sorry, but I believe Michael is only looking out for himself. I felt that I must warn you."

It was true that Michael could be ridiculous at times with his ambition and strict rules, but he wouldn't be bragging. He was just as likely to lie around all day eating spiritapples. Why was Saraquel lying? Regardless, Gabriel had to keep calm. The wink had him shaken up, and listening to Saraquel's irritating voice wasn't helping things. He turned back to Lucifer. "I will speak with Michael about all of this, and I will have an answer for you soon, Lucifer. Thank you for this opportunity."

"Please do. I wouldn't want an archangel trying to start a fight against me. I believe he is trying to do just that."

"I will find out. Shall I meet you here when I have my answer?"

"Arrayah will know where to find me. I will see you then. You are a fine archangel, Gabriel. It was a pleasure."

Lucifer turned to speak to the few remaining angels who were waiting for him, and Gabriel addressed Arrayah. "I need to go think. Maybe I should see you tomorrow." He couldn't help wondering if Michael could have been right about not trusting her. He didn't like this feeling at all.

"You don't have to explain." Her voice was soft and understanding. "Would you like to meet tomorrow at the Provender so you can show me your favorite place in all of Heaven? All of this didn't make you forget, did it?" She moved closer to him and smiled.

He thought of the wink and almost told her he had to cancel. But those alluring blue eyes were staring at him with an innocence that weakened him. His words came out in spite of himself. "Yes. I will meet you at the Provender, same time."

"I can't wait," she said, almost too enthusiastically.

Gabriel fixed a smile on his face and took off toward the cosmos. He needed to find Michael immediately.

XIII

Lucifer was on Terra, walking back and forth on a grassy rise that would serve as a makeshift platform. Later that day, he would be holding a meeting with the angels of the upper tiers. He was expecting seven seraphim, twenty-five cherubim, sixteen thrones, and one virtue in attendance—exactly forty-nine angels from the top four orders. It would be Lucifer's first large gathering about the changes to come. He imagined them spread out on the field, watching and listening in rapt attention. He paced on the grass and practiced his speech, rehearsing the words in his head so they could come without thought. This had to go perfectly.

From the corner of his eye, Lucifer saw Arrayah's shimmering gown as she floated down from the sky. She landed softly and sauntered directly toward him.

"It's lovely to see you, Arrayah."

"I need to speak with you."

"Let us talk in depth after the meeting. I am busy now. Have you done what I asked?"

"Yes. I'm meeting him at the gate today. I believe he is falling for me."

"Is there an angel who wouldn't?"

Arrayah lowered her chin and her eyelids closed. "He trusts me."

"I chose to partner with you for a reason. The power of beauty cannot be questioned."

"You would know even better than I. Is there anything more powerful?"

"I believe there are seven more powerful."

"Our virtues?"

"All in due time. You have many gifts, Arrayah. Use them. Don't come back without him." Lucifer began to pace again and waved a hand in her direction. "You are dismissed."

Arrayah turned to leave, and Lucifer once more pictured the crowd before him—their anger, their disbelief, their skepticism, but also their hope. Their hunger for something more. He had already spoken one-on-one to most of the angels who would likely attend, and now he was gaining momentum as the word spread. There would be some who thought he was wrong, some who just wanted to hear what was going on to stay in the loop, some who had a slight interest but needed to hear more, and some who were completely on board with full support.

By the time the day had passed and the meeting time had arrived, he was fully prepared. His armor gleamed. He stood tall and straight. He was what every angel aspired to be.

At the appointed hour, the crowd of angels all stood near each other, engaged in debates and endless chatter. Lucifer waited to begin while angels descended from the sky. He continued to wait until the suspense was at its peak. "Welcome, everyone!" He smiled and spread his arms wide as if humbled by the attendance. "I'm happy to see so many familiar faces. I would like to thank each and every one of you for coming. It is an absolute honor to see you here."

He put a hand to his chin and appeared thought-ful, then raised his head and took a deep breath. "I know many of you have heard things that may have come as a shock to you. They may have frightened you, they may have interested you, but I hope they have inspired you."

Some angels looked around in confusion. Others seemed appalled. But many were nodding along.

"I am no different from any of you and I don't claim to be. There is only One who does claim to be better than you. I hope what you have heard has inspired you to demand the truth—whether it is good or not. I didn't invite you here to tell you how to think. I invited you here to answer questions and openly discuss something that affects each and every one of us. Something we have never questioned. Ever. It comes down to this: is God who He says He is?'"

Lucifer pointed to Heaven and began to pace. The audience was mesmerized. "I, for one, don't know if I still believe Him. All I know are the facts. Facts of existence that He tells us He invented. Why is it that the more we find out and the wiser we become about this universe and the way things work, the more discredited His words become? Everything must have a beginning, yet apparently the laws of the universe don't apply to Him. Do any of you know why that could be?"

Lucifer dropped his hand, stopped pacing, and fell silent while he scanned the crowd with challenging eyes. After a few moments of pure silence, a seraph named Abbeus spoke up. "Since He is our creator, we must have faith in Him. He created the laws of the universe, so they are as He would have them be, and they don't really apply to Him."

Lucifer scanned the faces in the crowd. "That is a good point. I know many who feel that way. How many of you have felt the same way?" He raised his own hand. "I know I have. Anybody else?" Hands started rising in the air. "It's the normal way to think because that is what He has always told us. But what we have all found is that faith can be based on ignorance."

Lucifer looked straight at Abbeus. "What if I told you that I was here before God? Would you believe me?"

"Of course not," Abbeus huffed.

"What if I said that tree over there has always been there, but it never grew from a seed?"

"Well, I guess it could be possible. But I've never seen anything like that."

"Neither have any of us. But God wants us to believe that He has always been here without ever beginning. He wants us to believe in impossibilities of the universe that we have never seen. We must not be ignorant enough to ignore the truths that stare us in the face. We must at least question His story."

"But God made everything around us! His words have confirmed it, and it is evident in the beauty and miracle of all of creation. It is wrong to not believe it!" The words Abbeus yelled from the front of the crowd were voicing the concerns of the entire audience.

The next moments, Lucifer knew, would be critical. "I'm not telling you what to believe. I'm telling you to think for yourselves as strong, intelligent angels. God is the one telling you what to believe. What is your name, my good angel?"

"Abbeus."

"You are a seraph, correct? So you are near God all the time?"

"Yes, I am."

"And all day you worship God and you do nothing for yourself. That's right, isn't it?"

"Well, praising God gives me fulfillment. He is the reason for my existence."

"That makes sense. He must do things for you with all that praise you give Him. What does He do for you exactly?"

"He gives me life, light, and glory. I get the honor of serving Him. I get to be near Him."

"I'm asking what He does for you personally."

"This is absurd. God does not need to do anything personally for me."

"Why not? You have devoted your life to Him."

"Well, He really doesn't do anything for me only. I do speak to Him though."

"I see. How often do you and God have face-to-face conversations?"

Abbeus didn't respond immediately. He finally answered, "Not often. God is in the heart and soul of every faithful soldier at all times. God surrounds us and is a part of us."

Lucifer nodded compassionately, his words silken. "Well, He is quite busy, so that makes sense. Just estimate it for us since you are closer to Him most of the time than we all are."

"I really don't know. He speaks to me in my head quite often."

Some of the lower-ranking angels looked at Abbeus with wonder, but Lucifer laughed lightheartedly. "I don't mean in your head. Of course, you know how often you speak in person."

Abbeus looked around at the angels near him. Finally in a quiet voice, he said, "Never."

Lucifer gasped theatrically in unison with the crowd. Abbeus awkwardly looked away. Lucifer shook his head in mock disbelief. After a moment, he solemnly observed, "I'm sure He has His reasons." He met the seraph's eyes with his. "Right?"

Abbeus lowered his head. Immediately, a voice rang out from the crowd. "He doesn't even speak directly with the seraphim?"

Angels broke off into their own conversations amongst each other, and Lucifer lost control of the crowd. This was exactly what he wanted. Abbeus slowly made his way up toward Lucifer. When he got close enough, he whispered with his perfect white teeth exposed. "How was that?"

"Perfect, Abbeus. You will have your reward in my ranks."

A familiar voice called out. "Lucifer! I have someone I would like you to meet." Lucifer turned from Abbeus toward the two he most hoped to see. It was Arrayah and a rather large archangel—Gabriel. As always, she had perfect timing.

What followed went exactly as Lucifer had predicted—Gabriel unwittingly played his part as beautifully as Abbeus had. Their conversation led into the real speech he had prepared. When he was finished, the sky was full of angels flying toward Heaven, rushing to spread the word and recruit new converts. Gabriel seemed reluctant to join, and he asked for an additional day to consider the offer, but he would come around. Lucifer had faith in Arrayah's powers of persuasion. Once he had Gabriel, Michael would soon follow—or be crushed and cast aside.

Lucifer turned to speak to the other angels who were waiting for him, but he couldn't help but notice the way Arrayah looked at Gabriel. It was the way Thyaterra had always looked at him. The look that made him feel invincible. He used to get this feeling from God.

Gabriel left, flying back toward Heaven, and Lucifer excused himself from the remaining angels. He headed toward Arrayah and took her by the arm to guide her off to one side. "You have done very well. With his fighting prowess, Gabriel will be a great asset to our cause. I'm sure his reputation is accurate."

"I think he saw you wink at me."

"No, he didn't. What makes you think that?"

"I don't know. Sometimes I feel like I've known him forever."

He folded his arms. He towered over her. "What does that mean?"

"Nothing."

Was she getting soft on him? At his unflinching appraisal, she sucked in a breath and lifted her chin. The look of anxiety was gone.

"It is fine," he said at length. "He is perfect for our little problem with Michael."

"Gabriel has become fond of me very quickly. But he's not as ignorant and easily manipulated as I had originally thought. Now I'm not sure he is the best way to go about getting to Michael." She hesitated. "I don't want to hurt him unnecessarily, Lucifer."

Lucifer's arms tightened, his fingers digging into his biceps. "I will decide if something is no longer the best way. And please don't tell me he matters to you. Are you not still with me?"

She looked conflicted. Was she going to be a problem?

"Of course, I am," she said. She pried away one of his hands, held it in her own, and smiled.

She was cunning, and it infuriated Lucifer that she thought she could manipulate him. But he needed her skills turned on Gabriel. He would let it pass. "Good. You know how important you are to me." He went in closer to her and touched the soft skin below her chin. Her skin flushed. "I need you, Arrayah. We are so close to our revolution."

XIV

The next day Gabriel met Arrayah by the flowing green grass of the Provender. He wasn't as ecstatic as the day before. The sky had darkened, and an ominous, hollowed-out feeling was overtaking him.

"God's light has certainly dimmed," he said by way of greeting.

"Maybe God is abandoning us," she said.

"It's possible, but it feels more like we are abandoning Him."

"How have you been since yesterday?"

"Come with me." He took her by the wrist and leaped up, wings unfurling. She barely had time to extend her own and flap them in time with his. He let go after a few seconds, and they drifted apart to soar, wingtips almost touching. They flew over the grounds where the Paradise Games were held. The fields and arenas took up over five hundred miles. He loved it here, taking in the sweet air, and he started to feel better. For a moment, his troubling thoughts went away completely.

They didn't say a word—only looked at each other every now and then. Gabriel finally started descending near an opening hidden in an enormous grove of trees. From above, they could see miles of trees laden with fruit, and beyond these were rows of vegetables and giant patches of flowers all neatly separated into their own areas across the ravine. Their arrangement was impeccable. Unlike the imperfections of Terra, everything here was orderly and pristine.

"Have you ever noticed the order of all of these?"

"I have never really thought about it, but now that you say it, they are perfect," she said.

"Isn't it amazing? They are all grown in their own specific place for a purpose—all the pears next to pears, all the spiritapples next to spiritapples. Everything is meant to be exactly where it is."

"It's pretty spectacular to look at."

They hovered close to the ground next to a gap between trees.

"Follow me," said Gabriel.

As they landed, he walked her through a path that was not easily spotted from the air. They were amidst orange trees and were near the place where Michael had first spoken of his dream.

"These are my favorite of all the foods and fruits of Heaven. Would you like one?" As he said it, two white rabbits hopped away from his regular tree.

"Oh, cute. Sure, I'll try one," she said. "Why do you like oranges so much?"

He grabbed two, peeled them, and handed her one. He walked slowly, and she followed through the grove. The sharp, sweet scent of citrus was thick in the air, and the branches created a canopy overhead.

"Well, they are delicious, first of all. And they are juicy, sweet, and easy to eat."

"Nice. Did you come up with that yourself?" She was smiling.

"Certainly." He tried to sound playful in return, but it was not coming easily today.

"Is that it? I mean, I agree they are really good." She bit out a juicy chunk. "But there are many amazing fruits in Heaven."

"There's another reason too. Come here."

He led her to an iron bench situated in the middle of the grove. The bench was simple and unadorned, a rarity in Heaven. He had put it here, in his favorite place, a long time ago. He spent more time here than in his own home.

They sat there on the bench for a little while eating their oranges and smiling back and forth. She laughed when he bit into his orange and juice squirted into his eye.

After he wiped his eye, he looked at her and knew his grin said it all. He couldn't help enjoying himself around her.

"Come over here. I want to show you the other reason I love oranges." He walked her even farther down the path, which was becoming narrower. It was still surrounded by perfectly symmetrical trees heavily laden with fruit.

"You have noticed the layout of this grove, with the fruits, flowers, and vegetables all being in their places, right?" said Gabriel.

"Right."

"I've spent much time in all of these fields and orchards. Each of these trees or plants is in its designated spot and none are mixed with other kinds. Just like with the angels and how our order of things has always been until recently."

"I'm sure it was that way for a reason at one time. Hopefully, things are changing."

"Well, the oranges are much like you and me." Gabriel stepped to the side and revealed something unique.

That little, remote corner of the grove yielded a small bush with three flowers. One was red, one pink, and one white. It was completely encircled by orange trees. Arrayah gasped when she saw it. No other flowers were even on that side of the ravine, much less in the middle of an orange grove. It shouldn't be there. It was an imperfection in Heaven.

"They are absolutely beautiful!" exclaimed Arrayah, almost breathless.

"I think everything is meant to have its place. Some are just meant to be different. I don't believe it is a mistake like some would think."

She stood there taking in the remarkable flowers. "I agree with you. What are they?"

"I don't know. In a place full of the most magnificent fruit in Heaven, a lowly type of flower found its way to grow in their company. It is nowhere else in Heaven to my knowledge."

"I have never seen or heard of it either." Arrayah stooped down to smell one. She breathed in, and her eyes closed.

"The oranges took these flowers in, and that is why I love them. They exist to be themselves and grow where they have been planted though it seems an unlikely home." He smiled. "I come here all the time to remind myself that maybe I have a place too. Maybe I'm an imperfect type of flower."

He picked one of the flowers and accidentally pricked his finger on one of the thorns. He grimaced and handed it to her carefully. "These are the only ones I know of in Heaven. Do you want to give them a name?"

She peered at the odd thorns and then poked one, reacting the same way as Gabriel and jerking her finger back. "Yes."

"What will you name them?"

She reached for Gabriel and slid an arm around his waist. "Well, I see it like this. I think the flower needs to get more credit. The flower found a way to thrive away from its natural place, to be with the oranges when others couldn't. It rose up by itself to be something different. Something amazing."

Gabriel hoped she was talking about him as well as the flower, but in the back of his mind, he thought she might be referring to Lucifer. He couldn't get the wink out of his head. He was getting lost in unpleasant thoughts when she spoke again.

"I will name it rose," she said, touching one softly. "Just like you rose up from the lowest tier to become a leader in our new ranks. These are roses just like you." She tapped his nose with her finger. "What do you think?"

He couldn't help but smile. "I think it's a beautiful name."

"You know what else I noticed?"

Gabriel moved his hands slowly down her sides. She was so delicate underneath that silky dress. Blood was racing through his veins and his heart sped up, but he did his best to keep his voice level. "What?"

"This rose has thorns to protect itself because it's fragile, so one must be careful with it."

He was sure she was talking about more than the rose at this point. "Not everything needs to protect itself.

Sometimes others are meant to protect." She was shaking slightly, and he could feel it. He wondered if she felt him tremble too. "Just as I will always protect you." Her guard was down, it was clear in her eyes, and she was as lost in the moment as he was. Her eyes drifted shut, and the rose slipped from her fingers as she leaned toward him. They kissed. They kissed for a long time. This was the best moment of his existence. Better than his first victory in the games. Even better than the first time he met his best friend.

"Gabriel! Gabriel, are you in there?"

Ironically, that same friend's voice ended this moment. Arrayah and Gabriel separated, and Arrayah stood there in a stupor as his arms withdrew. She really did care for him. It was obvious from the way she looked up at him. She had to know he would always be there for her, and the wink from Lucifer must have meant nothing. She felt what they were building between them too.

"Gabriel, can you hear me?"

"I'm sorry," Gabriel said quietly to Arrayah.

"Don't be," she whispered.

"Maybe we should ignore him."

"Yes, maybe we should. Do you know who it is?"

"It's Michael."

"Oh." She perked up with a more serious look. The moment was gone. "You should answer him."

Gabriel turned from her with a little disappointment. He knew she was right although he thought it odd she changed her mind so quickly. "I am over here, Michael."

After a few more shouts back and forth, Michael found them.

"There you are," Michael said. He saw Gabriel was with someone. "Excuse me; I am sorry. I didn't know you had company."

"No problem. I wanted you two to meet properly anyway." As Michael got closer, Gabriel said, "Michael, meet Arrayah again. Arrayah, this is Michael. Maybe we can get along this time and not drive her away." Gabriel laughed, hoping to cut the tension.

Michael and Arrayah walked toward each other, and he reached out for her hand to shake it. When they locked eyes again, Michael froze just as he had done by the reef. He seemed almost petrified all over again.

"Are you all right?" she asked. Gabriel was sure she was used to angels staring at her because of her beauty, but Michael's stare was so intense that it rapidly became awkward. He turned away from her but had yet to look Gabriel in the eyes.

"Excuse me. Yes, it is an honor to see you again," Michael mustered.

"Michael, is something the matter? You acted like this the last time you met Arrayah."

"Oh, no. I'm fine and all is well."

"Are you sure?"

"Yes, it is no problem. I mean there is no problem." It wasn't like Michael to stumble over his words. Gabriel didn't believe it. Michael had become nervous.

"Well, I have heard a lot about you, Michael. Gabriel tells me you are his best friend, and I'm glad we can talk peacefully this time."

Michael had been looking at the ground, the orange trees, the newly named rose, anything and everything except Arrayah or Gabriel. Gabriel looked back at her to see if she had noticed.

"I would say Gabriel and I are more like brothers than just best friends. I will always look after his best interest." Then, finally looking at Gabriel, Michael said, "I am the older, wiser one."

Arrayah returned his smile, and Gabriel shook his head. "Older and more boring, you mean." They all laughed, and the awkwardness of the moment was gone.

"I'll give you that," Michael said.

"So what are you doing out here, Michael?" Arrayah asked.

"I hate to interrupt you two, but there is something I would actually like to speak with Gabriel about in private. Would you mind?"

"Oh, no, go ahead. I don't mind at all."

"Are you sure?" Gabriel asked.

"Positive."

Gabriel and Michael walked down the path toward the gap in the trees where he had entered. They stopped just before exiting by one of the hedge arches that served as entrances to the many miles of crops. Michael pulled Gabriel aside by his collar. His body language changed instantly.

"Gabriel, the time is upon us. God's light has dimmed, and there is a great separation amongst all of the angels of Heaven." Michael pointed up to the Great Mountain. The light of God was so altered. It was as if God was now gone and the afterglow was all that remained to light Heaven.

Arrayah's words came out of Gabriel. "Maybe God has left us."

"Gabriel, He would never leave us. He will be with us for eternity no matter what."

Gabriel wasn't so sure anymore. He wished he still felt Michael's confidence.

"I need your help, Gabriel."

"With what?"

"I'm starting a resistance group of angels for God. Something bad is happening in Heaven, and we need to do something about it now. God is going to need his loyal followers united."

"We are just archangels, Michael. We are the second lowest of the nine orders in case your big head has forgotten. What could we possibly do?"

"I know what we are. We are still angels just like all of the hierarchs that you praise more than your own Father."

"I don't praise them! I respect them. There's a big difference."

"You have always wanted to be like them. You want to be something important, Gabriel? You already are; the only one who doesn't know that is you. Well, here's your chance to finally prove it to yourself. Join me, and let's lead Heaven back to God."

"I can't right now, Michael."

"You have something more important?" He frowned and lowered his voice. "You are my brother no matter how much we argue. You know this, don't you?"

"I love you, Michael, but I can't join you right now."

"You won't is what you mean."

"You couldn't possibly understand." Gabriel couldn't abandon Arrayah or ignore Lucifer. His mind was all twisted up about what was right and wrong. He simply didn't know anymore.

"Gabriel, God told me to find you. I am here to help you."

"I don't need your help."

"Well, I need yours, Gabriel. There's something else I have to tell you too, but I need you to stay calm."

"I'm calm. Go on."

"It's Arrayah."

"What about her?" Gabriel could feel the hairs on his forearm stand on end.

"You are in danger. She is not to be trusted."

"You don't know anything about her. Don't start this again." Gabriel unsuccessfully tried to clear a lump in his throat.

"You have to trust me, Gabriel. I'm telling you the truth. God sent me here to protect you; I know that now."

"From Arrayah? You have to be kidding."

"Just listen to me. We need to leave."

"No, you need to leave. I knew you would act like this because you have no one. Even Lucifer knows that you have no one but me, and he has never even met you! You are just jealous of me, and I'm telling you to stop acting like this!" He immediately regretted talking about Lucifer. However, it actually felt good to reveal that he met the highest angel in all of Heaven. For once, he felt more important than Michael.

"Lucifer? What does he have to do with this?" Michael straightened and backed a step away from Gabriel.

"Yes, Lucifer. I have met the great cherub. He has some interesting things to say, and they aren't just some made up warnings about what God has shown him. Have you ever thought that God may be lying to us, Michael?"

"Is that what the highest cherub of all the angels told you? Does the betrayal go that high?" Michael's shoulders and hands dropped to his sides. He closed his eyes and began to pace and rub his temples.

"I'm not going to talk about it right now, but let's just say I have the chance to be far more than an archangel if things are to change."

"This is so much worse than I thought." Michael walked right up to Gabriel and grabbed his arms. "Gabriel, you need to be wise and listen to your heart. You know what is right. God is our Creator, and He has set rules for the angels—just, fair rules for the best for all of us. There will be consequences for this betrayal. Don't you see? You have to see that!"

Gabriel jerked away from Michael's grip. "Maybe I'm sick of rules! Maybe I don't want to be controlled!"

"Gabriel, they are there for our own good as well as everyone else's. You know this!"

"No. I think they may be there to hold us back. I'm starting to think that Lucifer may be right about God being a liar." Gabriel was surprised to hear himself say that and part of him wanted to take the words back, but they were already out. He hated being pulled in two directions.

Michael was shaking his head in disbelief. "Don't say that. Gabriel, please. Do you hear yourself? God knows what is best for us even when we don't."

"If God is saying that Arrayah is not what is best for me, then He is wrong. I have never been happier in all the years I've been here than I have with her the past two days. She is sweeter than anything Heaven has to offer me anymore. I can't leave with you." With that declaration, Gabriel stared at Michael with all the conviction he could muster.

Michael looked back with compassionate eyes. "I can see how much you care for her. She is the first to capture your heart. I understand. But this is dangerous, and I need you to listen to me. I know something about Arrayah."

"What do you know?"

"Gabriel, I am your brother and I love you." His voice was kind but firm. "I have always only had your best interest at heart and you know that. You've always been able to trust me, and nothing is different now. I need to get you away from her, just for a while, and you need to stay away from Lucifer entirely. She is making you too blind to see the treachery that is going on around you and all over Heaven. She can't be trusted."

Gabriel felt like he was going to burst through his clothes. "Save the concerned brother speech! What do you think you know that I don't?"

"Will you just trust me, please?"

"All I see is that you're trying to be better than everyone, and I think you're jealous of us. How dare you say she can't be trusted? You don't even know her! Now get out of here." Gabriel turned to walk away.

"Gabriel, stop. Stop!" Gabriel stopped but kept his back to Michael. Michael took in a deep breath and continued. "You are right. I don't know her. But I'll tell you what I know about her. I know that God sent me here to help you. I had no idea you would even be here. I was just told to find you. I have never met Arrayah, that is correct, but Gabriel, hear me now: I have seen her before. I wanted to tell you this at the Canyon Reef, but I hoped you would stop seeing her without it."

Gabriel slowly turned around and looked Michael dead in the eyes. Gabriel had no words, but his heart was filled with curiosity and fright. Michael was acting far too gentle for his comfort. Something was very wrong.

"Gabriel," Michael said, "she is the only female from my dream. She is the one that burned."

Gabriel remembered Michael's description of the formerly beautiful angel, charred and crying in a fuming landscape of ash and darkness. He felt as if his knees would buckle, but he managed to keep his stance.

"I could never forget those eyes," Michael continued, "or that face because I watched her transform. She screams in agony and her skin turns black, Gabriel. She loses her beauty and turns into something I've never seen before. Something not of Heaven. It was the worst thing I have ever witnessed. I'm telling you that whatever she does or is doing, she is on the wrong side and I have seen the consequences. And they are severe! She will fall from the grace of God."

Gabriel stood with that same silent stare, taking in everything Michael had said. The cold had taken him over as he pictured Arrayah suffering. He couldn't bear the thought of pain coming to her. He knew who she was, and there was nothing she could do to make her deserve what Michael described. It had to be wrong. Either God was wrong or Michael.

"Go, Michael. Just go."

"Gabriel—"

"No! Leave now before I make you leave!" Gabriel shouted with every last bit of air in his body.

"Gabriel, I only want to help you before it is too late." Michael held an outstretched hand toward Gabriel.

"Help yourself and get out of here while you can!"

Michael sighed and put his hand down. "You must let her go. Only she can save herself, and I won't let her drag you down with her."

"I'm not your responsibility!"

"You are my brother! Arrayah is not your responsibility. If Lucifer is the one in charge of all of this, then she belongs with him and not with you!"

Gabriel lunged forward with fury surging through him. He grabbed Michael's chest armor and with a mighty heave threw him as hard as he could. The strength his anger gave him was greater than anything he had felt.

Michael flew straight back and crashed through the trunk of an orange tree, splintering it into kindling. The impact uprooted it and sent the top of the tree spinning sideways even as Michael continued into the next tree. He smashed through seven trunks before flying through a hedge arch and sliding through the grass some two hundred yards from Gabriel. He very nearly fell off the side of the ravine, but his fingers clawed into the ground and he slid to a halt with his boots dangling off the edge. Gabriel started walking back over to Arrayah before Michael had even come to a stop.

He found her sitting on the bench, hands in her lap and a look of disbelief on her face. "What was that? Are you two fighting again?"

"Sorry. Michael crossed the line." Gabriel was breathing heavily and trying to calm down but didn't know how. He felt tension all over his body. He craved a spiritapple.

"I thought he was your best friend."

"Not anymore."

He leaned over to breathe, hands on his thighs, and Arrayah grabbed him by the shoulders. She gently massaged his neck. "I am sorry, Gabriel. Is there anything I can do?"

Her touch was so soothing. "Yes. Take me to Lucifer. I have made my decision. I'm joining you both."

"I am so happy, Gabriel! I will take you."

"Thank you." Gabriel stared up at the dim throne of God. He wished then that its light would burst forth even if it meant he had chosen wrongly, even if he would face punishment. The light stayed dim. No help was coming.

"Gabriel, I wanted to tell you how much I love this place. I will never forget this day no matter what happens." She grabbed his chin and looked at him. "Are you hearing me, Gabriel?"

"I hear you."

"Thank you so much for the flowers. They will always make me think of you. I want to spread them all over Heaven." She held his face and kissed him again. He loved her soft hands on his skin. She pulled away with a sad smile.

"I will think of you all the time, Arrayah, roses or not. And I will never let anyone hurt you."

"You are a great friend, Gabriel."

"You are more than that to me."

The corner of her mouth twitched, and she peered down before she met his eyes again. "I need to tell you something."

"What is it?"

"I don't know how to say it. I want you to know how much I care for you, but—"

"I have an idea," Gabriel interrupted. He didn't like where this was going, and more stress was the last thing he needed right now. He wanted to focus on the good and forget about Michael, God, and Heaven. He had noticed the rose in her hand. She was holding it close to her heart.

"What is it?"

"Let's meet here after everything changes in Heaven. Let's spread the seeds of these roses as a symbol for everyone to be who they are no matter the circumstances. Let this flower be a symbol of our relationship. Let this bond us together forever."

Arrayah looked at him with a small tear in her eye. "Of course. I would love it."

"Good. I can't wait." At least that was settled. They had a plan for the future—more importantly, they had a future together. Whatever else she had to say, this was decided now. "What did you need to tell me?"

"Oh, I was going to say," she said, then drifted off. Her eyes closed, and she brought the rose to brush against her lips. A soft sigh escaped her. Her eyes opened, and a steely resolve was in them now. "I was just going to say that I'm really proud of you for standing up to Michael like that. I'm glad you considered Lucifer's offer. I'm happy you are joining us."

Something didn't feel right. "Are you sure that's it?"

"Yes. For now." She offered a slight smile and grabbed his hand.

"Let's get out of here."

"I really care about you, Gabriel. Do you know that?"

"I do."

They walked out of the orange trees, and Gabriel looked for Michael. He was gone. He must have left upset, and he must have left quickly because he left the seven uprooted trees on the ground in a heaping mess. That wasn't like Michael. Although Gabriel created the mess, Michael would have still cleaned it up if circumstances were normal.

Gabriel studied the fallen trees with a heart that felt more burdened by the minute, weighted down by every choice he made. Despair welled up from somewhere deep inside. He felt regret and still suspicion too, but he had made his decision. Arrayah squeezed his hand.

"Gabriel," she said, "it's time to stand up for what we believe in."

He didn't know what that was anymore.

XV

G abriel and Arrayah spread their wings and headed over the fields back toward the Marble Falls. They were going to meet Lucifer on Terra. By the time they had made their journey back to the green-and-blue planet, the number of angels gathered there had exponentially increased from the last time. Lucifer's message was spreading like a swift wind in the darkness. It was happening faster than Gabriel had expected. A large factor was the undeniable fact that God's light had dimmed and was continuing to dim with each passing hour. Angels throughout Heaven were seeking answers just like he was. Lucifer's ideas were popular, and what he said seemed to make sense.

Gabriel would have never found Lucifer by himself had Arrayah not known exactly where to go. She led him to a small mountain surrounded on all sides by thousands upon thousands of angels. On the top stood Lucifer, an ominous seraph, and a petite angel who appeared to be a virtue. She was dressed similarly to Arrayah only her gown was a soft pink. As they drew close, Gabriel saw light reflected by the necklace she wore inscribed with her virtue. He should have known her name because the virtues were well known in Heaven, but he didn't.

"Who are those angels with Lucifer?"

Arrayah flapped her wings to slow down and Gabriel caught the gust.

"Those are two of the most influential angels involved with us. They really are inspiring. Abbeus is the seraph in the middle. He is the only seraph God never considered a single year to be one of the four to guard His throne, yet he stayed loyal all this time. It wasn't until he met Lucifer that he even knew how mistreated he was. Lucifer had the giant seraph in tears when he explained why God never used him to represent His throne. Have you ever heard a seraph cry? It's like nothing you've ever heard."

Gabriel thought back to the seraph's voice in his head at the orange grove. She had said her words would soon be forgotten.

"Actually, I have. A seraph spoke to me in my head recently."

"Come on, Gabriel. That doesn't make sense." She looked at him with a questioning stare. "What did it sound like?"

Gabriel closed his eyes and pictured being right back there under his tree. He could smell the citrus in the air and feel the pulp on his forearm. It was like being right back at home, something he longed for right now. "It sounded like a beautiful but sad song."

He opened his eyes to see Arrayah close her mouth. She had heard the exact same from Abbeus. It was written all over her face. She leaned forward and glided toward Terra's rocky surface at the back of the crowd. Gabriel followed her and touched down close, brushing a feather from her right wing.

"Do you know what that voice told me? It was a seraph saying that soon the glory of God will be forgotten. Look around us. What if she was right?"

"Stop it, Gabriel." She turned to walk through the crowd.

"Wait, talk to me. I'm just asking what if!" Gabriel tried to grab her arm, but she whipped around and slapped his hand away before he could register the motion. He was unprepared for the fierce reaction or her speed. He recoiled at the slap and the look on her face, but she turned back toward Lucifer, unfazed.

"Don't grab me."

"I'm sorry."

"Do you see the other angel up there next to Abbeus?"

Gabriel backed away. His heart sank further thinking she referred to Lucifer. "There are two. Which one?"

"Her name is Delia. She is the virtue angel of chastity."

Gabriel looked up at Delia's pink gown. "What about her?"

"She is my sister. As close as you think you and Michael have ever been, it is nothing compared to what I have with her. I will stand next to her. She and I are on Lucifer's side to the end. Are you with us or not?"

Gabriel didn't know what to say. He wanted to stand up for his friendship with Michael but realized the only two times Arrayah had met him they fought. He simply nodded and let her believe what she wanted.

She was right though, Gabriel thought, as she led him toward the mountain. He had forsaken his brother for someone he had just met. Michael had taught him everything he knew. The first time he ever crossed swords was with Michael. The very blade Gabriel used against him Michael had given him as a gift. Most of the things he owned and cared for were either because Michael had given it to him or Michael liked it first.

As young archangels, they had climbed trees on the far western rim and then glided down, seeing who could float the longest. Michael was always better at it, mainly because Gabriel weighed more, but he let Gabriel win sometimes. It was no secret Michael was the most important angel in his life. Yes, they fought, but he couldn't think of a single time Michael didn't have his best interest at heart. What was he doing here?

As Gabriel and Arrayah approached, Delia was finishing her speech.

"Don't be left in the dark with the One whose light has burned out from the breath of His own lies! His light has dimmed for a reason. He knows His end is near. It is the time of the angels! It is the time of the new angelic order! It is our time, and I give you our leader. He's God's own chosen one, the highest guardian cherub, a wonderful inspiration, and a true friend to us all: Lucifer!" Her silky dress flapped in the wind behind her, outlining an exquisite physique, but she still didn't compare to Arrayah.

The crowd of angels shouted praises with a thunderous outpouring of emotion for their champion. They cheered for him as they did at his concerts. Gabriel was astonished to see crowds of seraphim, cherubim, thrones, dominions, principalities, and even three of the seven archangels—Azrael, Azazel, and Saraquel. With Gabriel present, the majority of his class was apparently on board with Lucifer's plan to oppose God. If every class became that way, God would no longer be in charge. He suddenly became light-headed.

Lucifer walked up with seeming grace and humility, and when he finally held his hand up, the audience quieted quickly. His effervescent wings were outstretched behind him. His face looked different from last time Gabriel saw him, darker somehow, but was no less perfect. What an attractive angel, Gabriel thought. Why would Arrayah be interested in a lowly archangel instead?

"We are not here to convince you one way or the other as to what you should believe or who you should follow. Forgive my dear Delia. She speaks with such passion from her own conviction." He glanced at Delia with a loving smile. "Look at her. How can you resist her? You are a truly splendid creature, and I thank you for your wonderful heart." She curtsied, and the crowd laughed at her charm.

Delia looked so much like Arrayah from a distance. Gabriel began to wonder if she could be the female from Michael's dream. The two could easily be mistaken. If Michael's premonition was true, then he hoped she was that angel. Arrayah turned and smiled at Gabriel as Delia curtsied, and a flush of guilt ran over him for wanting her sister to burn rather than her.

Lucifer continued, "We simply want every angel to hear the facts. God wants us to worship Him for eternity, serving Him and handling our appointed duties forever. Unfortunately for God, the truth has been revealed, and we know now that He is no longer who He says He is. We have become too smart and are no longer His children to manipulate and control!"

The crowd erupted. Lucifer clearly had the angels in the palm of his hand, and Gabriel wondered how far it would go. How many would stay loyal to God? Lucifer continued his speech, and as it went on, Gabriel watched as thousands more were converted before his eyes. It seemed to be effortless for Lucifer.

"I don't want to make this about Him however," Lucifer said. "This is about us! This is a celebration of what is to come!" The crowd roared even louder.

"Isn't Lucifer incredible?" Arrayah turned and batted her eyes at Gabriel. He felt the lump in his throat still there from his confrontation with Michael. He finally cleared it.

"He is."

Gabriel had so many questions. Normally he would turn to Michael. He couldn't get his brother out of his head or shake the look on Michael's face as Gabriel hurled him through the trees. He remembered their very first fight as young angels; he could still feel Michael's knuckles against his cheekbone. It was what inspired him to take up sparring. He would have never won the arms spar in the Ludus Paradisus if he hadn't been so determined to beat Michael. From even their worst moments came positive outcomes. What if Michael was right? He wanted to protect Arrayah, and Lucifer's words were like honey. But what if this was the wrong side? Either way, he was bound to lose someone he could never replace.

He looked at Arrayah's flawless features. She was listening to Lucifer, apparently captivated, but there were lines of worry around her eyes. He knew he was only there because of her. Before any of this happened, the seraph had told him to follow his heart and only listen to Michael. It was only Arrayah keeping him from leaving at that very second.

The source of light here on Terra was a glowing yellow sphere in the cosmos, but it was slowly fading away over the horizon now. Darkness was creeping across the sky. Soon all would be black and void of light. Gabriel's troubled heart felt the same way; a darkness was growing inside. Looking at the shadows sweeping across the mountain and beginning to engulf the gathered angels, a sense of horror and finality struck him. It was as if he were approaching a point from which he could not return. He didn't know how to stop it, but he had to try.

"Arrayah, what if Lucifer is wrong about all of this? What if God truly is the Creator and the Ruler of all things, just as we have always believed? Then what? What if Lucifer is the liar here?"

She did a double take. "Have you not heard anything? Even some of God's own seraph angels believe He is lying. If He's not lying, then why flee in the midst of this revolution? Heaven is dimmed because His light is gone! Why wouldn't He clear up the rumors and stand up for Himself?"

"Well—"

"No, Lucifer is right."

Lucifer shouted and then paused for effect, and the cheers from the crowd almost drowned him out.

"Maybe God is allowing this to happen to see who is truly faithful to Him," Gabriel said. "What if He is allowing all angels to make their own decisions, just like Lucifer speaks of, before He comes back and reveals the truth? What then, Arrayah?"

She gazed harshly at him and then turned away before whispering, "You can't possibly understand, but I am too deep into this now." Gabriel stepped in closer to hear her. "I know things you can't imagine. I know you can't understand what it's like to have someone as close to you as Delia is to me, but even if I thought Lucifer was wrong, I wouldn't leave her. Ever."

"I do understand that. The only difference is I feel that way for two people. One I barely know but I know is already a part of me." She looked down, understanding him perfectly. "The other has always been a part of me. I know what you saw between Michael and me was terrible, but he is my most beloved friend and my greatest rival. Most of all, he is my equal. I know in my heart when he is telling the truth, and I can't leave him just like you can't leave Delia." He placed a hand on her arm, and this time she did not slap it away. "Arrayah, come with me. Please. We can come back for Delia when we are stronger."

She winced. She looked up at Delia with loving eyes, but then her focus shifted to Lucifer. Her face hardened, and her back stiffened. "It is your decision about what you will believe. I cannot make you choose either way. But I will tell you this: I have made up my mind, so don't try to convince me otherwise if you are suddenly back on God's side!"

Lucifer still spoke behind their conversation, and the crowd roared every few seconds. Gabriel just wanted to go somewhere quieter. "You aren't as sure as you would have me believe. You didn't think it would go this far when all of it first started, did you? It's not too late to get out you know."

"I believe Lucifer!" Arrayah shouted. After a moment, she looked down. She wasn't sure. "And yes, it is too late to turn back now even if I wanted to."

Gabriel shook his head and became silent when he heard more cheers from the crowd. He turned his focus back on Lucifer's speech.

"I will lead you to our new order," Lucifer stated. His voice was smooth and bold. "We will be raised above the Lord God soon, and we will unmask ourselves when He tries to make a stand against us."

"That is only if He ever shows back up!" yelled an angel from the crowd. Other angels chimed in remarks, but Lucifer's voice was still easily heard.

"Oh, He will show back up, and when He does, He will have no idea how many are with us. I will confront Him about all of His many lies! Any angel who opposes us until then will be crushed along with Him."

After Gabriel heard that, he could no longer take it. His heart was telling him to fly away as quickly as possible and get to Michael, but there was one problem. The other portion of his heart was standing right next to him. He wouldn't leave Arrayah in the hands of Lucifer. There had to be a way to protect them both.

"Don't you see, Arrayah? Michael and a seraph warned me of what would happen before any of this started. I realize now they were right. Listening to Lucifer now, everything makes sense. He is not trying to make everyone equal or uncover lies. He is trying to exalt himself, and he is using his own lies to accomplish his agenda!"

Arrayah's face flushed crimson. "I can't believe you just said that. Did you not just throw your own best friend through a bunch of orange trees? Did you not just tell me you wanted to come see Lucifer so you could join us? Now, all of a sudden, you change your mind even after you have seen how quickly he is gaining power? That makes no sense, Gabriel!"

"My mind was never completely made up. I know now I am here because of you, and I believe I am supposed to save you from this. I have a very bad feeling about what is happening here. Michael foretold this, and he told me that he saw you in his vision facing the consequences. You were turning black and screaming, Arrayah. I didn't want to tell you, but that is what made me so angry with him today. I know Michael, and I know now that it must be true."

"What? Turning black?"

"I don't know exactly what it means, but you have to trust me. I can't lose you." He could see Arrayah was scared, and so was he. She was at a loss for words. "I have to believe Michael was shown that dream and we met so that I could save you. Nothing else makes sense."

Saraquel made a gap in the crowd not far from them, pushing angels aside with his long, bony arms. Gabriel realized he was headed for them when he heard his scratchy voice.

"Arrayah, Gabriel, is everything all right?" coughed Saraquel with a cloud of smoke emanating from his breath.

"We are fine, Saraquel. Just give us a minute, please," said Gabriel quickly.

"Is everything all right, Arrayah?"

Arrayah gave a small nod. Gabriel wasn't happy with the black-haired archangel, considering he had just answered the question. "I said give us a minute, Saraquel."

"I believe she can answer for herself."

Arrayah pulled herself together and straightened her posture. "I am fine."

"Are you sure? Is he bothering you?" Saraquel jerked his head toward Gabriel, and his stringy hair whipped across his face.

Gabriel clenched his forearm muscles in restraint. "That is enough. You heard her answer, so please leave us."

"I would watch your insolent tone around here, for you are not on friendly ground if you raise your fist at me, Gabriel." He coughed hard after he finished. His hiss was lower than Gabriel was accustomed to. He had a new air of confidence, and considering they both knew Gabriel was stronger if the situation became physical, Gabriel didn't know where it was coming from.

"You are insignificant to me, Saraquel, and should it come to it, you will see how insignificant."

"I take it you have made your decision not to follow us," said Saraquel.

"You are correct, and Arrayah is coming with me. You can tell Lucifer that we are coming for Delia as well." Arrayah sucked in a breath and pivoted to look at Gabriel.

Saraquel began to laugh. "Do you really think Lucifer is just going to let you take Arrayah from here? From him? You have no idea who you are dealing with. You know nothing about Lucifer." Again Saraquel wheezed through a coughing fit until he caught his breath. "You don't even know anything about Arrayah. She is as much of a deceiver as the Lord you follow." Saraquel finished with a challenging grin.

"I would watch what you say."

"Look at her. Do you think she cares about you? She only cares about herself. She's using you!"

Arrayah shut her eyes. She didn't contradict him. Gabriel noticed, but he didn't even turn toward her. Instead, he lunged and grabbed Saraquel by the throat. Gabriel leaped skyward, lifting Saraquel with him about thirty feet in the air before spiking him into the rocky hillside. Saraquel's body hit the ground so hard that the vibrations caused a shower of rocks to come sliding off of the mountain. Almost everyone turned around to see what happened. Gabriel wasn't sure if Lucifer noticed.

Saraquel crawled out of the crevice his body had created. Although wounded, he jumped into the air and flew straight at Gabriel. Gabriel dodged to the right at the last second and grabbed him in a headlock. "Apologize to her!"

Barely able to breathe, Saraquel choked out, "It is the truth, Gabriel. She has deceived you."

Gabriel tightened his grip on Saraquel's neck, his wings beating hard to keep them both aloft, and Saraquel began to tap on Gabriel's forearm.

"Now!"

"I am sorry, Arrayah!" gasped Saraquel.

"Say it again and mean it!"

"I am sorry."

Gabriel released Saraquel and pushed him away. Saraquel tore off holding his throat and shoulder. He flew straight toward the summit where the leaders stood. Below, Arrayah looked up in shock. As he glided down beside her, Gabriel didn't know how she was going to react.

"Gabriel, that was not smart! Thank you for standing up for me, but you must go now. Saraquel is going to get Lucifer and the others. You must get out of here." She pointed toward the heavens and then peered over to the mountaintop where Lucifer, Delia, and Abbeus continued to address the crowd.

"I won't leave you here with them," said Gabriel.

Arrayah shoved him hard. "Please! You must leave now. You don't understand how powerful Lucifer is!"

"I am powerful too. I won't leave you, Arrayah."

"You don't understand. I've seen Lucifer do things."

"What?" A crowd was watching them, and in the distance Saraquel was nearing the summit.

Arrayah's eyes were dark and wide. She whispered so the onlookers couldn't hear. "He showed me something you wouldn't believe."

"What do you mean? What did he do?"

"I don't know. It couldn't move though. It wouldn't wake up."

"I can barely hear you. What wouldn't wake up? I don't understand."

She shook her head, looking suddenly terrified, and pushed at him again. He stood still as she continued to shove ineffectually. She finally just fell against him, crying softly on his shoulder.

"I'm sorry," she said under her breath.

"You have nothing to be sorry about."

After a few minutes, she raised her head up, and he knew she was looking at the mountaintop behind him. "You must get out of here now," she whispered.

"I won't leave you here with him. I would rather Lucifer do something to me than to keep deceiving you."

"Why do you care so much about me? Worry about yourself." She wiped the tears from her face, panicked eyes flitting from the mountain and back to him.

He knew she wasn't waiting for an answer, but he had one. "Because I love you."

Arrayah's eyes fixed on his, and for a moment he felt that a veil had dropped—that a wall, one he had not even realized was there, had crumbled down for but an instant. He saw her. Then she looked away at the mountain.

"Well, I don't love you. I lied to you from the beginning. Saraquel was telling the truth. The only reason I spoke to you was because Lucifer told me to get close to you to control Michael."

Gabriel could feel his eyes beginning to well up. "You don't mean that."

"Trust me, I mean it."

"I know you don't."

She looked at him again, and her expression was cold and distant. "I do, Gabriel. I would never love an archangel."

His heart felt ready to break. He held his composure together and flashed a paper-thin smile. "I don't believe you. This is real between us. I know you can feel what we have."

"We have nothing." Once more, her eyes darted to the mountain, and she started pushing at him with renewed strength. Her voice rose to a scream. "Go, Gabriel! Leave me alone!"

"Please don't say that."

"I mean it! You are nothing to me, and if you don't leave now, I will never speak another word to you again!"

Gabriel could find no more words. His chest plate suddenly felt three sizes too small. It was crushing him, and he couldn't breathe. He turned away from her to hide the tears about to spill over, and without another word he launched himself toward the black, star-strewn heavens. Darkness had fallen.

XVI

Lucifer looked out over his new followers and felt a tingling sensation across his body. His outstretched wings shivered as he thought of how far he'd come. There was a name for this delicious feeling: power. The seed had been planted, and he stared out at the fruits of his labor—thousands upon thousands of angels on his own wondrous world called Terra.

He felt a tiny vibration in the ground beneath him. "Did you feel that?"

"What?" said Abbeus from ten feet behind him. Delia shot over from the other side of the summit.

"What is it?"

"It's nothing, Delia. Back up."

Lucifer noticed the crowd was concentrating on something off to his right in the distance, but he couldn't tell what it was. He began again. "It has become dark on

Terra just as it has in Heaven. I now urge you to continue what we have started and bring all of your closest angels back here for our next meeting. Thank you, everyone! Remember, we know now why He is hiding!" The crowd roared. After the long cheer dwindled out, massive clusters of angels broke away toward the heavens like flocks of birds taking to the skies. All in all, another successful meeting. The revolution was spreading. His power was growing. He could feel it to the very tips of his wings.

"Mighty Lucifer!" Saraquel came tearing up to the summit, panicked. He had dirt on his armor and face and nearly ran into Abbeus. "Gabriel is over there with Arrayah!"

"Oh, excellent. He has come to tell me he is joining us. What happened to your armor?"

"It was Gabriel! He told me he is going to oppose us head on."

Lucifer tensed up at the thought of resistance, but it was especially insulting coming from lowly archangels. He wouldn't let this spoil his high from the wonderful meeting. "He said this?"

"Yes. He threw me into the ground, Lucifer!"

"You will be fine." Saraquel was visibly hurt by his reaction, but Lucifer had no time for weakness.

"He also said he would be taking Arrayah."

"Where are they?"

"There." Saraquel pointed into the distance exactly where Lucifer had noticed the disturbance. His wings snapped to full extension, and he plunged off the summit. He heard Delia shout for him to wait, but he had no time for her either. He raced over the remaining crowds.

Lucifer came upon Arrayah watching something up in the heavens. He thought he saw a tear drip from her face as he neared but couldn't be sure. He was distracted by the distinct flapping of wings behind him and turned to see Saraquel and Abbeus following. When he faced Arrayah again, she regarded him with a bright expression on her upturned face and a cheerful smile. Too cheerful.

"Where did Gabriel go?" he asked.

"I don't know."

He landed abruptly next to her and didn't tuck his wings. "What do you mean, you don't know?"

"He just flew away."

"What happened? I thought you had him under control."

"Well, I guess not," she said. Lucifer saw the six-winged shadows of Abbeus and Saraquel behind him and turned to them as they approached. "Excuse us for a minute."

"Of course, sir," they said almost in unison.

He waited until they had walked some distance away, and then he leaned in close to her. "What did you just say to me?" He kept his voice low. His wings curled around to cast her in shadow and hide her from view. She looked terrified. She knew too much to betray him now.

In a near whisper, she said, "All I meant was that I think he had something to do. He doesn't like me that much anymore. I told him he was ignorant for questioning your—I mean our—findings on God."

"Of course, he likes you. Don't be a fool. You should have succeeded."

"Maybe he just doesn't show it. I tried, but I guess he's not interested now."

"Saraquel said he is planning to oppose us."

"They argued and fought. I couldn't hear exactly what was said."

Lucifer watched her coldly. He felt a powerful pull from her life force. It was the only one comparable to Thyaterra's, and he had seen thousands of angels lately. If she was spouting lies, he wanted to catch her in one. If she was betraying him, he wanted her to crack. He waited some more. He could feel her nervous energy as he stared her down. She was an amazing creature and special to his cause but not too special to destroy if he had to. Fortunately for her, she didn't so much as blink.

"Did you find out anything about Michael?" he finally asked.

"I do know that they got in a fight today."

"Over what?"

"I don't know."

His wings trembled in anger, and his feathers stood up unintentionally all around her. She let out a gasp. Something must have changed on his face. He twisted his neck to pop it, and this action gave a quick relief.

"I'm disappointed in you." He kept his voice calm. He paused to think what to do next. "No matter then. He is no longer needed." He tucked his massive wings in tightly and spun to walk away.

"Good," she murmured behind him. There was unmistakable relief in her voice. He stopped in his tracks, turned back around, and stood directly before her.

"Why is that good?"

"I meant nothing by it."

"Do you care for him?"

She tilted her head as if amused and gave a careless laugh. "Of course not." It came too late though, and the look in her eyes told him something else. Without thought, his wings shot out violently to their full extent.

Arrayah took a step back. "He is an ignorant brute. He is harmless, that's all. I care for you." She regained her lost step and then walked up to him. She embraced him, the side of her face resting against his gleaming armor. Her eyes closed, perhaps to shut out his penetrating stare. Either way, it calmed him down, and he knew now what he was dealing with. He could handle her. He could handle all of them. Thyaterra always made him second-guess his own judgment, but no other angel would do that to him again.

"As do I, Arrayah."

She raised up to place her head on his shoulder. She rested her hand over his chest, but he could feel her looking up at the same place in the sky that she was staring at when he found her.

XVII

Gabriel forced himself to keep flying until he could reach somewhere to land and pull himself together. After shooting up the tiers of the Marble Falls, he veered over to the Great Forest and dropped down next to one of the giant pine trees. He landed hard, dropping instantly to his hands and knees. Then he began to pray, which he didn't do often. He probably prayed less than any other angel in Heaven. Even he couldn't deny that having everything he knew about God, Heaven, and the angels be challenged felt wrong.

"God, if You're still there—no, I know You are still there. Hear me now. I have lost my best friend. I've abandoned the angel I love. Now I have made many enemies. I am alone, and I need Your help. If You are who I have always believed deep down that You are, then You will come back and tell me what to do." He lifted his eyes to the dimmed light of God's throne. "Please!"

He waited, but there was no answer. "Please, God. Give me a sign!" Nothing. Gabriel sat there with his head in his hands. He wondered why he had been created at all if this was all he was meant for. His armor read, "*Miles Gloriosus et Nuntias Dei.*" He knew why it said Glorious Soldier. It was the "*Nuntias Dei*"—Messenger of God—that he didn't understand. He couldn't even get through to the angel he loved. In fact, the only person who thought his opinion was important was Michael.

Gabriel used to wonder why there was practice combat when there was never any real combat. At times, he would feel it silly to be a great warrior angel. Now he could see he was being prepped for this particular time his whole existence. God knew this was going to happen. Maybe he was supposed to fight for Arrayah. Gabriel didn't understand God dimming His light, but he trusted Him nonetheless. And he was suddenly filled with a renewed sense of purpose. At least holding onto hope was better than facing the realities of a hopeless end.

He was about to rise to leave when he heard the snap of a twig near him. He jumped to his feet, ready for combat, and looked around the thick pine tree. He caught sight of an angel walking away from him and ran forward in pursuit. After ducking under a couple of tree limbs, knocking off some leaves and needles, he went straight through a smaller branch. As it snapped off, he popped out on the other side to realize there was no one there.

He was not used to the darkness that had taken over Heaven. It had never been this dark. Not even close. He was frustrated by his poor vision, and the darkness made him feel alone.

"I know you are here, so come out and fight!" he yelled. "I can hear you moving!"

He waited for a second, and the rustling noises faded until silence again settled on the landscape. A voice began to speak.

"Will you make enemies of everyone now?"

It was the same voice from the orange grove, the one he was beginning to think was a dream. He would recognize it anywhere. "I have already made enemies out of everyone, including my best friend. I don't know what I am doing anymore."

"Don't worry; Michael will forgive you. He has a pure heart. He was only concerned for your well-being, as am I." The seraph's lilting voice was again mesmerizing.

"Why is everyone so concerned with me? I am only an archangel."

"Sometimes the most influential come from humble beginnings, Gabriel. Michael cares because he is your friend. I care because I know what you can be."

"So you believe I can save the angels too, I guess. Well, that's just great."

"I believe you can and that you will become much more than you realize. But you must also believe in yourself," said the seraph.

"I'm not concerned about me. I care about what's going to happen to Arrayah. How can I save her?"

"Remember what God has written on your armor, Gabriel. That is who you truly are. You must realize it. Everyone cannot be saved."

"Who says they can't?" he demanded.

He felt the seraph's presence disappear as before.

"How do you know what is written on my armor? I have never even seen you. Hello?" He waited for a response, but none came. This time he was not surprised. "Of course, you're gone," he muttered as he crumbled to the ground. He sat against a tree again, resting his arms on his propped knees.

He ran his thumb over the words inscribed on his chest plate. "Glorious soldier and messenger of God," he mouthed. He closed his eyes for a minute to think. Exhaustion and fevered thoughts overcame him. Time was lost. An image of thousands of angels weeping flashed through his head.

He opened his eyes, not knowing how long he had been there. He needed to find Michael—to apologize and warn him about Lucifer. He needed Michael's help to save Arrayah. Gabriel stretched his wings and took off toward the heavenly city. He soared over the field, turning it golden yellow, and flew up the jeweled layers of the Great Mountain before landing on the ledge. As he neared the closest pearl gate, he saw for the first time there was no dominion guarding it. He pulled his wings in until the lower feathers brushed his calves. He shoved the gate open enough to squeeze through and headed for Michael's home.

Michael lived in the city in a house elevated about halfway from the gates to the throne level on the south golden ramp. His house was made of stone and was the least grandiose of the homes around it. It was only one story, and the only thing that made it stand out from the rest was its unremarkable nature.

In the yard were two tall white oaks like the ones from the White Woods of the north near the Lake of Purity. There were footprints very close together in the soft soil at the base of one of the trees. Someone had been spying on Michael. Did Lucifer have someone watching him?

Gabriel knocked on Michael's front door. No answer. Gabriel was still drained from everything that had taken place, so he decided to wait at the door. It seemed the easiest course of action. He plopped his large body down on the raised step on the porch, and his armor clanked against the stone. He leaned back against a thin pillar.

He lay there for hours, thinking about what he would say to Michael when he finally came home. He really was sorry for how he had treated him. He hoped Michael would not only forgive him but forgive him quickly. He needed him.

Then his mind raced back to Arrayah. He thought of what he could possibly say to her the next time he saw her. He had to snatch her from Lucifer's clutches. Perhaps she and Saraquel were telling the truth and she really had been fooling Gabriel the whole time. Maybe none of it had been real. In his heart, he knew there was more than she had admitted. She was under an influence that was not of Heaven. Even if she kept saying she felt nothing, he didn't believe it. If she were to pay the consequences for transgressing God, then Gabriel would go to God Himself on her behalf.

He pictured her screaming and turning black as Michael had described. He watched as the light in her beautiful blue eyes went out and her writhing in pain as her body transformed. He winced as her skin charred to ash and her wings and hair were consumed by fire. He could smell them burning. She was burning up right in front of him, and there was nothing he could do. She screamed his name as she burned—*Gabriel! Gabriel!*

"Gabriel, Gabriel! Wake up! What are you doing here?"

Gabriel jerked awake, startled. Michael's looming figure looked down at him. He needed to shake off his visions of Arrayah, but it took him a minute to pull himself back to reality. Then he smiled up at Michael. Michael's face showed no emotion. Gabriel was pretty sure he was still angry. He didn't blame him.

"Michael, I'm glad you're back. Look, I've thought about what you said and you were right. I am sorry for the way I treated you. I—"

Michael stepped over him and opened his door. His voice was as flat and unfeeling as his expression. "I'll be right back. I need to get something." He walked in and shut the door behind him.

Gabriel stood and waited at the door. Michael seemed to be unforgiving, contrary to the seraph's words. He must have hurt Michael physically as well as emotionally. This might be harder than he had hoped. After a few minutes, Michael returned holding a massive sword in his left hand. An ornate inscription ran down the blade about the spirit of God, and a large star shone on the end of the pommel. The blade itself was over ten feet long.

"Whoa, take it easy. I said I was sorry. I didn't think I hurt you that bad." Gabriel scrambled back off of the porch, his foot meeting air on the steps and causing him to stumble before he regained his balance.

"Oh, really? You are sorry, are you?" Michael stalked down the steps.

"Yes, brother. I didn't mean to hurt you. And I should have listened to you from the beginning."

Michael advanced, raising the large blade. He lunged forward and Gabriel flinched. The sword's tip stopped an inch short of his chest.

"Good, brother! I forgave you the first time you said it." Michael revealed his right hand from behind his back and tossed a large orange. Gabriel caught it purely by reflex, then laughed as Michael's words sank in.

"Oh, and don't worry," Michael continued, "you could never hurt me. It felt like a stiff wind had knocked me over, not the glorious soldier of the archangels."

"Right. You stood your ground about as well as a stalk of wheat."

Michael propped the sword on his shoulder and started back to the house. "I saw you flinch, by the way."

Gabriel showed no sign of hearing. He was wrapped in thought about what Michael had just said about him being the glorious soldier. "I know what I must do," he said.

Michael turned. Only the trace of his smile remained.

"I must fight against Lucifer to save Arrayah."

"Hold on. What are you talking about?"

"A seraph has spoken to me twice now. The first time she warned me that many would turn from God and to trust my heart. It turns out she was right. The second time was earlier today, and she told me to remember what is written on my armor. It says "Glorious Soldier," so I must defeat Lucifer in battle to save half of the angels, including Arrayah."

"Your armor also says *Nuntias Dei*. Don't get ahead of yourself, Gabriel."

"How many messages have you ever seen me deliver? I am a soldier, Michael."

"Lucifer is the highest of the cherubim. I don't think picking a fight with him may be the best option right now. Just be patient."

Gabriel shook his head. "You have said yourself that I would be responsible for saving over half the angels of Heaven. How else could I do it if not with fighting?"

"It is not for you to decide. God will let you know what to do when the time comes." He clapped Gabriel on the back. "Either way, I will be there with you."

Gabriel peeled the pristine orange and let the rind fall to the ground at Michael's feet. "Well, I didn't listen the first time to the seraph, and that was the wrong choice. I won't make the same mistake twice. I am going to confront Lucifer and bring Arrayah back. I know where he holds his secret meetings. I could use your help to keep others from getting involved, but either way, I am going, so don't try to stop me."

Michael studied Gabriel for a moment and then picked up the rind from the ground. He placed it in his tunic pocket. "I didn't get my sword out for nothing."

Gabriel broke into a smile. "Let's go." He sprinted out to the street, and Michael followed without hesitation.

Gabriel ran down the golden streets toward his home, passing the seven archangels' houses. Each one represented the personality of its inhabitant. Azazel's was overreaching, with lavish fixtures, fountains, statues, and columns. Uriel's was conservative in size and ideas but made of the finer things. Raphael's was very cozy and welcoming, surrounded with many flowering plants and trees and a garden often visited by animals. Azrael's property was paved and void of life, not so much as a blade of grass; the house was very tall and made of solid grey stone. Saraquel's home was a mix of styles drawing from each of the other six archangels' homes. After passing all of them, he came to his own house. It was a bit messy, and the yard was cluttered with books, writing quills, archery targets, and, of course, fruit peels. A pool of semi-clean water sat in the front yard, and the house itself was made of wood and brick.

He stormed in and came out shortly after gripping a weapon similar to Michael's, only a little thicker at the base. It wasn't clean and polished like Michael's sword. In fact, it had a little mud on the blade, but it was elegant nonetheless.

"I can see you still take care of your sword." Michael grinned.

"Not everyone is as particular as you. I think my sword prefers to be a little dirty. It shows that it is seasoned and not sitting around doing nothing, like yours."

Michael chuckled. "I attend the games every year just like you. Lead the way, Glorious Soldier."

"Yes, but it's what you do in between the games that keeps you sharp. That is why I am victorious."

"Ah, yes, and humble too," replied Michael. He followed Gabriel to the city's gate on the south end, and as they walked out, Gabriel jumped up with outstretched wings and soared off toward the Field of Tranquility. As they zoomed over the luscious field, the swaying wheat was overcome with blue light.

Michael caught up to Gabriel. "How many followers has Lucifer accumulated?"

"Too many to count now."

"That many?"

"Yes, but I just want you to keep the others from getting involved. This is between Lucifer and me. I will deal with him myself."

"I will do all I can," Michael said. "You better know what you are doing."

Gabriel kept his face blank even though he felt sharp tension all over his body. He was more than nervous. This might be the most disastrous course of action he could take. He was going to confront the highest of the cherubim, the most powerful angel in all of Heaven.

They flew for several minutes before Gabriel finally answered. "I don't."

XVIII

S ome of Lucifer's most intrigued followers had started to become inseparable from him. After each meeting, a group of angels would probe him for hours with questions and dispense general flattery, but there was one angel who was particularly of interest. He was the archangel Azrael. Most of the angels who flattered him wanted to work their way up Lucifer's ranks but not him.

Azrael often isolated himself. From what Lucifer gathered, he enjoyed seclusion; they had this in common. He was opposed to all authority and ordered law, even more so than Lucifer. Azrael did not like to be told what to do. He was an easy convert, but Lucifer had bigger plans for this angel. Lucifer had discovered the antivirtue wrath, a source of great power, and this angel was full of it. He could feel it welling inside Azrael every time he was near. Azrael was unhappy with his duties as a leader of the lowest class of angels, but more importantly, he strongly resented another archangel, Raphael, for reasons Lucifer had not fully discovered yet.

Azrael rarely sought out company, but after his latest speech, Lucifer noticed him lurking close by. It was as if Azrael had been following him for a long time, but Lucifer just picked up on it. The last time they had spoken, Azrael called many angels fake and pompous but reserved special venom for Raphael, who was apparently the epitome of everything Azrael shunned. He was social, friendly to everyone regardless of rank, and popular among the lower class for it. Azrael believed he saw through Raphael's mask. He felt Raphael was not honest about who he was deep down, so not only did he not respect him, he also couldn't stand him. Lucifer understood this but felt there was more to Azrael's hatred. He saw two antivirtues were strong in this angel: envy and wrath. A useful combination.

Lucifer walked over to him. He had been waiting to use an angel for a specific mission. He had thought Saraquel would have to do, but now he realized that Azrael was perfect for it. "It's Azrael, isn't it?"

The awkward archangel in a dark cloak was hunched over. His face was hidden in shadow. "Yes. Your words were divine today, great Lucifer." The high, unpleasant pitch of his voice grated on the ears, but it was fitting of this abberrant angel who always seemed to hide. The biggest puzzle for Lucifer was the fact he couldn't feel Azrael's life force at all. Ever since he had chosen to leave God, he had become keenly aware of the source of life in those around him. Every angel had one, though none as strong as Thyaterra, yet this angel had none. At least, Lucifer couldn't feel it. Odd. This angel could have been following him for days and Lucifer would have never known of his presence.

"Tell me the desires of your heart, Azrael."

Azrael's body contorted each time before he spoke, and it was never the same movement. "I want to see God's Heaven destroyed. There is nothing for me there."

"Why do you feel there is nothing for you?"

"It disgusts me. They pretend that everything is perfect. They hide behind glossy eyes of bliss and smile to each other like they are as perfect as God. They all wear masks, but I know their true desires. They think they are better than their leaders and peers. Angels only care for themselves when it comes down to it. They will take everything they can."

"Who are 'they'?"

Azrael slouched over and let slip a quick smirk he couldn't hide. Lucifer smiled encouragingly. Azrael stood up tall, and Lucifer noticed the Latin word *messor* engraved in his armor as his dark cloak pulled open at his chest. "The archangels, Lucifer!"

Lucifer's smile grew twice as large. "Your class of angels is proving to be quite interesting for only seven of you."

"I know what you are capable of. I have shadowed you for a long time. I know what you have done to animals when you are alone with them. I too have taken life on Terra."

Lucifer felt a spark of rage, but he subdued it as best he could. There was no life force coming from Azrael. He needed to find out more about why. "Come with me."

Surprisingly the archangel didn't hesitate. Lucifer jumped fifty feet in the air and spread his wings, soaring straight for Heaven. Azrael tailed him all the way to the canyon near the Hanging Gardens on the inner island of Heaven. They landed and walked through a passage that led to the underground caverns of the Great Mountain. The smell of fresh flowers covered the area like a fog; the ground here was carpeted with them. Lucifer despised the smell. He glanced back at Azrael, who puckered his nose at the floral odor as well. Who was this angel?

"The stench is becoming stronger up here," Azrael said. "I prefer the grittiness of Terra."

"Things are about to get exciting in Heaven. Are you excited?"

"I am," replied Azrael. "Where are you leading me?"

They entered the cavern tunnels, and the flowers gave way to cool stone. The temperature dropped as they headed farther in. "I want to show you something. You mentioned you have taken life on Terra. Tell me about this."

"I tracked animals, mostly small ones. I broke their bones until they no longer breathed."

"Why did you do that?"

"I saw you do it. I want to be able to do it to an angel."

"Let me guess. Raphael?"

The bitterness in his eyes was confirmation enough. Lucifer walked deeper into the Great Mountain. "What makes you think it is possible? Have you tried this in Heaven?"

"I don't know if it is, but I have been unable to catch an animal in Heaven to attempt it. They run from me like they know what I am going to do."

"They are God's creatures. Maybe they do know." Lucifer led Azrael to a corner of a large cave where the body of a lion lay lifeless. Azrael approached it as Lucifer continued. "I, however, have been successful in Heaven. I believe the same principle can be applied to taking the life of angels."

Azrael's eyes lit up the dark cavern. Lucifer saw without a doubt that there was a flicker of remorse for the cat, but Azrael quickly buried the emotion with a cold stare. "Did you know that Raphael has led some angels into hiding? He asked me if I wanted to join them. If I find him, you can try it on him. What do you think? He represents everything that is wrong with Heaven!"

"You are special, Azrael. There is a unique aura around you that I can feel. I am assigning this task to you. I want you to be the second to take life in Heaven."

"Why me?"

"I have to be honest with you. I didn't take kindly to the fact that you followed me, but now you know more than any other angel about life and destruction. I could easily take life from you now, but I fear you have barely a soul to take. There is no life force around you as with other angels, and this intrigues me greatly."

"I am sorry for following you. I just had to see who you were behind the mask. I wanted to see what you did when no one was looking. I was fascinated."

"Do you think everyone has a mask?"

"Yes. How many roles do we play throughout the day? You play a leader to the angels, you play a friend to your class, and you play a subordinate to God, just to name a few. I only wear one mask now, a mask of sanity in a corrupt universe."

"Are you ready to take life?"

"If it is Raphael's."

"You must separate the life force from Raphael if you are to destroy him. Do you know where that is?"

"I don't know what you mean."

"It is at the base of the wings of every angel. You must sever them from above. Do you not feel drawn to the necks of angels?"

"I have no feeling left at all. I am numb."

Azrael and Lucifer walked deeper into the caverns, and their voices echoed off of the walls. The smell was much better here, and Lucifer took a deep breath of the thin air. Azrael was in pain like Lucifer. He could smell this too, like the fear in his animal prey. None of their previous pain mattered anymore—the task at hand was much bigger than their personal vendettas.

Lucifer stared off into the distance at the light glowing at the entrance to the cave and realized how far they had come. Then he focused back on the cloaked archangel's hunched form. The angel's awkwardness came from the writhing pain he had held in for so long and in such isolation. The torment oozed from his body like an infected wound that had never healed. How many years ago had Raphael wronged him? Whatever had happened, Lucifer was the key to unlatching his shackles. Azrael's agony was a precious gift. He would use the archangel to ignite his war. He would use him to unmask his secret without bearing the consequences himself.

"We will steal a piece of God's Heaven. With one blow from your scythe, you will have your life back from Raphael. Are you ready to take back what he has stolen from you?"

"More than you will ever know."

XIX

Michael and Gabriel shot down the Marble Falls and split the water below with a loud splash. They plummeted through the deep body of water. When they burst out on the other side into the cosmos, Michael halted in mid-air, hovering like they did when they were young.

"This is where my dream took place, Gabriel! I had no idea how vast it was."

"It was here? This is where Lucifer has been coming."

"The angels looked like fireballs shooting through the atmosphere. I can still hear their screams as they transform into something unholy. I can still smell the burning wings."

"You're scaring me, Michael."

"I'm sorry. I have a strange feeling about this."

"You seem to be getting those in abundance lately," Gabriel said.

"I know. They have also been right so far."

Gabriel shrugged. "Can't turn back now."

He led Michael straight for Terra. Michael looked around at the many planets and stars around them, trying to take it all in. Gabriel was feeling quite anxious at the moment, so he didn't really feel like commenting.

"Is this where Lucifer's been having his rallies?" asked Michael as they neared Terra.

"Yes. He claims it for his own."

"It's not his to claim."

"Well, he definitely controls it for the time being."

"The time being will be short. He won't control anything when this is all over."

They entered the atmosphere, and Gabriel felt an urge to fly down and simply scoop Arrayah up and take her away. He knew he had to convince her to leave willingly, yet he was tempted to just take her. There was one large land mass on the planet, and they headed for the portion of its dry ground where Lucifer held his meetings.

The land was a beautiful mix of greens, whites, and browns, highlighted by the sky's deep blue. As they neared the hill where Lucifer spoke, Gabriel noticed angels were scattered around. Gabriel and Michael searched the area, hovering in the air for quite some time. They could not find Lucifer, Arrayah, or even Saraquel anywhere.

"I can't believe how many angels know about this," said Michael. "What is this place?"

"This is where the angels of the rebellion come. Lucifer speaks to them and leads them from here. The numbers have grown rapidly since God left."

"God isn't gone."

Finally Gabriel touched ground. Their search from the air was turning up nothing. He stopped a worker angel and asked him where to find Lucifer.

"The great seraph Abbeus will be able to tell you. I just saw him," said the angel.

He pointed out a small group of angels surrounding a much taller seraph. Gabriel recognized him from the summit speech. He started walking in his direction with Michael by his side.

Gabriel nudged Michael and spoke under his breath. "I am about to speak with the first seraph who joined Lucifer's army. He was with Lucifer addressing the crowd before. He gives me one of those strange feelings you're always talking about."

As they neared, Gabriel noticed that the seraph did not have his eyes covered with his two middle wings. Michael seemed to notice as well and slowed down to cautious steps.

"How long has this angel been with Lucifer?" Michael asked.

"I am not sure."

"Oh, it has been a long time, trust me. This seraph has none of God's light anymore."

They approached, and Gabriel lowered his head with a respectful bow. Abbeus flew in their direction, and a moment later his six fully extended wings brought a shadow upon them as he landed.

"Abbeus, I am Gabriel, and this is Michael."

Michael followed Gabriel's lead and bowed slightly before he looked the angel up and down.

"How may I help you?" The seraph declined to return the bow. He kept his chin up and posture straight, avoiding Michael's eyes. He had an air of arrogance that Gabriel was immediately perturbed by.

"I would like to speak with Lucifer. Do you know where I can find him?" Gabriel asked.

Abbeus studied Michael and took his time to speak. There was a slight upturn to his nose as if he smelled something foul, and a half smile curled his lips before he faced Gabriel. "Yes. He was very disappointed to hear of your decision as was I. But I am sure Saraquel had something to do with it."

"Saraquel needed to mind his own business," Gabriel said.

"I heard there is some hostility between the two of you, but let me assure you that you will be well taken care of should you change your mind. I would suggest sooner rather than later." His voice, as was common among the seraphim, was oh so enticing. "Saraquel is no problem. He has already forgotten about it."

"I have never seen the face of a seraph before," Michael interrupted. "It must be liberating to no longer bear the burden of God's glory."

Abbeus ignored him, but Gabriel knew that he heard every word.

"It must have been hard for you to fake your loyalty all of this time," Michael continued. He was taking the focus away from Gabriel. Michael habitually took the pressure off Gabriel in uncomfortable situations, and although at times Gabriel resented it—as if he couldn't handle himself—he didn't mind this time at all.

"Ah, you must be the famous Michael. I've heard so much about you." Gabriel thought Abbeus seemed rattled but was trying to hide it.

"Yes, I am. I've heard nothing about you. How does it feel to be the only member of the seraphim to betray the living God?"

Abbeus looked shocked that Michael had the nerve to speak to him that way. Abbeus was preparing to say something, but the seraphim were naturally reserved, so it took a while. His upper two wings stiffened, and his chin lifted further. Before Abbeus could respond, Gabriel broke in.

"My decision was not based on Saraquel. And I appreciate your offer, but I must respectfully decline."

"I am sorry to hear that, Gabriel, but I am sure you will think otherwise in the future."

"Time will tell who will think otherwise," chimed in Michael.

Abbeus turned to him with his feathers standing straight up. He lowered his face down to Michael's. "It did become very cumbersome to constantly praise God when He treated others like they were more important, and I am sure you will experience much of the same. Worshipping Him is a bore and a chore! No one is important to Him for long."

"I would guess He knew what you would become," said Michael. "In fact, I'm certain of it."

Abbeus shrugged the comment off with contempt. He stood straight again, regaining his composure the best he could. "He will regret He showed favoritism when He had the throne. Oh, and Michael, if you still believe that I am the only one of the seraphim to, how should I say it, alter my way of thinking toward God, then you are more naïve than I had imagined."

As Abbeus stared at Michael, there was a look in his eyes that Gabriel had seen before when Azrael stared at Raphael. It was a dark, penetrating look of anger without a shred of forgiveness. It made his stomach crawl.

"If that is so, then I feel sorry for them as well," Michael said. "Now, are we wasting our time, or do you know how we can find Lucifer?"

"I would recommend that you join us before it is too late, but from your disrespectful tone, I fear it may be too late for you already, archangel. I will summon Lucifer. May I ask what this is regarding? I feel I must ask considering the rather large weapons the two of you have decided to grace us with."

"I would prefer to speak with Lucifer about the matter," said Gabriel.

Abbeus paused. "I assume this has something to do with our precious virtue, Arrayah. Let me oblige you." He flew off in the opposite direction.

"I never met an angel above me that I couldn't stand and had no respect for—until now," Michael said.

"If you liked him, you will really love Lucifer. Try not to be too smitten."

"I can't wait to meet him."

"I'm not sure yet what I'm going to do, but I will do my best not to put you in harm's way."

"We are already there. Just be ready for anything, Gabriel, and try not to lose your temper. You must disguise your feelings for Arrayah, or they could be used against you."

Gabriel realized that despite everything he couldn't wait to see her again although confronting Lucifer was more important at the moment. "I will do my best."

After a while, they saw Abbeus returning with three other angels. Gabriel's blood began to flow like a wave crashing against his heart. He was an instant from storming Lucifer when he noticed one of the three walking with him was Arrayah. He clenched his fist and hid his fury to his best ability. His fingernails sank into his palm.

Their eyes met across the distance, and he noticed that she was wearing many more jewels than she had before. His heart plummeted. She looked so beautifully innocent yet so corrupt. Who was she, really? He still felt he knew.

"Lucifer is watching you two stare at each other. Quit, Gabriel."

Gabriel snapped his eyes over to the grand angel. Lucifer, ever the consummate performer, approached the warriors with the same personable welcome he always bestowed. The third angel was Saraquel, who seemed to be mimicking Lucifer's walk and posture.

"Gabriel, it is so nice to see you again," Lucifer said with a grandiose gesture of welcome. He wore an impressive new grey cloak that swung with the movement of his body. Gabriel wished it would cover the obnoxious jewels on his chest armor. "I regret that I was unable to speak with you the last time you were here. However, the past is the past. Let's discuss our future."

"Hello, Lucifer. Hello, Arrayah." He concentrated his look on her. A coldness he had never noticed surrounded her. "Where's your sister?"

"She's giving a speech by the river behind us." She held his stare for a few more seconds and then looked away.

Michael stepped forward and gave Gabriel a quick, stern look before addressing Lucifer. "The future looks dark for you and your followers, Lucifer. You should ask God for His forgiveness now, and maybe He will show you mercy."

Gabriel had never seen an expression of surprise on the great cherub's face, but Lucifer looked momentarily taken aback at Michael's boldness. He eventually smiled. "Michael, what a pleasure. I have longed for a chance to speak with you. I have heard of your undying faith in God. It is admirable."

"The pleasure is all yours," said Michael.

Lucifer studied Michael's armor and remarked, "*Dux Bellorum*. I have no doubts you are indeed an excellent war leader."

"Your compliments are as hollow as your empty heart, Lucifer."

"Oh, but I have a big heart, Michael. I care about you as well. I do not mean to be so blunt, but did you know that you are one of the very few who is unable to accept the fact that God is not who He claims to be?"

"That's a lie."

"I, too, was disheartened, more than anyone, but we all had to accept the truth. Now it is simply time to do something about it."

"You will soon see that your influence is not as mighty as you believe, dear Lucifer, and your plan to exalt yourself will come crashing down quickly and painfully," said Michael. Gabriel didn't like where the conversation was going. It was too fast. He wanted to be alone with Lucifer to confront him without endangering Michael. Every time he looked in Arrayah's direction, she had her head down almost as if she pretended not to be there.

Lucifer laughed and looked at Abbeus and Arrayah. Abbeus smiled, and Arrayah stayed silent and didn't make eye contact with anyone. "Forgive me if I disagree," Lucifer replied smoothly. "And this is not about exalting me. It's not about me at all. It's about every angel in Heaven."

"We both know that it is about you. I just want you to know your side is the minority. You may have angels too scared right now to oppose you, but you will be surprised at the loyalty to God in the end," Michael said.

"My intention is not to frighten. It is merely to inform. I don't expect your mind to grasp the overwhelming evidence I have against God, but if you would like, I can explain it to you in simple detail," said Lucifer.

"I'll pass."

"I would hate for you to miss out on such a grand opportunity, but it seems that you have made up your mind. I would love your loyalty to shift. I will give you far more to believe in and many rewards for doing so."

"I believe in the true God, and your lies will not be forgotten when He returns to His throne. I would never follow you, Lucifer."

"I am sorry to hear that." Lucifer then turned to Gabriel. "I have very high hopes for you, so I hope you didn't come here to disappoint me as well. Where do you stand?"

"That is what I came here to discuss. May we speak away from all of these angels? Perhaps we should travel back to Heaven."

Gabriel felt safer on common ground. Arrayah started to step forward but didn't. Gabriel felt in his heart she was not on the side that she wanted to be. Something held her back.

"I don't believe going back to Heaven will be necessary," Lucifer said. "I have something to show you if you would be so kind as to humor me."

"Lead the way," Gabriel said. As Lucifer and Gabriel opened their wings, Michael started to follow them, but Gabriel made a quick motion with his hand in Arrayah's direction. He wanted Michael to stay with her. Michael understood and turned back.

Lucifer led Gabriel out of Terra's atmosphere. "Try to stay close," he said as he pierced through deep space. Gabriel could barely keep up. Terra grew tiny behind them and then almost disappeared. He felt the temperature drop more and more as they traveled away. After a while,

Lucifer slowed down, but they had covered much distance in a short amount of time. They were approaching another planet, which hung in space like a dusky red ball.

"Everything you see around you belongs to me, Gabriel. What is visible is barely a speck of what is around us. The vastness is past your comprehension. Billions upon billions of stars, and I know everything there is to know about each and every type here. I would like to give you this red planet as a symbol of what I can offer you as a leader in my ranks. Red is symbolic of the passion our new Heaven will need. It is symbolic of the new life I can give you. Is there anything you would like to know about all of this?"

Gabriel realized he no longer needed to stay calm. It was finally just the two of them. "I know all I need to know. I know none of these planets are yours to give. I know you will pay for all you have done."

"When I saw your sword, I feared you didn't really want to speak in private about my offer. It is a mistake to challenge me, Gabriel. I can take away life just as quickly as I can give it." Lucifer's tone was new and different. It was something beyond threatening.

Gabriel didn't know what he meant, but he didn't care. "You are the one making the mistake. God will not let you get away with this."

Lucifer stiffened his shoulders. "Oh, really? Where is your mighty God? I don't see Him. Does that sound like a God who cares? Does that sound like He is even in charge? He has left, and you have no idea where He has gone!"

"I am not here to discuss God. I have come here for Arrayah, not for you or anyone else." Gabriel's flapping wings felt three times heavier than normal. "I won't let you take her down with you."

"Arrayah came to me before she even met you. She had questions your feeble mind could not even form, let alone answer. I merely gave her the information she yearned for. Something you could never give her."

They were very near the red planet, and Gabriel stopped following him. "You filled her head full of lies, Lucifer!"

"Your God is the one who is full of lies! Anyone who worships Him is a fool, and I will bow to no one, nor will she."

"Leave her alone, or I will make you, you worthless cherub!" exploded Gabriel.

"How dare you threaten me, lowly archangel? I have been exceedingly generous with my offer to you, but my kindness has its limits. You have no idea the power I possess," growled Lucifer, his face darkening and his hair curling back from his forehead.

"For the last time, tell Arrayah of your deception and let her go!" His body wouldn't allow a louder yell. His voice cracked.

"If it weren't for me, Arrayah would have never even spoken to you. You met her because of me, you ignorant fool. You actually thought a virtue would care for you? She will never leave me for a pitiful archangel!" Lucifer laughed and faced Gabriel with his arms spread, daring the archangel to come at him.

Gabriel didn't hesitate one second.

XX

Gabriel unsheathed his sword from his hip, and the blade sparked on its metal scabbard. He rushed Lucifer at full speed and swung with all his strength, putting his entire weight into the blow. Lucifer lifted his armored forearm and, impossibly, stopped the blade's advance as it crashed down. It was like striking one of the seraphim statues—there was no give whatsoever. As the metals clashed, more sparks lit up space like a heavenly fireworks display.

Gabriel was in shock that Lucifer could block such a blow, and it slowed his reflexes. Lucifer grabbed him by his chest plate and started to spin him around. After one full revolution, Gabriel head butted him in the nose and tried to struggle free, but it only infuriated Lucifer further. He launched Gabriel toward the red planet with such force that the sheer velocity and pressure prevented him from opening his wings as he pierced the atmosphere. He plunged through space like a stone through water.

He hit the ground with enough power to cause a massive crack. A huge cloud of red dirt flew up, blinding him, and he could hear the fissure ripping through the surface of the planet, slowly at first and then faster and farther away. Though he could barely breathe, Gabriel forced himself to roll to the side in case the crack opened up beneath him. Lucifer torpedoed down to land no more than ten feet away from Gabriel. Another dust cloud blew up around him, and a second crack leaped along the ground, but Lucifer kept his feet. His tall, lean body loomed over Gabriel's face, blocking the light behind him, and his armor sparkled even through the dust cloud. Gabriel's wings felt broken though he knew they couldn't be.

"You give this message to Michael. If he dares to oppose me, I will destroy him. The same is now true for you. Arrayah will be right next to me when I overthrow God. I will make her my highest angel, and she will forget you ever existed if she hasn't already, you pathetic worm. She is probably laughing at you right now." Lucifer turned his back to fly away, snapping his wings back out.

Gabriel pushed himself shakily to his feet and charged at Lucifer with all his remaining strength. Lucifer spun at the last second, his wings whipping around, but it was too late. He turned to meet Gabriel's thick shoulder right in his stomach. They shot into the air with the blow, but Gabriel couldn't believe the resistance that was still coming from the lean angel. He had never dealt with such strength in all of his thousands of matches.

Lucifer stopped their movement in midair and again took hold of Gabriel. He dashed forward with a loud downward flap of his massive wings and threw him with a vicious grunt. Gabriel hit the ground with such force that an enormous quake split the surface where the first fissure had started. He split through the planet's initial wound and kept going, the throw sending him deep into the ground. He could feel rock breaking against every inch of his body as he plunged. He could hear the crack ripping through the ground off into the distance. It kept going like nothing would stop it. Gabriel tried to hold to consciousness, but as he felt his body slowing its descent, rock now wedged tightly all around him, and everything went black.

Awareness came back gradually and painfully. He slowly opened one eye at a time and had to jar his arm free to wipe the dust from his eyes. His whole body felt devoid of moisture. An eerie silence surrounded him, and his whole body was lodged in rock except for his free arm. Not the best situation, he thought. An intense soreness made him realize he may have been there for some time. He began to fight his way up and out of the crevice, using his free arm to drag himself and knock the rock loose around him until he could scramble upward.

When Gabriel emerged, he was covered in rubble and dirt. As he licked his dry lips, he found his entire face was blanketed with a layer of dust. He had never been so uncomfortably hot or beat up in his long existence. He peered over at the extensive crack his body had made and could not see where it ended. Lucifer was nowhere to be seen.

Gabriel decided to head back toward Terra but did so slowly and stiffly. His legs felt like boulders, and he thought they had the worst of it until he opened his battered wings. Even short flaps felt like someone was pushing down on a handful of bruises with each motion. The feathers that covered them pointed in different directions now. Though he wouldn't normally care, he couldn't help reaching back to brush them into place when he realized he would see Arrayah shortly. At least he hoped he would. Lucifer could have taken her far away by now.

He shook the red dust out of his hair and beat it off of his palms, wondering how he could have let Lucifer get the best of him. How could he be that powerful? It was unbelievable. That type of strength was not angelic.

As Gabriel moved through space, he heard a faint whistle. Someone was near. It was the sound angels made when they were in distress or simply needed to summon someone. He calmed his nerves, flew toward the sound, and tried to return the signal but found his lungs could scarcely draw enough breath. A few minutes later, he saw Michael flying his way.

"Gabriel!"

"I'm so glad to see you," Gabriel said with all the energy he could muster, which hardly amounted to a whisper. "I need you to fly me back to Terra. I have to get back."

"You look terrible, brother. No chance. I need to get you back to Heaven as soon as possible. There will be another time to finish this, I promise." Michael started to put his arm around Gabriel, but Gabriel attempted to pull back. It was a feeble effort.

"It may be too late! I need to get her. I can handle him. I just need another shot."

"I know, and you will have your chance. But not today. Right now we must get home so you can heal." He put his arm around Gabriel more firmly but not enough to hurt him and started to help the battered angel fly. After a few hundred miles, Gabriel was finally able to fly on his own as his body healed itself. With much convincing from Michael, he realized he was in no shape to challenge Lucifer again. Not right now. It was a long way home from the red planet, and at the pace they were going, it seemed to take an eternity. It gave both of them plenty of time to think. When they arrived back in Heaven, they aimed straight for Gabriel's home so he could recuperate.

"I guess I should have had a better plan, huh?" Gabriel gave a painful chuckle as they walked through the gate of the Great Mountain.

"You are the only angel I know who would make jokes after something like this." Michael tried to keep a straight face but had to laugh.

"What's Heaven without laughter?"

"Laughter heals everything. We'll talk later," said Michael in a gentle voice. "Get some rest, Gabriel."

"I will, brother. Thank you."

"Of course. I'm the boring one. If I didn't look after you, where would I get my fill of excitement?"

Gabriel chuckled and labored up to the door. At the top step, he turned around.

"We have to do something. If we don't, who will?"

"I know. Get some rest."

Gabriel stumbled into his home and heard Michael let out a soft sigh just as he closed the door. Peering out the window, he found that Michael was already in intense prayer that looked a lot like pleading. Maybe God would answer Michael, but from the knot in his gut, he feared they were on their own. Maybe they deserved to be. Either way, it was time to fight for God and start His army. Gabriel was certain of one thing—Heaven would never be the same.

XXI

Gabriel and Michael began traveling throughout Heaven, searching for angels to rally for God's army. They started with their own street. They knew that stopping Lucifer would require an all-out war in Heaven, for Lucifer's army was massive and would be difficult to overcome. They canvassed one street after another for hours seeking out comrades and true believers. Gabriel had far less success than Michael. He could not get other angels to even stop and listen to him.

"You're just prettier, Michael. That's all."

After a number of angels heard Michael out but gave no firm commitments, they decided to go to God's throne. It was time to raise the stakes.

God's light was so dim that there was a permanent dusk blanketing Heaven. It was impossible to ignore. Gabriel found it heartbreaking. Nonetheless he managed to stay focused as he followed Michael up the long staircase to the platforms of the thrones and seraphim.

The laws that prohibited flying in the city were insignificant in the face of the current crisis, and none of the angels who would have enforced them were even at their posts. Angels were flying all around the city. Chaos had taken over Heaven. Most of the seraphim, cherubim, and thrones were gone, but they approached the ones who remained on the upper platform before the throne of God.

"Are you ready for this, Gabriel?"

Gabriel thumbed the inscription on his armor. "I'm the messenger angel, remember?"

"Oh, now you are? Not too long ago you were all about fighting."

"Watch how it's done. I was made for this."

Gabriel outstretched his hands and shouted, "Join us, hierarchs!"

A few of the angels turned his way with awkward glances, others with looks of resentment before they all continued about their business. Michael's crossed arms suggested he was unimpressed.

"Like I said, you're prettier. Go for it." Gabriel bowed and swept to the side.

"Who here is still loyal to God?" Michael demanded with a raised voice. He sounded so authoritative that even Gabriel straightened up. Almost everyone looked in his direction, and a few even stepped forward. "I know that many are confused about what is going on."

"We're not confused," a cherub said. "The only thing we are confused about is who you are."

"I am a loyal follower of our true God. I am Michael." He gestured toward Gabriel with confidence. "And this is my brother Gabriel. What is your name, mighty cherub?"

"I am Lustar. What we also know is that Lucifer has rallied many of our kind to join him in a powerful revolt against God." He was a robust figure decked out in cherubim armor, complete with a chest plate of solid gold. His head and body seemed oversized. His hair was dark blond with thick bangs that covered his forehead like the columns covered the wall estates.

"Yes, he has, which is exactly why I am here. I am looking to gather those loyal to God to march on His behalf and stand up against Lucifer," said Michael.

"Do you even know who Lucifer is, archangel?" Lustar looked Michael up and down. Gabriel was impressed by the size of his forearms more than anything. He must be great at the arms spar. "Do you know what he is capable of?"

"Yes, I do. I know that he is more powerful than any angel in Heaven." Michael finally tucked in his wings.

"So what is it you think you can do? What can your army accomplish? He has most of the angels in Heaven behind him already," said Lustar. Lucifer had made this a common misconception, and now most angels believed it. Gabriel found himself wondering if it was true—if Lucifer already had more angels out there in the cosmos than were left in all of Heaven.

"I know Lucifer is powerful, but I also know that God is more powerful. Right now, Lucifer is making it seem like God has no following. There are so many angels who are unaccounted for. Now, who will join me? We need everyone, including leaders. Right now," Michael announced. The nearby angels hesitated, looking around at each other. No one responded. Their fear of Lucifer was apparent. The silence was almost painful.

Finally, Lustar spoke. "Why would any of us follow you?'

"I am not asking you to follow me. I am asking you to follow God. I am asking you to stand up for our Creator."

The angels' expressions showed shame, fear, confusion, and even anger. Lustar appeared unmoved. "Since you think you are so close to God, tell me why He has abandoned us in this time of crisis."

"I cannot answer that. But I know there is a good reason."

"That's what I thought," said Lustar. He turned to walk away. The crowd was starting to talk, some of them looking away. If he lost Lustar, he would lose everyone.

"What do you think, Lustar?" Michael asked.

Lustar turned around. "I think you know nothing."

"I think the same thing. We have something in common. No one knows anything, for that matter. I'm not the smartest angel here among these brilliant minds of the first tier. I do however choose to believe in something bigger than myself. I also don't think it is abandonment. I think we simply don't understand what He is doing. That's all." Michael had a way with words. It was very different from Lucifer; not as elegant perhaps, but effective nonetheless.

Lustar paused, considering. Then he said, "Why would a perfect God allow us to feel such heartache?"

"He has a plan that we cannot understand."

Lustar stood straight and seemed to have grown ten inches. "No. Why would He allow things to go wrong? If He were truly who He is supposed to be, then He would confront Lucifer now and not allow all the rest of us to feel this way."

"I choose to believe He has His reasons. Maybe it is for us to learn. Maybe it is for us to prove our loyalty so He can see who truly believes in Him. I don't know. All I know is that I am going to fight for Him. Are you with me or not? Are you with God?" Michael raised his voice again and made eye contact with as many of the angels as he could.

The crowd was still divided and hesitant. They moved around and spoke to each other quietly. At least this time they were all engaged.

"What is the point of this existence if we have an Almighty God who causes suffering?" Lustar asked. "Why would He allow us to suffer? No, He is backing down and abandoning us, and Lucifer has exposed Him. It is too hard to believe in Him anymore. That is why—"

"I will join you," a throne interrupted as he moved forward from the crowd. Gabriel recognized him as Anistar, an angel who had never been a leader but was known for his deep loyalty to God. He was frail with pale skin, and he looked older than most angels. His armor was bedecked with purple velvet, gold embellishments, and red rubies. After he stepped forward, two more thrones joined him, and then a seraph named Grandathos said, "I will also fight for our God with you."

Gabriel couldn't believe it. It was a start.

Grandathos's middle wings covered his face like the other seraphs', so it was disconcerting to see him walk forward toward Michael without bumping into anyone. Seraphs were tall and intimidating, and Grandathos was no exception. He had massive wings, and his presence alone demanded attention. Thirteen others followed suit immediately after him, and Gabriel's wings quivered in excitement.

Thus Michael started their army. Lustar stayed behind with many others, but they now had seventeen on their side. The new troop marched up the steps together before Grandathos stopped Michael.

"God is not up there anymore."

"Did God say anything before leaving?" Michael asked.

"No. Nothing."

Michael said a prayer to God. As he prayed, Grandathos drew Gabriel to the side and spoke with a lowered voice. "Your calling is undeniable. I am following your friend who spoke, but I came because I saw you."

Gabriel couldn't fathom why Grandathos was so impressed with him. The fact he couldn't even see the seraphim's face didn't help Gabriel feel any less awkward.

Michael finished praying, and they began to descend the stairs. Michael explained in detail what he felt was happening, which sparked debates between the other angels. Michael seemed to have more answers than any of the angels above him, and they all felt it was odd that he knew so much as an archangel. Grandathos didn't have much to say; he just followed Gabriel, a little closer than he would have liked.

Gabriel realized from their questions that many were simply confused and scared. They didn't understand why God couldn't be reached. Had he abandoned them? Michael assured them that God would soon return and those loyal to Him would not suffer the consequences of the division. Gabriel wasn't so sure. All he could do was hold onto hope. He talked with Anistar, the pale angel who had first volunteered; he spoke of his belief that not one single angel from the class of the powers had left God's side for Lucifer. This was astonishing considering every other class had half or more who had strayed. The powers class was large—over two hundred thousand angels. Many felt their persistent loyalty was a rumor, but Gabriel wanted to find out. He told Michael of Anistar's faith in the powers, and a plan was set.

The powers were a very quiet class of angels. They were warriors as their given duty, and they worked directly with the principalities. The principalities reported to the powers, and the lead powers kept records of every significant event that took place in Heaven. Gabriel was surprised to hear from Anistar about all that they had allegedly documented already throughout this time of tribulation. They were much more informed than he would have thought on what had taken place.

According to Anistar, Michael and Gabriel needed to seek out the powerful leader, Rametheus, who had played a large role in the powers' unity. His strong loyalty had served as a guide to others in his class. Through a small circle of friends, Anistar kept in contact with the powers, and he felt that Rametheus would be willing to see them.

They led their newly formed group outside of the inner island and east of the Great Canyon. From there, they flew toward the Endless Highlands. Anistar had heard a rumor that the main group of the powers had settled in the highlands in one of several secret dwellings they had throughout Heaven. No one in the company knew how many they actually had.

They traveled along a small creek that ran between two large hills covered in soft, cloth-like grass. The creek emptied into a small body of calm, murky water with another huge hill on the opposite side. A fifty-foot-tall gate had been constructed in the base of the hill and led directly within; the hill itself was the size of a small town. Some of their party flew across the pond while others walked around, and they regrouped by the gate. It was much quieter here than in most of Heaven. In fact, Gabriel realized there was no noise at all. There was not a breath of wind, and not even the water moved. With all the chaos going on, the tranquility of the place felt haunting.

Michael, Gabriel, and the seventeen angels approached the door, and Michael rapped it with his knuckles. Not one second after the knock, the door opened with a creak of its hinges. One of the powers stood there to greet them. He was large, at least five feet taller than Michael, and metal shards of armor adorned his muscular shoulders, one bronze and the other silver. Behind him, Gabriel saw an entire community within the hill, its structures made entirely of wood—wooden floors, buildings, and countless pillars and columns for support.

"We would like to speak with Rametheus," Michael said.

"I'll take you to him," the power replied without a second of hesitation. It was like he knew they were coming. With a clank from his armored feet, the angel turned to lead the way within.

Gabriel found the powers to be an odd class of angel. They all looked very similar, sharing the same physical characteristics. The powers themselves were the only ones who could name each other based on face and voice alone. They were also quite muscular compared to the average angel. The male powers were usually bare chested, with shards of metal that covered various body parts, depending upon their ranks. The higher they ranked, the more armor they had and the more elaborate its designs. Gabriel had known a few and always felt they had no personality.

The female powers were similar except they had solid metal covering their upper torsos and usually some portion of their arms. As Raphael had once put it, they were "exciting to look at." Gabriel had to admit that the entire class had amazing bodies even if he was fonder of the daintiness of the virtues.

They followed the power into the hill and began to see others going about their business in this hidden community. Several hundred torches with endless blue flames dimly lit the entirety of the underground city. Gabriel savored the smell of hickory smoke that seemed to envelop the place. It was a short escape from the nerves, and a sense of hope built inside him with each step. They needed these angels on their side.

The group walked on amber-stained flooring about eighty yards and then up three steps to an amphitheater that looked designed for large gatherings. A strange gazebo in the far-left corner looked out of place. Gabriel and the others crossed an arched bridge that took them over a thin, neon-blue stream that split the city in two and then up a flight of stairs that led to the largest building in sight. The hillside's entire city seemed built around this wooden nucleus. Four flaming torches shone on each side of the doorway. A few of the powers stood in dark shadows nearby, but their role was uncertain.

"He is in there. Only one of you can go in," the power stated in a nonnegotiable tone.

Michael turned around to face Grandathos, Anistar, and the others. "I will go speak with him on our behalf if no one objects."

"*Nuntias Dei*," said the power. Gabriel's mouth fell open, and Michael pivoted back around. After a short silence, the power pointed at Gabriel.

Gabriel's head felt half its weight. "I think it would be better for Michael to go in. He'll be better with words for your leader."

"You are the one he wants to see." He pointed directly at the words on Gabriel's chest plate. Gabriel had never heard so much about this silly inscription in all his life. It was becoming annoying.

"It must be you," continued the sturdy power.

Gabriel glanced over at Michael, who looked just as perplexed.

"Michael?"

Michael evaluated the angel, but the power's eyes stayed on Gabriel. He wasn't budging. Ever. "Well, if that's what he wants," Michael said. "Just be yourself, and let Rametheus know we need them to join us. Badly. No pressure."

"No pressure at all," returned Gabriel. He walked up at least fifty wooden steps that never creaked until he came to a door with a ten-foot carving of a lion. He started to knock, but he was apparently expected; it was ajar. He pushed it open.

Gabriel was taken immediately by the sheer presence of the power at the end of the large room. His mystical wings exuded light and had some of the largest feathers Gabriel had ever seen. They were the color of aged ivory, spattered with touches of grey. Of course, Gabriel thought, he expected no less of a spectacular angel for someone who could get him almost over two hundred thousand followers with one conversation.

The honored power stood behind a table that had two carved cups and a wooden pitcher between them. His beard, hair, and eyes were all brown, and he wore large shards of metal on his shoulders. He was muscular and stood with perfect posture and an air of confidence even greater than most powers.

Gabriel noticed a large stack of armor piled neatly on the floor beside him. Anistar had said that Rametheus was the oldest of all the powers though he didn't look it; he was undoubtedly the most respected. He was soft-spoken considering the influence he had on the powers; however, when he spoke, it was of great importance, and they listened intensely.

"Are you just going to stand there, or are you going to say something?" Rametheus said in a low, husky voice.

Gabriel hoped he hadn't already messed this up from his awkward stare. "Hello. I was just admiring your wings."

"Thank you. They were once all white, but few angels were here back then. Welcome. I am Rametheus. Join me for a drink."

"Thank you." Gabriel walked over to the table and pulled out a chair. "Were you one of the first?"

"Lucifer was first. I was the seventh."

"Did you know him well?"

"We called each other brothers back then, but that was long ago. We are no longer brothers."

"Good. I am Gabriel. I am an archangel. I have come to speak with you about the dissent among us." The chair was borderline uncomfortable, but he had remembered the only line Michael told him to say, so now he felt better.

"Heaven is no longer as it once was."

"No, it is not. Few have stayed loyal, and we have come for your help."

"What can I do for you?" Rametheus grabbed the pitcher and poured green liquid into Gabriel's cup. Steam rose from the spout of the pitcher. He then handed the pitcher toward Gabriel instead of the cup. Gabriel didn't know what to do with it. Rametheus was looking at him like Michael did when he was about to scold him, and Gabriel realized he was supposed to pour him a glass as well. Gabriel willed his shaking hand to relax for a smooth pour.

"Thank you," said Rametheus, pleased.

"It is you who should be thanked. I have heard from our following that none of your class has succumbed to Lucifer's lies. Is it true?"

"I cannot be certain if that is true, but we have not had the misfortune of losing anyone's loyalty to him. Each and every power is still with us."

"I have heard you have been the driving force behind the loyalty of your angels. I have come to ask for your aid in rallying more throughout Heaven in order to build our own army to oppose Lucifer."

"I cannot take credit for the powers. These angels are strong, and I am proud to lead them. I am bound to stay with my order and keep them protected." He took a slow sip from his cup.

"I understand your desire to keep them strong, but from what I have heard, you have done your part. I ask that you join me in sharing your strength with others. Help us save them from the path of destruction Lucifer is leading them down," Gabriel said.

"Lucifer is cunning. Always has been. I know the soft angel that hides behind those enchanting eyes." For a moment, Rametheus smiled thoughtfully, but it disappeared. "However, he is still cunning, more so each day. Do you not care for your nectar? It is good for strength."

Gabriel looked down. He had forgotten it was there. "I am single-minded. I am sorry for being rude."

"Go on with your plea," Rametheus said.

Gabriel sipped his drink. "The hour is late, and Lucifer is gaining power extremely fast. Too fast. We need to gather angels and let them know they have a choice. I have a small group of first-tier angels with me already waiting outside. We would like you to join us."

"Are these hierarchs following you?"

"We are all in this together. Angels have questions, and I give answers to the best of my ability," replied Gabriel. "But no, they follow Michael. He is the real leader here."

Rametheus studied Gabriel for a solid minute without saying a word but simply sipping his nectar.

Gabriel waited. Finally, Rametheus said, "Do you know why you were sent in here instead of this Michael?"

"I was actually wondering quite a bit about that."

"Brattack saw what your followers see."

"He pointed at my inscription." Gabriel gestured at the engraved words without looking. "*Miles Gloriosus et Nuntias—*"

"He was pointing to your heart," Rametheus interrupted. "These angels follow you for a reason. I see it in your presence as Brattack did. You know who you are, and others see more strength in you than you can even fathom. If I go, the powers will come with me. We stay together. Our power is in numbers."

This angel was contagious. Gabriel could feel it. No wonder his class stayed loyal. He made angels feel secure in themselves within the first few minutes of meeting him. Of course, Lucifer was also adept at that. "Thank you. I would have it no other way. I'm curious—how have you kept your kind so loyal?"

"We have had some of our brightest and most faithful angels amongst the powers sit in on Lucifer's meetings from the beginning. They brought back the information to discuss its validity within our class before Lucifer had a chance to send one of his followers to approach any of us. We make decisions together as a family, and we stick to them together as a family. We are for God and God alone."

"I wish I could say the same for the archangels. We only have seven archangels, and we are split. It's incredible what you have done."

"It is not what I have done. We listen and look through each other's perspectives first. Then we consider with our own eyes and hearts. It is easy to see through our own perspectives. Wise angels see through the eyes of others. Communication is our answer to disagreement. When a decision is made, we believe it is the right one, and we stick to it."

Gabriel could see how easy it was for angels to follow him. He wished what this angel had described held true for all the classes. "I respect that. When will you vote on whether you will join us?"

"We already have. We've been waiting for you. It was decided two days ago."

CHAPTER

XXII

L ucifer had gained so much power in Heaven and influenced so many angels that God's original Heaven no longer existed. Lucifer was determined to keep it from ever being restored. He was ready to confront God with the new message embodied within his army.

Azrael approached Lucifer on Terra draped in a long, black hooded cloak. His eyes were dark with one of Lucifer's favorite antivirtues, wrath. The angel dragged a wooden cart behind him filled with black garments and on top lay his long scythe. Following him were at least fifty other angels with similar carts; these angels all bore pieces of black cloth on their armor.

"They are ready, Lucifer."

"Good. Pass them out, and let everyone know this color symbolizes the absence of God's light and the lies he has told. The weapons?"

"Saraquel is leading hundreds of worker angels in Abbeus's cave as we speak. The dominions designed weapons according to our specific need. They are being mass produced now."

"How long?"

"It should not be long now. A day at the most."

"And Azazel?"

"He is with the principalities as you instructed. The Provender will be more than ready."

"You've done well. You will have your revenge with Raphael."

Beneath the shadow of his hood, a white smile formed.

"We will all gather in Abbeus's cave before we head to the Provender. Any angel who is not there will now be our enemy. Make sure the word is out."

"There will be few against us, Lucifer. I will."

Azrael led his wagons south to the cave of Abbeus. It was an ominous place protected by a body of water with vast fields beyond. The massive mountain's face had been hurriedly carved to feature the likeness of an enormous Abbeus leaning on his seraphim sword. The entrance was through the black hole of one of his eyes, reached by flight or a winding path up the cliff side. Once through, it opened to a near-endless gathering room surrounded by fire and ash. Even farther in, tunnels into the rock provided raw materials. Lucifer knew it was the perfect place to produce quickly the number of weapons he needed.

He awaited his groups at the cave, which had already amassed the majority of angels in Heaven. He had separated his angels into three groups. Delia led one that was close to five hundred thousand, and she had three of the thrones working for her to keep order and help with communications.

Abbeus's group contained the seraphim and the working-class angels of the bottom tier. He led over six hundred thousand with the help of two seraphim and two dominions appointed by Lucifer. The seraphim at the front struck fear into the lower-class angels; none had their eyes covered, and they had all six wings outstretched, which made them appear far larger than any other angels in Heaven. Lucifer had instructed them on this. The seraphim hovered smoothly over the body of water in front of the many thousands behind them, as endless as the mist that covered the distant fields.

Lucifer's group was, of course, the largest of them all. He had over two million angels by this time, made up of every class of angel other than the powers. Saraquel stayed by his side, and Lucifer had six of his closest cherubim angels helping lead the large force. Others were passing out weapons. Each angel who entered took one. After every last angel entered, he turned around on the raised platform to address his army.

"You are the overwhelming majority of our population! The angels have spoken! The new heavenly order will take what is rightfully ours from God and banish Him for all of His lies. This is now our Heaven! The throne is now our throne, and I am proud to be your leader in this grand time of change. Who hears what I am saying?"

The crowd erupted. As he peered over the crowd, blazing fires around them lighting up their features in dancing reds and yellows, he could feel the energy build. When he raised both arms, the cheers grew still louder. Unlike his concerts, he knew this praise was for him alone, and he basked in it. The crowd slowly quieted as Lucifer lowered his arms.

"We will show no mercy to those who oppose us. God has shown no mercy in His relentless onslaught of rules and regulations for our entire existence. We have our own rules now!" Lucifer looked out across the upturned faces and saw anger, resentment, and most of all utter determination to overthrow God and claim the new order by force. Perhaps it was the sheer heat in this enclosed space, but his blood felt ready to boil. "Use your weapons with the zeal that I have brought up in you. This is our new family now! We must protect it by any means necessary. God is not ready for what is to come. To the Provender!"

G abriel, Michael, and their seventeen followers stood waiting in the middle of the amphitheater with Rametheus. They were completely encircled by thousands of powers, who looked like perfect soldiers as they waited quietly for Rametheus to speak. They were in lines formed by rank with precisely two feet between them on all sides. The higher the rank, the more armor they wore. Each ordered row waited with an air of ready tension, like a finely tuned instrument about to be played.

"Well done," Michael whispered as he leaned back toward Gabriel's ear.

"It was already decided. It had nothing to do with me."

"Well, whatever happened, I am glad we have these guys. Look at them."

Gabriel peered over the impressive class and almost wished he were one of them. "Pretty incredible group."

The front angels were festooned with shards of metal while the powers in the very back had little of their bodies covered. All of the attention was directed at Rametheus. Gabriel again noticed the gazebo in the corner. On a chair inside it sat a small, old female angel. She was definitely a power from the look of her outfit and strong presence, but she was by far the frailest and oldest he'd seen. Her hair was solid white. Her body was completely covered.

"Fellow powers! The time has come. We will gather the weak and give them strength as we have always done. Gabriel the archangel will show us the way. He is strong and just. We will face this revolution with discipline and humility. Where do you stand?" shouted Rametheus.

Gabriel felt awkward and unworthy and quickly shouted, "With Gabriel and Michael!" Michael smiled at his response and almost laughed, but Gabriel could see that he was also humbled by it. He would have made a joke about it otherwise.

Rametheus either didn't hear him or ignored him. It didn't matter, really. Gabriel would still follow Michael. The crowd answered with a crashing thunderclap as the handles of their huge axes struck the wooden floor in perfect unison. It shook the entire city in a single beat. Gabriel peeked over at their followers, and Anistar, the throne who had joined first, turned to meet his gaze. He grinned and nodded his head in approval. Rametheus turned his attention to the group of nineteen, and just then the mysterious seraph Grandathos, who stood high above the others, uncovered his eyes from beneath his crossed middle wings. The white light from his face illuminated God's new army in a blaze of light. Brilliant sparkles bounced off the shards of metal worn proudly by their new companions. Gabriel felt a rush of excitement course through him and shook it out through his wings. It felt amazing.

Their army begun, Gabriel and Michael soon departed the hillside retreat of the powers. They continued traveling throughout Heaven, recruiting everyone they could. Friendships had been ripped apart by the division, and many loyal to God blamed angels on the other side—particularly Lucifer, Abbeus, and Delia since they were causing most of the conversions. Gabriel and Michael used this to their advantage when they could. To others, though, those three were the most inspiring of the revolutionaries, and then words of loyalty to God fell on deaf ears.

Gabriel's method of recruiting was different from Michael's. He was naturally loud and at times intimidating even when trying not to be. He started out by speaking boldly around the streets of the inner city. He wasn't far from his own home when he yelled, "If you have loved ones who are turning away from God to follow the cherub Lucifer, then join me and let's bring them back! Before it's too late!"

A female angel stormed across the golden pavement to him and fell sobbing onto his shoulder. She soaked it with tears, and Gabriel let her finish and catch her breath. He invited her into his home, listened to her story, and comforted her. A group of passing angels saw this happen, and they came in as well. That was how he won angels over: he showed them there was still something they could do to help their lost loved ones, and he shared his passion and determination with them. He knew he would never give up on Arrayah. He would reach every angel he could, and they would take a stand for their loved ones. It was really all they had left.

Heaven's order was no more. It was complete chaos. It was darker than Heaven had ever been and only getting darker although Gabriel felt his spark of hope inside was getting brighter. Soon every angel around had been recruited by one side or the other. Both sides had a variety of groups, some more radical than others. Neither side really knew who had more followers because there was such a division among such vast numbers and confusion ran amok. At least that was what Gabriel told himself. Deep down, he knew how outnumbered they probably were at this point.

Gabriel's group was mostly made up of angels who were upset that their loved ones had turned to Lucifer's revolution. Radical groups for God, which had been marching around like rogue armies lacking unity or leadership, joined them quickly. They spread the message that God would soon return and the angels of the new heavenly order, as Lucifer's side called it, would reap the punishment they were bringing upon themselves for their betrayal of God.

The group Gabriel met near the Blue Crystal Geyser of the south corridor was the most radical of all. When Gabriel and the others approached, the group was aggressive, threatening, ready to fight. Rametheus flew up in the air with his powerful wings, catapulting his large frame into everyone's vision.

"Join us in our loyalty for God! Gabriel," Rametheus said, peering down and pointing at Gabriel before he fixed his penetrating eyes back on his audience, "and Michael are true leaders. Together, we can stop Lucifer and his army from destroying Heaven and the angels we care about! Nothing is more important than taking a stand for the ones we love in this fight against Lucifer."

Gabriel couldn't have said it better himself. Rametheus had heard him about Michael after all. All eyes shifted to him and Michael and assessed them. Gabriel finally felt like a leader. Like someone angels could follow. Arrayah had provided him with the universal inspiration that all angels could relate to—love. Rametheus knew it too. Even if she didn't ever give it back, he was forever changed. The dramatic display of strength and sympathy worked, and the group of radicals joined their cause.

Michael spread the message among those loyal to God that they should not have animosity in their hearts, for that is not what God would want, but some didn't listen. They were fueled by anger and feelings of betrayal. Michael hoped to bring those on Lucifer's side back over to the loyal followers—as did Gabriel, starting with Arrayah—but Gabriel knew the influence Lucifer held over others. He was beyond charismatic and should not be underestimated.

"It's time to put an end to this," Gabriel said to Michael. He was looking over their accumulated ranks of angels, which numbered in the hundreds of thousands.

"Many more groups like these have amassed outside of the city. We must bring everyone together and confront Lucifer because I have heard rumors he may be escorting his entire following back to Heaven."

"If he hasn't already," interrupted Rametheus.

Gabriel's stomach dropped, but he tried to hide his worry. He knew they needed so many more angels than they had. "We will be fine," he said.

"You are not worried are you, Gabriel?" Rametheus was smiling.

"Of course not. You know, you are a great speaker, but I must say when I heard all you had accomplished, I thought you would be taller." Gabriel smiled back. As usual, Michael didn't seem to know how to react when Gabriel didn't hold his tongue.

Rametheus just smiled more broadly though. "I'll take that as a compliment. Thank you, Gabriel."

Michael looked relieved. "I think we should divide the group in half. Rametheus, will you lead an army northeast? Gabriel and I will go northwest."

Rametheus looked to Gabriel, waiting for confirmation. It still caught him off guard. He nodded when he realized what Rametheus was waiting for.

"I will," Rametheus said.

"We will meet south of the city after covering our sides of the inner island. We will run into each other eventually. Is that all right with you, Gabriel?"

Gabriel had no trouble hearing Michael's sarcasm, but Rametheus thankfully didn't catch it and waited for Gabriel's approval again. After the confirmation, Rametheus said, "We will see you there. God speed."

Michael waited for him to step away. "Seems you have a fan, Gabriel." Then he flew out over the large army and hovered in their midst as he spoke. "Half of you will follow Rametheus and the powers northeast. The other half will come with me northwest. We will bring Heaven back to our Father!" He swooped down and flew directly through the crowd, driving a line between the masses of angels. "This side will join Gabriel and me. This side will go with Rametheus."

Rametheus led his group east through the streets and then north. It was made up mostly of the powers. In fact, even the few powers who were supposed to go with Michael followed Rametheus instead.

Michael and Gabriel led their thousands of angels around by the West Pearl Gate, picking up stragglers and small groups of angels along the way. They had heard rumors of groups of angels outside the city gates looking for guidance and hope amid the chaos. Others were in prayer together, beseeching God to once again share His presence. Gabriel heard of other groups who were taking advantage of the lack of duties by entertaining themselves at popular places of leisure. He knew exactly where he would go—the Canyon Reef.

They would fly over the fields beyond the gate first and look for prayer groups gathered there. Gabriel would definitely let Michael do the talking on this one. The thousands of angels led by Michael and Gabriel poured through the gate like ants from their mound and spread wide, waiting for their leader to issue orders. Michael worked his way to the front of the crowd and addressed them.

"We will march to find every angel in need of support until this ends. God answers our prayers, and I thank you prayer warriors for staying strong." After he spoke, he leaped off the edge of the mountain and soared down with the elegance of an eagle. Immediately behind him came an awesome avalanche of angels that covered the sky as they poured over the cliff. They landed on the ground with such force that it shook. From there, they headed west and very soon found a prayer group in the grasslands just west of the White Woods.

The prayer group covered almost every blade of grass. It seemed as if every angel who left the city through the north side went there if he or she didn't know what to do. Gabriel knew it was imperative they get to the four corners outside of the heavenly city before Lucifer did. God's light was so dim that angels yearned for God's glory back and missed Him dearly. Even Gabriel realized he did, and his relationship with Him was miniscule. A small part of Gabriel still felt liberated by the feeling of freedom unconstrained by rules, but he fought that urge. He knew other angels wouldn't.

To Gabriel's surprise, Michael waved him forward. "It's time I follow you for once. Get up there and make them believe in you as I do."

Those were the best words Gabriel had ever heard. He flew up over the angels in prayer and called out. "I know many of you are scared and miss God very much right now. God is testing our faith and loyalty. There is another who is trying to raise himself above the living

God, and he is the reason for all of this chaos. God will soon return to put him in his place. I can see by your actions that most of you have made the choice to stay loyal."

The majority of angels had their heads raised and were listening intently. Gabriel continued. "It makes me proud to see how strong all of you angels have been through this dark time. We need each other to stay strong. Without my brother Michael, I would have fallen for Lucifer's lies. It makes me proud to see my brothers and sisters standing up for good. I invite you to join us as we march in these last hours for God! Let's give Him a reason to come back to us!"

Nearly every angel got up off his or her knees and shouted. Many of them raced over and joined the massive crowd behind Michael. Others came a little slower. Very few stayed in their spots. Gabriel looked down at Michael and gave him a wave forward, inviting him to lead the mob. Michael looked up at Gabriel with a smile and then marched ahead.

Gabriel and Michael led the angels west to the Great Canyon Reef. They neared the estates of the Canyon Wall, where angels were diving from the wall down into the reef below. Thousands of other angels were in or around the reef, lounging on the sand or playing in the surf. Many who had not joined a side were using God's absence as an excuse for leisure. Gabriel had to admit there was no better spot for this in Heaven than the reef. Some angels wanted to pretend nothing was happening as Gabriel so often did. If things had happened differently, perhaps at this moment he would be swimming in the water or sleeping under an orange tree. How could he judge?

Michael instructed some of their followers to spread out and round up as many like-minded others as they could as quickly as possible. As Gabriel watched Michael talking, a sudden urge took hold of him to go into the nearby White Woods. He had no idea why. It made no sense. He walked closer to the beach, trying to ignore the feeling, but it only sank deeper, lodging in the pit of his stomach. He needed to go there. The woods were calling him. He knew he had already questioned too many things before this. It was time to make a change and start believing.

"Michael, I will be back soon," he said. "Take control here." He flew away toward the woods, taking off before Michael had a chance to respond.

"Where are you going?" Michael shouted from a distance.

"The White Woods."

The woods were nearby, and he reached them quickly. He started his descent into the midst of the white trees and landed without knowing where to go. The forest was thick with trees of all different heights and shapes, but they all had the same basic structure. The base and limbs of the trees were a pale, frosty white, sticking out like icicles, while the leaves were rich shades of green, red, and brown. Gabriel was in a remote section of the woods that was dense with plush foliage. The light, already dim, was even darker here beneath the canopy of the trees. He slowly walked around. He was looking for something and could even feel it drawing him closer, but he didn't know what he was seeking.

He could hear movement. Very subtle, quiet movement, like a rustling of leaves in the distance. To his left, the grass was bent. Someone had just been there. He followed the direction of the bent blades and traveled deeper into the woods. "Hello?" he shouted. "Anyone out here?" His hands were shaking, and he couldn't control it, which was odd since he wasn't nervous.

Out of the shadows, an angel flew toward him as quickly as a branch was pulled back and released. He slammed into Gabriel, sending him tumbling over the ground like a skipped stone. The mighty angel, a cherub, followed after him and pinned his arms to the ground before he had even stopped moving. He was strong—not like Lucifer but powerful nonetheless.

"What are you doing here?" the cherub yelled in Gabriel's face.

Gabriel did not raise his voice in response. "I am here looking for angels to join God's army." He surprised himself with his own composure. Not long ago, he would have reacted with a blow to the angel's head.

"You should not be here. Leave us." As he said it, Gabriel saw another angel peeking out from behind a tree. He heard the rustling of leaves all around. He then saw a virtue angel and thought instantly of his love. She looked like Arrayah from a distance, and her necklace glistened in the light. Then he saw another male six-winged angel near her and realized these weren't just ordinary angels. Out of the five he could see, three were cherubim, one was a virtue, and one was a seraph. A powerful group.

"These are the final hours of God's absence," Gabriel said in a loud voice, making sure the others could hear him as well, "and we must decide whose side we are on. God will soon return, and those who follow Lucifer will be punished while those who stay loyal will be rewarded."

"Look at me! We are on no one's side." The cherub pushed Gabriel's shoulders into the ground before he rose up to loom over his face. With that, a new seraphim angel walked from behind a tree and uncovered her eyes. Gabriel squinted and raised his hand to shield himself from the light. The importance of this struck him hard. Here was a seraph who was still close enough to God that His light had not yet faded from her face. Michael had educated him all about it. She had to be the only one who still reflected God's glory.

"It's all right, Jasifer," she said as she made herself visible. The cherub slowly backed off. As the seraph walked forward, many other angels made themselves visible. "What is your name, angel?" she asked.

"I am the archangel Gabriel."

"You should leave," said Jasifer. He was much larger than Gabriel, which was rare, and wore a metal plate of armor conformed to his body. He turned to the seraph. "We should send him away."

"If he leaves, he could inform Lucifer of where we are."

"I am not with Lucifer," said Gabriel.

She paused to look him in the eyes. "You aren't, are you? I am Thyaterra." She was tall, lean, and radiant, with fair skin and blonde hair. She had been Lucifer's closest companion for many years. Most angels knew of her.

"Nice to meet you."

"It is nice to meet you as well. You are an archangel? What brings you here?"

"We have started a following to oppose the revolution. We seek angels to join us."

"Do you know who you are up against, Gabriel?" Her voice was surprisingly kind.

"Yes, I do. Lucifer, the highest of the cherubim, and he has many followers now. Millions, I'm sure." Whispers could be heard from angels behind him. There were far more of them than he had realized.

"Yes, he is the great cherub, but he is also the most powerful angel in all of Heaven, and God has left us for now. We came here hoping that He would return," she said.

The angels gradually made themselves visible. Gabriel realized this was the hiding place for all of the cherubim, most of the thrones, almost all of the virtues, and some of the seraphim who hadn't joined Lucifer. There were less than half of the upper classes left. They didn't seem to have any interest in joining Lucifer. They were simply hiding.

"I know that you fear Lucifer's power is too great now, but God's power will always be greater." He felt Michael's presence as if he was speaking for him. "We mustn't let Lucifer gain power and numbers while we stand in limbo. We have amassed a large following for God, and we will stand up to Lucifer until God returns. And He will return soon."

The angels looked at Gabriel, and he knew what they saw was faith and not fear. It was confirmation. Whether or not they accepted his message, he knew he was in exactly the right place.

"What makes you so sure that He will be back? How do you know that Lucifer will not overtake Heaven completely?" Jasifer asked.

Gabriel's eyes went from Thyaterra, who was looking down at the ground, to Jasifer, who was staring a hole through him. A silence blanketed the woods as Gabriel searched for the words. They waited for him to speak, all of them, but he didn't know what to say. The confident feeling that he had found his place was fading.

"Because I have seen what happens when this is all over," Michael said. He stepped around from a tree behind Gabriel and came to stand beside him. He stared right back at Jasifer with pain in his eyes. "The fallen angels will writhe in an agony I cannot even explain."

"You followed me," Gabriel whispered without thinking.

"How would you know?" retorted Jasifer. He stepped closer to Michael. "This is ridiculous! Who are you?"

The angels were whispering to each other, sounding urgent and anxious. Gabriel felt uneasy and knew they needed to hurry. Michael went straight to the point.

"I am Michael the archangel. God showed me."

Jasifer looked around at the other angels. "He showed you? God showed you what? You are an archangel!" He laughed and a few of the others joined in. "We don't have time for this nonsense."

Thyaterra walked forward and touched Jasifer on the shoulder. He backed up, and she approached the two of them. She focused on Michael. She was not laughing.

"Did God really show you this, archangel?"

"Yes, He did."

"How?"

"In a vision, a dream."

The other angels surrounding them grew quiet. Thyaterra moved slowly toward Michael with a soft expression until she was close enough to touch him. Searching his face, she found only sincerity. She looked down as a tear fell from her eyes and then slowly raised her head. Gabriel studied her every move, and he saw in her pain an echo of what he felt for Arrayah. It was comforting to know he wasn't the only one, yet it was a painful reminder of all he stood to lose.

"Oh, Lucifer," she whispered. "It's true. What have you done?" Her eyes closed, several seconds passed, and then she looked back up at Michael. "You are with this angel Gabriel?"

"Yes."

"We can stay neutral no longer. The seraphim will join you. Lead us to your army."

Many more seraphim emerged from the woods and gathered around her. There was no hesitation. Some were male and some were female, and Gabriel was overwhelmed to see so many up close. They all moved so gracefully he couldn't take his eyes off them. There were so many more than he had ever imagined.

Meanwhile a virtue angel moved her way to the front, holding the hand of another behind her. She stared up at Gabriel like she knew him. "The virtues will also join you," she said. Then four others appeared. They represented the virtues of diligence, patience, kindness, charity, and temperance. Well, according to the necklaces they wore. Gabriel couldn't help but realize the only two missing were Delia and Arrayah, chastity and humility.

The thrones followed right behind them. They were a large group of angels, draped in robes and jewels like the rest of their kind and popping out from the shadows of the white trees like rabbits. "As will we," said Betheczar, one of their most influential leaders.

The cherubim all seemed uneasy as they were waiting for Jasifer, who was the last of their leaders to speak. Most of the cherubim had already moved closer to the group of followers, but none had spoken. They were awaiting Jasifer's decision and Gabriel knew it.

"We will all stay together then," said Jasifer finally. Thyaterra smiled at him, and he nodded humbly back. Gabriel let out a sigh of relief he had not realized he was holding.

"Lead the way, archangels," Thyaterra said.

They walked through the woods to the southwest toward the Great Canyon Reef. Michael strode beside Gabriel, followed by thousands and thousands of angels. It was an impressive group. When they neared the edge of the dense forest, the two flew up through an opening in the trees, and a vast cloud of first- and second-tier angels followed.

When Gabriel and Michael approached the reef with a massive army soaring gracefully behind them, the angels who had been waiting for them to return stared with disbelief. Two archangels were leading an enormous flight of high-ranking angels. It was an image not soon to be forgotten in the minds of the loyal. Heaven had truly been turned upside down. What you did, where you came from, what you looked like, and even what class you belonged to—these things no longer mattered. Every angel was equal. It was apparent in that moment to everyone that they were all in this together. Gabriel could see it on the faces of the angels below him, and his hope grew ten times inside him.

As Michael, Gabriel, and the hierarchs swooped down, the other scattered angels hurried back from recruiting those lounging around the reef. Gabriel and Michael landed at the shoreline, and the crowd of hierarchs floated down all around the Canyon Reef, touching down on the sand or in the water wherever there was space. The number of angels was too many for Gabriel to guess. Behind them, the canyon falls thundered down, but no one was diving off them or even sleeping on the sand—they had everyone's attention now.

The seraphim stayed close together as they flew in, thousands of six-winged beings as white as snow with touches of grey. The cherubim followed, all of them in impressive armor adorned with jewels. Some were tall, some short, some were thick and others thin, but they were all intimidating. The thrones were mixed with the rest of the hierarchs, but the glow of their golden crowns made them easy to spot. As the group of hierarchs landed, hundreds of other unconvinced angels who had been splashing around the reef now hurried over. Instantly Michael and Gabriel's army had grown significantly.

When Michael landed, Gabriel gave him a look of approval though he wasn't surprised that Michael had felt the need to watch over him once more. "Thanks for being there. You saved me again."

"You would have convinced them. I just wanted to help you speed it up." Michael smirked, and Gabriel knew something was coming. "And anyway, you always drag things out."

Gabriel chuckled. "You're a terrible brother."

"That's more like it. You are too."

Michael approached Jasifer, and Gabriel's focus shifted to a virtue angel walking up in a flowing, light-blue dress. She had long brown hair, and she wore a necklace like Arrayah's that read *Diligentia*. She had round cheeks and kind, turquoise eyes.

"I am Gabriel," he said.

She gazed into his eyes. "I know. I have heard of you from Arrayah, my sister. It is nice to meet you. I am Merithah."

"Sister? But I have seen her sister, Delia."

"There are two of us."

"Oh." Gabriel held his tongue for once, realizing that Arrayah had talked so much of her relationship with her sister Delia but had never mentioned Merithah.

"I know what you are thinking. Arrayah protects Delia, not me. Our relationships are different. Delia is in love with Lucifer and won't let him go. That is why Arrayah is involved."

"Because she also loves Lucifer?" He didn't want to ask it but couldn't help himself.

"She loves you, Gabriel. She told me about you the last time I saw her."

Gabriel didn't know what to say. His mission suddenly seemed less important than going to Arrayah immediately. "She's spoken of me?"

"Oh, yes. She said all good things. You and Lucifer have been all she's talked about."

Gabriel cringed. His mission became clear again. "Have you seen her lately?"

"The last time I saw her, she was telling me about Lucifer's new way of thinking. Then she talked about you. She wanted you to join them and said her feelings were becoming strong for you. There was something she needed to tell you, she said, and then she had to go."

"I have seen her recently. I was hoping she might have left him by now. We need to get her away from him because I know in my heart she is better than this. I don't want something to happen to her, and she is not safe with Lucifer."

"Is she in danger?"

"All of the angels following Lucifer are," Gabriel said. "I believe she wants to get away from him, but she is frightened."

"I hope we can help her, but she won't leave Delia. I miss her already."

"We will save everyone we can, including Delia."

Merithah's smile dropped away. "Delia can't be saved."

Gabriel was unnerved by this reply and wanted to press her for more, but the angels around the water looked anxious. It was time to move. Some of the larger battle cherubim appeared particularly unhappy, especially Jasifer. A throne angel accidentally splashed him, and he picked the angel up clear out of the water and deposited him on his other side. The throne never said a word except to apologize for the splash. Perhaps Jasifer didn't like to get wet.

Michael approached, all business again. "Let's go, Gabriel."

"I agree."

Michael and Gabriel led that army of angels all over the inner island of Heaven—from the Granite Falls above Paradise Canyon all the way around the Great Mountain through the White Woods, the Mountains of the Canyon

Reef, the Rolling Hills of Peace, and past the Field of Tranquility—as they gathered even more angels to join in their campaign. Large groups of angels were at each popular site. Near the Field of Tranquility, Michael halted the army with the help of Gabriel, Thyaterra, and even Jasifer. He flew up to address the crowd once again.

"We have found so many lost angels in a very short period of time! We will still be well outnumbered. We have a long way to go in order to stand up against the masses that now follow Lucifer, but it can and will be done!" Many in the crowd were unmoved and a large number looked worried, but Michael flapped his wings and spoke to them with such confidence that it was hard to say he was wrong.

Gabriel had an idea and grabbed Michael's shoulder. "I do not want to split up, but at this point, we need to cover as much land and gather as many angels as we can. We have two small groups that will be led to hunt for more. One will head east, and one will head south. We will all meet back here as soon as we have covered the second circle in each of our directions. What do you think?"

"I think you are right."

Gabriel looked over at Jasifer. "Jasifer, you are a powerful leader, and many look up to you. I know you don't think highly of me, but I ask you for your help in leading a team east. I believe there is no one better."

Jasifer's stony expression finally softened. "I thought you would never ask. Mind if I take a few cherubim, sir?"

Gabriel nodded and smiled. "Please don't call me that."

"Sorry, sir." He flipped around. "Let's go!" Jasifer leaped into the air, and twelve other cherubim followed close at his heels.

Gabriel noticed the crew was a little intimidating. Probably too intimidating. "Merithah, would you and the virtues join them?"

She looked up at the cherubs taking off. "Of course. They may be a little rough around the edges, but it's nothing a little virtue softness can't fix." She winked at Gabriel and turned to gather the others. The four angels agreed. When they flew off, Gabriel noticed how fast they were—faster than any angels he'd seen besides one. He remembered flying with Arrayah. It comforted him to know that if it came down to it, at least she could fly away from danger. It must be one of the many gifts of the virtues.

Michael said, "Quick thinking. I'm not sure anyone would have talked to that rough bunch without the virtues along."

Gabriel left his thoughts of Arrayah and quickly came back to the conversation. "Sometimes a female's touch is all you need."

Michael laughed. "Not what you need. Well, let's go."

Thyaterra took it upon herself to lead some of the seraphim south toward the lower rainforests in search of more angels. She said the seraphim would have no problem attracting attention. It was the act of actually getting angels to follow them that she wasn't sure of.

"Meet back here after covering the second circle straight south, and we will do the same," Gabriel called to Thyaterra as they left.

"We will!"

"I hope Rametheus doesn't disappoint us," Michael said, flying alongside Gabriel.

"I know you are not beginning to doubt yourself. We are on the right side, remember?"

"Yes, we are. That is why you are my brother, Gabriel. You keep my head straight." He grabbed him by the shoulder and pulled him in for a quick hug. Michael lowered his tone to a whisper near Gabriel's ear. "You are the backbone of this resistance. Don't forget. These angels look up to you for strength and confidence. Without it, things could fall apart."

"I understand. Everything God told you has come true. You still believe that right?"

"With all my heart. He also told me that you would be responsible for saving half of the angels. Remember that?"

They continued east, skirting the base of the Great Mountain. To rest their wings, they walked across the fields. The air started to get cooler. A slight wind began that Heaven had never experienced before. Soft smoke rose in the sky and gathered together to form clouds. Many angels stopped walking and looked up. Something was coming soon; Gabriel could feel it.

"We must keep on!" Michael shouted to him. "We are running out of time. We need to save as many as we can."

Gabriel jumped in the air and flew over the crowd. He shouted to everyone to keep moving. He told them God was coming back.

They did keep moving. Only a few fell behind. After a little bit of walking, just south of the Great Mountain and before the Hanging Gardens, they reached the grounds of the Provender. It was as thick and lush as ever, the grass was damp with dew, and the far end was dense with fog. It made Gabriel think of the games.

As they started across it, an angel fifty yards to Gabriel's left was suddenly catapulted in the air with a spike driven through both wings. It happened so fast that for a moment they all just stared. Then Gabriel heard the spring of a mechanism in the ground next to him and the angel to his right was knocked to the grass, shrieking, a jagged jaw of metal clamped onto his leg and wing. Much of the army froze in place, others took to the skies, while a few went to free the injured. Gabriel stared into the fog, trying to tune out the cries of pain. He could see exactly what he hoped he wouldn't. They were all out of time.

XXIV

S traight ahead beneath the fog, a massive, dense line of angels—over five miles wide and seemingly endless in depth—stood in opposition. They were about a mile away across the large field of grass where the sporting events had always taken place. It was ironic, Gabriel mused darkly, given the good nature of the games. They had taught angels to battle for fun.

"Those aren't the angels we're looking for, are they?" said Gabriel, staring straight forward.

"No, I don't imagine they are," replied Michael.

The entire dark group in the distance carried weapons. Even the classes of angels that didn't normally wear armor were outfitted with breastplates, shoulder guards, helmets, wrist guards, and leg guards. The few who didn't have at least one black piece of armor wore a piece of dark-black cloth on some part of their bodies. Many were covered with the color.

Heaven had never seen the pitch black that they wore because there had never been such a complete absence of light. It was like they had embraced the darkness with this color. They had somehow found a way to make it and lots of it.

Gabriel noticed seraphim and cherubim hovering throughout the opposing army, acting as connection points for communication with the six angels in front who led them. At the helm was Lucifer, easily distinguishable even at this distance. He was relaying messages through his network to his entire army. The highest cherub was clearly not only powerful but frighteningly intelligent. Gabriel took to the skies to avoid the traps and snares, and Michael followed him.

"Everyone must stay here!" Michael shouted. "Step carefully and tend to the wounded. We will confront them civilly if we can." Gabriel's intentions weren't exactly the same, but he would try to stay calm for not only Michael but also for the rest of his followers as well. Being a leader had its downfalls—like maturity and responsibility.

An angel broke from the crowd and flew up to him. It was Raphael. He had neatly groomed facial hair now, so Gabriel hardly recognized him.

"Gabriel," he said. "I want to apologize to you. I have made mistakes in my past and have still been quick to judge others. I want you to know that I am sorry."

Gabriel appreciated the apology, but it wasn't the best time to say the least. "It is quite fine, Raphael. I apologize too. I never gave much effort to doing the right things."

"I fear something bad is going to happen, something terrible, and I think I may know why." The angel's skin seemed to have aged a thousand years. His face was lined with worry.

"Let's talk about this another time." Gabriel tried to focus on the opposition ahead, which was slowly approaching.

"No, Gabriel! I need to tell you now before it is too late. I told a horrible lie years ago about an archangel to tear him away from someone that loved him deeply. I was selfish because I wanted her for myself, and it worked. She never believed him again and left him to his seclusion."

"Amitiel?"

"Yes. My closest angel knows nothing of my lie. She is the angel of truth and knows nothing of my lie! But he does, and I fear him now. Azrael is over there. I know it."

"It is fine, Raphael. I'm sure you were forgiven long ago."

"Not for this lie. I don't think I can ever be forgiven for something like this."

Raphael might be right. Gabriel thought of the hatred burning in Azrael's eyes when he spoke of Raphael. "We have all made mistakes."

"I haven't told you what it is I did. I need to say it, and you'll understand."

"I do understand. It doesn't matter what you did or said. We have a forgiving God. If Azrael hasn't forgiven you after all this time, he will be the one who suffers, not you. Now I need you to calm down and help us out right now."

Gabriel had to believe God would forgive anything because if Arrayah was to go through what Michael said, he needed to believe she would be forgiven. If not, he didn't know what he could believe in. "I need you to fly as quickly as you can to find Thyaterra and Jasifer and the others. Lead them to us as soon as possible. Can you do that? Think of Amitiel; she is with us too. Do it for her and focus."

Raphael seemed to come to a decision and drew a deep breath. "Of course, Gabriel. Anything I can do to help."

Raphael was considered one of the friendliest angels in Heaven, and Gabriel knew his charming demeanor could possibly help make the meeting they needed to have with Lucifer civil. However, Raphael wasn't himself, and it was important to make sure Thyaterra and Jasifer were brought back with their armies quickly. Michael could think whatever he wanted, but Gabriel had a feeling Lucifer's army wasn't looking for peace.

"Are you and Raphael done?" asked Michael. "Lucifer and his leaders are walking our way. We should meet them peacefully."

Gabriel held his tongue. Lucifer didn't want peace. As the six of them approached, they dodged certain spots in the field, and Gabriel realized how far the secret traps must stretch. No, this had been planned for a long time.

"They sure are walking funny, aren't they?" Gabriel said dryly. "Let's go, but watch your step."

Michael instructed their followers to stay where they were, and he and Gabriel dropped down to the field and began walking to meet their counterparts. When they were almost halfway between armies, Gabriel noticed that the six were made up of Lucifer, Abbeus, Saraquel, Arrayah, Delia, and, surprisingly, Azrael. Lucifer and Arrayah were in the middle with the others flanking. Gabriel and Michael stopped and waited for them.

His attention shifted from his fellow archangel to his favorite virtue. "Arrayah," he murmured accidentally. Just the sight of her was a relief.

"Keep your cool, Gabriel. I want this to stay as peaceful as possible. We need God right now," said Michael.

God isn't coming, Gabriel thought. They needed Rametheus, Thyaterra, Jasifer, and every last angel they had gathered. Gabriel spared Michael his doubts. The six drew closer, and Lucifer led the way, nearing Gabriel. Gabriel felt energy pumping through every part of his body.

"Gabriel," Lucifer said, spreading open his arms. "It's good to see you back on your feet."

They all laughed except Arrayah, who faked a smile uneasily when her companions looked at her. Gabriel cared more about her reaction than anyone else's. She waited for them to turn away from her and mouthed, "I'm sorry." Her apology was cheapened by the absurd number of jewels on her gown.

Lucifer's wings were missing feathers near their base. Gabriel had never seen one missing feather on an angel before, much less the entire base where the cherub's wings met his back. The base was a pinkish hue with a scaly texture, and it looked painful. Something was terribly wrong with him. His hair had changed to a long, dark black, and his eyes were a deep, dark brown, like burnt wood.

Lucifer gave three slow handclaps as he danced toward Gabriel. "So, where do we go from here, archangel? And here I thought Michael was going to be the biggest spike in my side. How did that angel enjoy the spike in his by the way?"

"What do you want, Lucifer?"

"I want something you can't give me, Michael. You archangels are playing admirably big roles in this for both sides, but you are still insignificant. These two, however, won't be for much longer." He gestured to Saraquel and Azrael.

Azrael stood shrouded in a massive dark cloak, yet even his hidden face couldn't disguise the hatred in his eyes. What was Lucifer putting in their heads?

"Azrael, I know you are angry," Gabriel said. "I know you hold onto jealousy and hatred for Raphael because of her. You don't have to do this, you know. He is sorry." Azrael quivered with disgust. Gabriel focused back on Arrayah. "Every last one of you can be forgiven for this."

"It's interesting you say that, Gabriel, because as you stare at Arrayah, we all know you are the jealous one. I can help you with that you know."

Gabriel strained to hold himself back. Lucifer only smiled.

"End this, Lucifer," Michael said.

Lucifer slumped his arms and shoulders with exaggerated animation. "Ah, but it is such a fine day, and I would hate to spoil it. You know, I'm feeling benevolent. I will still allow you to join us before things get out of control. What do you two say?"

Gabriel listened, but his thoughts about Arrayah tortured him. Why did she not leave this twisted creature's side? "Arrayah, you don't have to follow him. You owe him no allegiance. I love you and want the best for you. This is not it, and you know it."

Arrayah's confusion and uncertainty had already been plainly written on her face. Now, as she looked at Gabriel and then over at Lucifer, he saw fear for the first time in her.

"That is so touching," Lucifer said. "Your feelings are such a priority of ours. Still, unfortunately for you, Arrayah has made her choice." His voice changed from its pleasant silkiness to a scratchy hiss. "I will not tell you again that she is no longer your concern."

"I wasn't talking to you," Gabriel said. Michael gestured to him to calm down. He did, with difficulty. Arrayah wouldn't even look at him again.

"We have two sides with conflicting beliefs, Lucifer," Michael said. "I think we should keep them separate until God returns."

"Where is your God, Michael? You seem to know Him so well. It seems He is scared to show up, even at this very late hour." His voice was still noticeably different than Gabriel had ever heard. Even Abbeus and Arrayah turned in surprise at his scratchy inflections. Saraquel ducked a little toward Lucifer's back.

"You can't see yourself, but everyone else can. You have no idea what you have become. God is allowing all this for a reason. You will soon see."

Abbeus fully outstretched his six wings. "We are replacing God's throne with Lucifer's. It is superior for a superior leader. The new heavenly order will take effect as of this day's end. Lucifer is our new god. The old one will be dealt with upon His return, should He ever do so."

"Your dramatic gestures are unnecessary. Your six wings do not mean much to me except that they will burn longer. Nothing is happening until He returns," said Michael.

"I believe it is," broke in Lucifer. "My angels are prepared. We have power and knowledge neither you nor anyone on your side comes even close to possessing. You leave us with no choice but to initiate the final resolution, which we are fully prepared for." As he spoke, his face darkened further as he noticed another group of angels emerge in the distance. Gabriel turned to see that they were led by a seraph. There were many more angels than had been with them before, close to two hundred thousand. Although great, their numbers still paled in comparison to Lucifer's.

"It looks as if you have added another insignificant group to your tiny army. Congratulations," said Saraquel. He was holding one of Lucifer's wings. He seemed to have grown taller since their last meeting, yet he cowered behind Lucifer. He was surprisingly arrogant in his speech for an angel hiding behind his master.

The new addition of angels moved to the front line of Gabriel's and Michael's army. Lucifer's face harbored a frown when he realized who was leading the new addition of angels. Six feathers fell from Lucifer's wings and landed softly behind his feet. Gabriel saw them drop and then followed Lucifer's line of sight to Thyaterra. Right next to her were Bretabian and Raphael. They must have been close already. For a moment, a light almost like compassion shone in Lucifer's eyes.

Then Lucifer's body shivered and his voice shrieked. "The time for talking is over! Bow down and give up your army! Your God is no longer in control here!"

Lucifer grabbed Arrayah. Gabriel began to tense up. Lucifer threw her behind him a little too roughly, and she yelped. Gabriel stepped closer with clenched fists.

"You are fine, Arrayah! Back up, archangel. We've been through this once already." Lucifer drew his sword. "I know she has you all choked up inside because you are weak, but stand down or it will cost you your whole following." He grabbed Arrayah by the wrist and jerked her back onto her feet. "Arrayah, come here and—"

Gabriel rushed at Lucifer and tackled him by the legs, slamming him down to the ground on his back. Lucifer's head hit the ground so hard it sounded like it had cracked open.

"No, Gabriel!" cried Arrayah.

When Lucifer hit the ground, it was the single move that triggered the start of the war. The entire front row of Lucifer's millions of angels came tearing down the Provender, screaming. Their swords were drawn, armor clanking, dust and grass flying up under their feet. Some angels jumped in the air to travel faster while others ran and leaped over traps. A deafening roar rang throughout all of Heaven as they charged across the field, headed straight for Gabriel.

L ucifer drove his elbow up into Gabriel's forehead like a hammer blow, and Gabriel was momentarily stunned. The sky and the field switched places. Cool grass brushed his face. Pushing himself up with one hand, he saw God's side charging from his direction. The sky was so thick with angels that many were forced to run across the field; he could feel the vibrations through his palm. Buried traps and snares clamped shut on angels' legs or drove spikes through their wings, but the armies rushed on. Michael also rushed to his aid, but Saraquel and Abbeus grabbed his wings from behind as he reached for Gabriel. Gabriel stretched out his hand but never made contact. In a flash, the two armies collided in the air and on the ground with a crushing force that shook the Provender. Saraquel and Abbeus took cover as angels crashed together all around them, dropping Michael in the process. It sounded like thousands of explosions going off all at once. Sword hit sword and armor rammed against armor in a steady rain of blows. The war they feared most had begun.

Mere seconds had passed. Where was Lucifer? Gabriel looked but could not find him. All around him, angels from both sides tumbled into each other with astonishing speed. As wave after wave collided, the contact seemed like it would never end. He then spotted Lucifer, who had been swarmed by the radical group they recruited near the geyser. The fight was a blur of flying arms, wings, and weapons. A dozen black-armored angels swooped up on Gabriel, and he drew his sword and blocked a flurry of blows as they passed. He knocked two of them out of the air, and the others kept on, smashing into another cadre led by Bretabian. Gabriel could hardly focus. Angels were screaming in anger and pain all around him. It was the loudest Heaven had ever been.

Sparks flew from striking metal, and small fires lit the grasses. Soon the fields filled with noxious smoke. Gabriel felt heat beneath his toes and saw his boot was on fire. As he stomped it out, he noticed Azrael darting past him, his scythe drawn. There were angels all around and innumerable battles raging, but Gabriel felt compelled to stop him. He had an idea where Azrael was going.

"Azrael!"

He kept running.

Lucifer broke free from the angels piling on him, knocking them viciously away with mighty swings of his sword like he was cutting down trees. He leaped into the air and hovered about twenty feet up, and Gabriel looked up just in time to see the cherub rushing down at him with a vicious blow. Gabriel met the blow with his own sword, but the impact still knocked Gabriel's blade back into his own chest plate and drove him off his feet and into the ground.

Lucifer's armored boot slammed down onto Gabriel's stomach, forcing him deeper into the dirt, and his sword pressed against Gabriel's blade until the inner edge began to sink into his chest plate. Gabriel was pinned. He could see Michael fighting Saraquel close by, their swords locked.

Michael saw him. "Gabriel!" He broke the deadlock and kicked Saraquel in the side. Saraquel charged again, and Michael met him with an upward slice that spun him off his feet. Saraquel's necklace was cut and went flying, its Alexandrite stone landing near Gabriel's free hand.

Lucifer leaned low over Gabriel, his face a snarling mask of fury that was no longer remotely angelic. Unbelievably Gabriel's armor was beginning to dent in from the pressure, to crush him within it. Michael called his name again and ran toward him, but Abbeus tackled him from behind. Michael struck him twice in the jaw and rolled free. More blackened angels were flooding in around them.

Straining, Gabriel's fingers touched the chain of Saraquel's necklace in the grass. Lucifer leaned even closer, his eyes wild with rage and furious pleasure in this moment, his unfathomed strength crushing Gabriel. Gabriel grabbed the necklace and swung it hard, whipping the stone directly into Lucifer's eye. Lucifer howled and reared back, and Gabriel kicked him in the chest with both feet. Lucifer flew off, and Gabriel staggered up. He was seeing spots.

Through a blurry haze, Azrael was visible again for a moment, charging across the field. Gabriel jumped into the air and pumped his wings hard. He was nearly flattened again by a group of thrones flying by at breakneck speed, but he weaved between them.

"Gabriel!" Lucifer shouted from below. He began to leap into the air in pursuit, but Bretabian and several other seraphim came flying out of the fray. Bretabian raised a broadsword high and charged at Lucifer. Gabriel turned to search for Azrael again.

The weapons Lucifer's side was using were different from any design he had ever seen. They were various shapes and forms of axes, swords, and even scythes, but they all had one thing in common: a curvature of the blade. Lucifer's army wore ornate helmets and new armor, and many had large shields. They were prepared for full combat. This war's outcome was predetermined.

Gabriel picked Azrael out again, a dark figure flying low across the field. Looking farther out, he could see Raphael. Gabriel flew faster, dodging battling angels in the air, and soon closed in on Azrael. He dropped down and was about to block Azrael's path when something took hold of him from behind.

Lucifer ripped Gabriel violently from the sky, digging his own heels into the ground to stop the arch-angel's flight. Then he leaped forward into the air and hurled Gabriel into a line of charging angels from the opposite side. Gabriel smashed through eleven angels before he stopped sliding along the grass. The white on his clothing was covered in green stains, and he spit a rough chunk out of his mouth. He climbed shakily back to his feet, bracing his hands a moment on his knees. Lucifer closed in on him again, but Michael and an-other angel were flying in from the side. They lunged at Lucifer, but he spun and sent them both to the ground with a blow from his massive wings. Before they could get up, five other black-armored angels attacked with swords and axes.

Lucifer drew his ridiculously ornate sword and advanced on Gabriel. Only Lucifer would carry such an extravagant weapon, Gabriel thought. He was trying to summon up the energy to even draw his own.

Nearby, Azrael had reached Raphael, and it looked like they were having a heated conversation with Raphael as the aggressor. Gabriel forced himself to run toward them as Raphael fell to his knees with his hands together. He was probably pleading for forgiveness. Despite what he had told Raphael, Gabriel did not think he would receive it. There was only one angel in Gabriel's way—it was Lucifer. Gabriel would have preferred any other ten angels in Heaven.

"Raphael! Get up!" Gabriel shouted across the field.

"Raphael is gone, Gabriel!" Lucifer moved directly in his path. "Azrael has him now! There will be no more forgiveness—angels must pay for what they do. They will all be held accountable, including you." His eyes were blood red. A darkness surrounded him that Gabriel could not even explain. He realized now why Arrayah was so afraid. They did know something the rest of the angels didn't, and he had a feeling Raphael was about to find out what it was.

Gabriel ran at Lucifer with all of his might. Using just his wings, Lucifer sent a powerful gust of wind that knocked Gabriel on his back again. Where was this power coming from? He got up as Azrael raised his scythe over the archangel, his friend, on his knees. Gabriel charged again, and this time Lucifer tackled him to the lawn, gripping Gabriel so tightly that he couldn't move.

"Watch, Gabriel! This is what will become of all of you!" Lucifer held him on the ground and jerked his head back by the hair, forcing him to face Azrael's raised scythe. Gabriel struggled as he watched Raphael's mouth moving. He couldn't make out the words. The pain in his back and shoulder deepened as Lucifer pushed him harder into the ground.

In that northern grassland, Azrael's long scythe came down hard on the back of Raphael's neck in the small crease that separated it from his flexed wings. It was the same spot on the back where Lucifer's feathers had fallen out, the marginal coverts. Gabriel stared in horror as the blade ran straight along Raphael's spine, severing the soft tissue at the fragile base of his wings like a spiritapple being opened from its top. The blade sliced all the way down. Raphael let out a shrill cry that was deafening as it raced through the vast corridors of Heaven. His severed wings fell to the ground behind him, and he toppled over lifeless.

XXVI

E very angel stopped fighting as soon as they heard the shriek. The piercing cry was so intense that those nearby dropped their weapons and covered their ears. Lucifer let go of Gabriel to shield his ears, but Gabriel couldn't move to get away; they were so close to it that his vision blurred and his head rang. Gabriel tried to scream or at least thought he did, but he could no longer hear.

After a few seconds of staring over his bloody creation, Azrael looked over at Gabriel and smiled. It might have been at Lucifer—Gabriel wasn't sure—but it fueled a roaring fire inside him. The life that was once in Raphael was gone. The glow had disappeared from the two pieces of his body.

This was the secret that Lucifer kept. Angels could have their wings separated and life force drained by severing the marginal coverts down through the base. Now a countless number of angels had seen exactly how it worked. Worse, nearly every angel around him who witnessed this revelation was on Lucifer's side. This was planned all along, Gabriel realized. They knew to follow Azrael and see what would happen. They had been told this would be the turning point in Heaven.

Lucifer looked across the field at his masterpiece, Azrael. Lucifer had killed animals, but now he'd done something so much more important. He had convinced another to take life. Even better, he had convinced an angel to take the life of one of his own kind.

"Now you see what happens to those who oppose us!" he called to his armies. "You all have the power Azrael just displayed to his enemy. Now let's take the wings of every angel against us!"

Immediately all of his followers charged back into battle with a roar that echoed throughout Heaven. They began aiming for the top of their opponents' wings with bloodthirsty cries. Kaldeczar, the throne, held Uriel's arms as Saraquel sliced through his wings. Lucifer felt almost dizzy with anticipation of what would happen next. Heaven and the cosmos was theirs to take. Was God really gone for good? He grabbed a passing angel and ripped his wings off with his bare hands, tearing through the base like he was shredding paper.

"No!" screamed a voice behind him. As Lucifer
turned, a heavy shoulder crashed into his stomach and
drove him to the ground. It was Gabriel. He had forgotten
briefly about the archangel. No matter. His feeble tackle
would not accomplish anything. Lucifer twisted his arm
around the stubborn archangel's neck and pulled him up
to his knees. It was time to dispose of him once and for all.

"You've lost, Gabriel!"

"This isn't over, and I will not let you take her down
with you!"

"Well, you won't be around to see what happens."
Lucifer grabbed one of Gabriel's thick wings and worked
his fingers in for a strong grip. As he prepared to rip,
Lucifer was smashed into from the side. Gabriel flew
from his grip, and Lucifer slid on the ground for almost
a hundred feet with a large body on top of him. His right
wing dug a track in the ground, pulling up grass and dirt
the entire way. It was Jasifer. One of his own kind and
commonly considered the strongest of the cherubim.
Well, he knew the reality. There wasn't an angel in Heaven
that could match his own strength.

Jasifer's cherubim stormed through the crowd,
but their number was still insignificant. Seven of them
swarmed Lucifer as he lay on his back after Jasifer's
vigorous tackle. They were like the vultures that flocked
to dead corpses Lucifer left on earth. They thought they
had Lucifer pinned.

He reached deep within for the fury he needed. As they struck him, forced down his limbs and wings, and pinned him to the ground, he felt something raging up in him. For a moment, he thought of God's Son. He blacked out for a brief second. When his vision cleared, the cherubim were flying in different directions like an explosion had gone off. His arms and wings were fully extended, nothing was holding him. God had nothing compared to this power. He felt drugged on it, sick, unbalanced, but overflowing with strength. He was unlocking secrets God didn't even know. The power of his antivirtues was so much more destructive than God's virtues could ever be.

Jasifer had been knocked loose with the rest of them. Lucifer rose to his feet and saw Gabriel running at him again. Persistent fool. Lucifer easily sidestepped, grabbed Gabriel by the throat, and lifted him into the air. Jasifer charged again from the other side, but Lucifer caught him by the neck with his left hand. He held both of them up, squeezing until he thought he might close his fists and twist their heads free from their bodies. Lucifer felt weightless. He stretched his scaly wings to their full extension. It felt as if they were growing that very second. They extended so hard that the pressure hurt to the point of pleasure.

"Why is your God hiding?" he shouted. "Why hasn't He helped you yet? Call to Him now and see what happens!"

A black sea of his angels flooded the field behind him howling battle cries and cheers for Lucifer. The grass was littered by bloody wings and lifeless bodies. It was his dream coming to reality, and he truly knew God was gone. Now it was time to destroy the rest of those who opposed him. He listened to every shout of praise and knew he deserved them and so much more for what he had accomplished.

Gabriel and Jasifer grasped at their throats and flapped their wings desperately, trying to free themselves from Lucifer's grip. Lucifer squeezed the pitiful angels' throats more tightly. He felt like killing them both without delay, but he also wanted to relish the spotlight. Every angel in his vicinity was watching him single-handedly overpower two of the opposition's most powerful warriors. He wanted them all to see his strength. He wanted every single one of them to remember this moment always. God was overthrown, and Heaven was now his for the taking.

"I dare you to come back now, God! I dare you to show me the Son you think is worthy of overtaking me in rank!"

Saraquel stepped forward and looked straight into his eyes. The proud smile on the face of his most loyal follower said it all. Lucifer felt the energy of the two struggling angels in his grips start to dwindle. Saraquel's grin disappeared at something behind Lucifer, so he quickly turned to see what it was.

Thyaterra approached from no more than three hundred feet away surrounded by a large huddle of warrior angels. She was the type to attempt to fight, but she was always protected against her will.

A sharp pain suddenly went down Lucifer's spine, and he dropped the two in his hands and fell to his knees. He grabbed for the base of his wings and realized Jasifer had struck at his marginal coverts. How could he have been so distracted? How did one of the angels in his hands even obtain a weapon? He was furious, but as he looked around holding his neck to ease the pain, he realized Jasifer and Gabriel were gone.

Quickly he turned toward Thyaterra's circle of fighters. That dark fury rose up in him again although this time he did not black out. As they came at him, he knocked them down with crushing strikes and backhands to each body as if they were powerless stalks of wheat. When he had pummeled each to the ground, he walked among their groaning forms and ripped their wings from their bodies one by one, absorbing Thyaterra's screams. She ran at him, and he pushed her onto her back. His forearms were crimson with blood. He turned to look at her as he severed the last angel's wings. The ripping tendons of the angel seemed to be mirrored by Thyaterra's heartstrings, and he savored the feeling as both broke. Shiny tears poured from her like water from the Falls of the Canyon Reef. Finally, the last angel grew stiff and still, only an empty shell, and he turned once again to his lost love. She had left him when he needed her most. She deserved this.

"I told you it would end this way!"

She struggled to muster words through her sobbing. "You are disgusting, Lucifer! I don't know who you are, but you are not of Heaven!"

He wanted to rip her heart from her chest in revenge for what she had done to him. "You're right, I am not of God's old Heaven. I am a revolutionary."

"No, you are a deceiver. Do you know what you have become? Look at yourself! What happened to you?"

"Don't stand there and pretend you have no idea what happened to me!"

"I don't! Nothing can justify what you have done!" she shouted. "And now you will have to live with your decisions. How could you do this? Look at the blood you've spilled. Look at what you have made of Heaven and its wonderful angels!"

"You of all angels know exactly why this had to happen."

"Why, Lucifer? Because of your arrogance?"

"I gave my life to servitude for His love and got nothing except His betrayal! Love is a weakness bound to destroy the souls of the ignorant. Why would you love a disappointing God like Him?"

"Because He loves us too," she cried. "Love is the only thing that matters, Lucifer. You pervert its role in the heavens. You have done all this with pride and arrogance, not love!"

"Look around you! I am the one who was right!" He turned around in all directions, holding his arms out toward the bloody scene. "Don't tell me how to think. You have no answers!"

Injured, beaten, and lifeless angels lay everywhere, but so many continued to fight that beyond the body-strewn patch the giant grassland was barely visible. The vast majority of angels still standing or flying sported the black of his army. Thyaterra was watching something down the field now, and he followed her gaze to see Michael still upright and fighting, holding off six angels who were trying to take his wings. One jumped on him from behind and started delivering punches to his head. Michael was forced to the ground. Lucifer smiled, waiting for Michael's wings to be severed. Not far from him lay Gabriel, pinned with his face in the grass, covered by a dozen angels. It was ironic that Thyaterra's eyes found those two when Lucifer had lost them. Why was everyone drawn to these two archangels?

"You see?" said Lucifer to Thyaterra, and he turned back to face her. "Where is the pathetic God you love so much now? Where is His all-important Son?"

She closed her eyes and lowered her head. Lucifer felt something shifting inside and realized that even now he waited for her to join him. In his core, he still yearned for her approval. Was it possible he still yearned for her love? He could not let himself feel this. It was weakness. It must be destroyed inside himself. For about a minute, she looked down and softly prayed, and he waited, allowing her this time. She had lost everything. He could grant her this. When she opened her eyes, she looked not at him but over his shoulder.

"Yes. I do see," she finally said.

In the distance, coming from the east, the darkness uncovered a large group of angels who were new to the battle. It was an entirely fresh, pristine, powerful army. The large, tightly uniform group was led by a striking leader decorated in shards of glowing gold. Lucifer realized it was the one group he had been searching for, the class of angels he could never reach. It was Rametheus and the powers.

He shifted back to Thyaterra and saw her soft lips form a smile. "Why are you smiling?" he demanded.

She closed her eyes and whispered, "Thank you, Father."

The army of powers was clearly armed and organized. They flew in tightly ordered ranks, and as they neared, they swooped down to land in lines, seamlessly continuing their advance. They were fully armored with helmets and shields, and every single one carried an enormous golden axe. When all had landed on the field, Rametheus dropped down ten yards in front of his army and raised his golden axe high in the air. At this gesture, the angels pounded the ends of their axes to the ground twice in unison and let out a battle cry. It shook the heavens. They came down in two hundred vast rows of golden warriors stacked thousands of angels deep.

As the powers neared, three hundred thousand lower-class angels stormed down from the skies behind them to swell their ranks. They had been outfitted with swords from the powers' armory. As these armies neared, most of Lucifer's angels in black rallied to meet them. Lucifer vacillated between Thyaterra and the new army. He didn't want to leave her, but he knew he must lead this charge.

He wondered agitatedly why she looked so confident. He finally grunted and took off, flying straight at Rametheus. The bulk of Lucifer's massive remaining army charged as well, falling into rows behind him. These new angels needed to be dealt with, but their numbers were still not nearly enough to challenge Lucifer. He would make their leader bleed himself. He would stack his wings right on top of Gabriel's and Michael's.

XXVII

G abriel lay on the ground, struggling. The angels pinning him were about to slice off his wings, but then the powers arrived, their battle cry deafening, and most of the angels holding him charged toward the new threat. Gabriel seized the opportunity and kicked as hard as he could at one of the last two, connecting with his chin and knocking him back. The second dark angel tried to pin Gabriel again, but he used his wings to push himself up and then landed the most vicious right hook to the angel's jaw that he could remember. It reminded him of the only time he ever knocked out Michael.

He realized he was free and no angels were around him. Looking up, he said, "If that is You bringing the powers, Father, thank You. I'm rather fond of my wings. Perfect timing." He took to the sky to rejoin the fight.

"Gabriel!"

On the field close by, he could see Michael held by four angels while another prepared to sever his wings. There wasn't enough time to get there. Gabriel pulled his sword from its harness and threw it as hard as he could at the angel behind Michael. The sword rotated end over end and sank heavily into the right wing of his target. The angel dropped his sword and Gabriel immediately heard a cry, but it wasn't coming from the angel he hit. It was coming from the air above him.

A dark cloud was getting larger and larger in the dim sky. It began to separate like it was being pulled apart. The cry became louder and louder, and then the cloud dissolved into another army of angels. The rest of the powers who had not led the charge down the field were flanking the large numbers of Lucifer's army from high in the dark sky. They blew past Michael, buffeting all of them with a gust of wind and knocking the four angels down with strikes of their weapons. Sparks flew as their black armor was mashed in.

This new wave came on fierce and undeniable, and it took down many of Lucifer's angels from the side. The powers made a noticeable dent in the opposing army from both sides and gave God's exhausted followers time to energize again. Angels healed quickly, and this was a significant opportunity for Michael and Gabriel to regroup and coordinate the troops for their next attack.

Michael ran over to Gabriel.

"Are you all right, brother?"

"Are you?" replied Gabriel.

"Yes. Thank you for saving me."

"I just got lucky. Not even sure who I was aiming at."

"Yeah, right."

Gabriel was relieved Michael was fine, but he knew this war was far from over. How could this conflict even end without the slaughter of the rest of their angels?

"What can we do, Michael?"

"We will not take the lives of angels. We have to believe there is another way."

"Look around you! The lifeless bodies of our friends are everywhere!"

Michael said nothing.

Gabriel knew he didn't have an answer. "I will not stand back and let them destroy us all."

Ahead of them, Rametheus waded through rows of Lucifer's forces. He swiftly destroyed their armor with the heavy pierces of his axe. He led the powers yard after yard into the crowd of the enemy, but he didn't know the secret Lucifer was wielding. His forces didn't know to guard their wings.

As Gabriel watched, he realized that Rametheus, as strong as he was, was still probably the weakest of the powers. The powers were ripping through the enemy and gathering beaten angels into their ranks as they progressed. How long had the powers been in the sky waiting Gabriel wondered. It didn't really matter. It was an intelligent tactic.

Rametheus's angels cut a wedge through Lucifer's army, pummeling every angel in their way. They then broke formation and spread out, their weapons swung with destructive finesse. Rametheus flew through the air, crushing dark angels and sending them spinning to the ground. The powers performed somersaults and other maneuvers that confused their opponents. Gabriel watched in awe.

All of a sudden, he saw Arrayah. She was fighting, but it seemed more like pure defense. Gabriel tore off in her direction.

Her attacker landed a violent blow against her blade, which shook in her hands. "I saw you throw Jasifer that sword to escape Lucifer!" he screamed. Gabriel recognized the screech of Saraquel.

The anger Gabriel had held inside for too long felt like it was boiling over the top of his skull. He rushed at Saraquel. All of the pain from Arrayah, Michael, Raphael, and every other shred he could muster seemed to flow through his body as he wrapped his arms around Saraquel's body and drove him into the soft dirt. Gabriel pinned him and began raining down blows on Saraquel's face. For a moment, he saw Lucifer instead, and he lost control. He must have struck him a hundred times before his vision cleared and he realized Michael was pulling him off his fellow archangel.

Gabriel jerked himself free of Michael's grasp and grabbed Saraquel to flip him over. He wanted to take his wings. If the dark angels could do it, why couldn't he? He gripped the thick marginal coverts of the dazed and beaten Saraquel and prepared to rip them.

"You want me to be like Lucifer, Arrayah? Do you?" He saw the look of shame on her face—for herself, for him—but he could not stop. "I can be just as powerful! Is that what you are looking for?"

Arrayah said nothing, but Gabriel could see it all over her face. She was lost. She still would not turn from Lucifer's side. How could she still care for him after all of this? He wanted to rip off Saraquel's wings from frustration, but he wouldn't. He couldn't.

"Well, I'm not like him! I will never be like him!"

Gabriel released Saraquel's wings and let him fall to the ground. Arrayah was watching him, and although she still seemed lost, he saw now that she looked at him with the same admiration as when she looked at Lucifer. Gabriel finally understood. She loved both of them.

He turned to see how the powers were faring. Lucifer's angels had recovered from the initial onslaught and were now viciously carving the wings from as many of the shocked powers as they could. Rametheus nearly had his own severed, and he flew into the air, shaking off three angels who clung to his wings.

"Powers, guard your wings!" he shouted.

It forced them to fight defensively, to huddle back to back instead of pressing forward. The dark angels pressed their advantage, and the combat reached a new level of frantic violence. The chaos of battle soon became so vicious that some angels struck those on their own side. Lucifer was right in the thick of it, cutting a wide swath through the powers, ripping wings from downed enemies and throwing them aside with fury. His army followed his lead, tearing loose the wings of exposed powers or slicing them away.

Soon angels could scarcely fight without stumbling over the lifeless forms of fallen warriors. In desperation, the powers and the other remaining faithful beat the dark angels into unconsciousness or broke their limbs until they could no longer fight. Angels and wings dropped out of the sky in a steady rain, plummeting all around Gabriel, striking the ground in an endless rhythm. It was horrific. He looked around at the desolation that had once been a place of innocence. Even if they won, what kind of Heaven would be left? Arrayah was weeping. He felt his hope nearly gone.

At that moment, the dark skies were split open by the brightest light that Heaven had ever seen. It blinded Gabriel, and time seemed to stand still. He could barely make out Arrayah in front of him, and she covered her head with her face down on her knees. He fell to his knees and closed his eyes, tilting his face up toward the light.

"He's back," Gabriel whispered.

A smile spread across his face. The battle was over. Angels could hardly see the ground next to them. Heaven shook from a powerful vibration, and a warm wind swept through the grassland. The entire sky was lit with fire, and the cold turned to heat in an instant.

God's unmistakable voice began to speak, filling Heaven with its reverberations. His voice was the deepest thunder and consumed Gabriel's whole being. "You have fallen from Heaven, O Lucifer, son of the morning! You were the anointed cherub upon the holy mountain. You walked up and down in the midst of the stones of fire. You were perfect from the day you were created until iniquity and pride were found in you. You have filled Heaven with violence, and you have sinned greatly. Therefore, I cast you from the mountain of God, and I destroy you, O great cherub from the stones of fire. Your heart was lifted up because of your beauty, and you corrupted wisdom by reason of your intelligence. I will cast you and all your dark angels to the ground, for you have said in your heart that you will exalt your throne above the stars of God."

God's voice was so overpowering that when it finally stopped, Gabriel felt the energy from his body finally coming back in the silence. He had been frozen in place. Swords, shields, axes, and scythes dropped to the grass. Every angel was letting God's words sink in. Many were starting to cry. Some cries were of joy while others were of sorrow and guilt. Gabriel realized that it was almost too late for certain angels, including Arrayah.

Without thinking, he prayed to God, "Merciful Father, I know now what I am supposed to be. Allow me to speak with these angels as one of them and convince them to fall on their knees and beg for Your forgiveness before they face their consequences. My heart is with one of these angels. I cannot bear to see her fall without a chance at redemption because of this great deceiver! Many others deserve this same chance. Many of their hearts are actually still with You, O Lord! Some did not know what they were doing."

God answered Gabriel aloud for all of Heaven to hear. "Gabriel, I will grant your request to give these dark angels one chance at redemption. Those who ask My forgiveness will be saved, but those who do not will be cast out with their leader."

God's blinding light faded. The dark Heaven was again restored to its former splendor with God's light once more shining from His throne on the Great Mountain's summit. The angels slowly rose up, rubbing their eyes and re-establishing their equilibrium. As they stood, Gabriel flew up over them. Speaking as loudly as he could, he addressed the crowd, and he knew somehow that all were able to hear his words, even those who would have been out of earshot. They would all receive this chance. Gabriel decided to hold nothing back. His emotions poured out like a waterfall.

"Our God has returned to us, just as I and many of you knew He would. Many of you have been deceived by Lucifer and his leaders. I tell you now that it is not too late! I know how God is feeling. He loves you so much it is painful." He looked down over the crowd at Arrayah. "His heart is truly broken at the thought of losing those of you who have left Him. He hurts from your deceitfulness."

His eyes welled up with tears. Arrayah's gaze met his, and he wanted to go directly down to her. "He still loves you. He always has and always will. I say to you now, get on one knee and ask Him for forgiveness so that He may grant you mercy. He wants nothing more. There are angels here who love you too and want nothing more. Do it before it is too late. Do it now!"

Gabriel knew the way God felt about losing the angels because it was the way he felt about losing Arrayah. Gabriel could see from the sky that tears were sliding down her face again. Gabriel saw so much potential in her, but she desired Lucifer. Why else would she not ask for forgiveness? Why did she still resist?

All over the Provender, angels began to drop to their knees. Hundreds of thousands of angels started asking

God for forgiveness. As they did, Lucifer flew up toward Gabriel. Gabriel noticed Arrayah's knees that had almost buckled now straightened at the sight of him.

"Bow to your true god!" Lucifer shouted. "Those who follow me, know this—we shall reign in the cosmos until our return, which is much better than serving Him here as slaves. Do you not want to be the masters of your own existence? I certainly do! His power is based on tricks and lies! This is not over! We will reign!" Some angels in the crowd still cheered for him.

Gabriel began his descent toward Arrayah, and she gazed directly back at him with weary eyes. After a moment, she stretched open arms toward him. She seemed to want him to forgive her for her deceit, but she would not fall to her knees and ask God for forgiveness.

As he approached her, he said, "Did you throw the sword to Jasifer?"

"I did." Tears dripped from her chin.

"Why help us if you are still on his side? Why don't you ask for forgiveness now?"

"I don't deserve to be forgiven!"

As he reached her and took her into his arms, all of the angels that followed Lucifer and had not asked for forgiveness were banished from Heaven. Gabriel felt Arrayah being pulled from him and clung to her. Her mouth pressed to his ear, her breath was soft and quick. "I'm sorry." Her body contorted and he tried to hold onto her, but it was useless. The force of her departure was unstoppable. He could only watch as her weary, tear-filled eyes turned to shock and fear.

Screams and shouts filled the air. The banished angels' bodies twisted as they tried to withstand the awesome power of the pull, but it could not be resisted. It was impossible to fight. Arrayah's face went white with terror as she was ripped from his arms. Gabriel watched as her body spun, and he could see her reaching for him and hear her screaming his name. He heard her bones breaking.

"No! Arrayah!" She was dragged in a southwesterly direction so quickly that a blue flame flared in her wake. He ran toward her, but she was now out of sight. She was gone. His knees buckled, and he landed on the ground at the spot where she had stood just a moment ago.

He buried his head in his hands and started to cry. He could almost hear his own heart break like her shattered bones. Gabriel grabbed his chest plate like he was holding on for dear life. It felt like it was crushing him again.

One third of the angels of Heaven suffered the same fate as Arrayah. They were gone, all of them, in an instant. They had been sucked down the cliff of the Marble Falls together at an incredible speed. Those left behind saw sparks erupt into large balls of fire as the banished descended. Within seconds, they were all gone, and Heaven was once again filled only with true followers of God.

Gabriel's body went limp. He simply had no more strength. Then he heard God's resounding voice again in his head.

"You are strong, Gabriel. I love you, my son. There is one left among you who will suffer a different fate. Go find Azrael."

Gabriel stood up with a newfound strength. He started walking without hesitation, and he knew inside which way to go. As he went, God's voice continued in his head. God gave him specific instructions for confronting Azrael, whose fate would be different than the rest of the fallen. God had a plan for him. He would become the angel of death.

There was an energy like no other that drew Gabriel in. It was Azrael who was still on the field and down on his knees. On the ground, the dark archangel looked confused. Gabriel stopped right next to him.

"Azrael, stand up."

Azrael slowly turned his head to Gabriel. "What do you want?"

Nearby angels were staring and pointing, shocked that Azrael was still in Heaven.

"You will not be cast down with the others," said Gabriel. "You will suffer a different fate. You discovered what will be called murder and brought about death to an angel. Your envious heart caused you to perform an unspeakable act. You intentionally severed the life source of Raphael, knowing full well what would happen."

Azrael looked at him with disgust. "What do you know about it? Nothing!" he shouted. "Leave me alone!"

Just then the blood-soaked fields turned greener, the blood faded away, and the severed wings of the lifeless bodies moved on their own to their rightful owners. The wings reattached, and each one of the dead calmly opened his or her eyes. Wounds healed, skin brightened, and all of them woke up as if they had simply been dreaming. Gabriel looked back to Azrael, who wore a horrified expression that all the carnage had been undone.

"For your act, you will become the angel of death. God has already restored life into Raphael as you can see, and you will be the only one to bear the burden of this unspeakable act. God will not allow one of His angels to be destroyed under His protection in Heaven again. You will scour the universe for eternity bringing one thing to other beings: death. It has been ordained by God, and I am merely the messenger." Gabriel turned to walk away with a heavy heart.

"Wait," said Azrael, but Gabriel kept walking. "What beings? No! Lucifer showed me how. It was Lucifer's fault! He has been murdering animals and knew what I would do. He tricked me!"

In an instant, Azrael was sucked out of Heaven with a blue flame in the same manner as the fallen, but he was sent in a different direction. He was sent to the northeast, down the Granite Falls, into a place in the cosmos millions of miles from Terra where he would be alone for eternity without an entrance to Heaven. God had ordained it. He was to search for life throughout the millions of planets and stars by himself, bringing nothing but death.

Gabriel eventually stopped walking and just sat on the ground with a blank stare, trying to think of something he could do. Michael walked over and sat beside him, but for once, he had nothing to say. After a few minutes, Merithah approached with compassionate eyes. "Gabriel, are you all right?"

"Yes, I'm fine," Gabriel answered, staring straight ahead.

"I miss her too. It's fine to be upset," she said.

He stood up. Michael stood up too, but Gabriel didn't look at him.

"Where are you going?" Merithah asked.

"To get Arrayah." He started walking, and Michael fell in step beside him.

"You can't," she said.

"Gabriel, stop," Michael said. He put a hand on Gabriel's shoulder, but he shrugged it off and jumped up, wings unfurling. "Gabriel!"

He flew toward the Marble Falls, and Michael took off after him. Merithah flew after them both.

"Gabriel!" shouted Michael.

"Stay back!"

"Gabriel, stop!"

He didn't respond. Michael was faster in the air than Gabriel, so he caught up to him in the Field of Tranquility. It was still black when they got there from Lucifer and all of his dark angels who had just been ripped across it. They had never seen it black before. It was now turning blue-green as Gabriel crossed it and then finally back to its typical brilliant blue as the other two godly angels passed over.

Michael hugged Gabriel from the back and steered him down to the ground. They cut through the blue wheat like a sickle, sending blue spores into the air and then a spray of dirt. Michael held onto Gabriel as Merithah flew over to them.

"Get off me!" He struggled to free himself.

"You have to let her go," Michael said. He fought to keep Gabriel down. They were covered in dirt and wheat from the tumble.

"No!" Gabriel heaved himself up and shoved Michael off. Michael grabbed his leg before he could fly away and pulled him back down to the ground. He took hold of Gabriel's wrists and twisted them crossed over his chest, and then he leaned over his friend to hold him down.

"There's nothing you can do to save her!" yelled Michael. In a softer voice, he said, "I'm sorry, my brother. But there really is nothing you can do." Gabriel finally stopped struggling. After a moment, Michael let go of him.

Gabriel took a deep breath and rolled over on the ground. He and Michael just lay there, staring up at the sky and not moving.

"She can't be saved now," said Michael with labored breaths.

Gabriel watched the dancing blue stalks of wheat around them. It was like they had never been black. "I know," he said. After a long pause, Gabriel added softly, "Not yet."

Michael turned his head in Gabriel's direction but stayed silent. He was at a loss for words again, and Gabriel knew why. Michael couldn't understand. He was restricted by rules and laws but not Gabriel. There would always be hope.

"Gabriel, trust in God. That's all you can do," said Merithah. He wondered how long she had been standing there just behind them. She sat lightly on her knees beside him and brushed his hair back from his dirty face.

"I will, Merithah." He closed his eyes and felt a tear roll down his cheek.

Merithah wiped Gabriel's tear and lay down directly beside him and Michael. Her soft touch was comforting. She stretched out on her back and stared up.

The three of them lay there in silence for a long time, and it was quite peaceful after the havoc of the last hours. Gabriel suddenly noticed a feather float by on a breeze. It was pure white, long, and thin, with the distinct shape of virtue feathers—like the tip of a spear. Behind it was the most brilliant blue sky he had ever seen in Heaven. It made him think of all that was lost and all that was gained on this terrible, beautiful day. *What do we do now?*

Lucifer felt his bones strained to the breaking point, but he didn't resist. He was consumed with a blue flame that was not quenched as he passed through the water beneath the Marble Falls. He was drawn from there into the cosmos. He had lost all control of his body, and now he was going to collide with his lonely planet, Terra. Behind him, an endless onslaught of pulsing lights blazed through the cosmos, each angel an individual inferno.

The balls of blazing fire ripped through space at incredible speeds, headed straight for the silent planet. Lucifer entered the atmosphere first, flashing his way down and into the rocky terrain; his collision shook the planet like an earthquake, and Lucifer's entire body felt broken from the impact. Dust and debris blanketed the sky. The lavish green grass that covered this part of the planet was seared for miles around the large crater created by his impact.

To his surprise, he found that as he settled in the crater he had only a few broken bones and he was still brilliant white without even a single burned feather. Heavy, grey smoke rose from him as he started to cool like a stomped-out fire. The thick smoke enveloped and overtook the dust. He stretched his large, powerful wings as he did after a long sleep, and the soreness was severe.

Before his wings could fully separate, he reached up with a glowing hand and noticed his abnormally long, wiry fingers. As he reached out and up for the crater's ledge, the ground shook nearby when a second blue fireball crashed down. Lucifer began to pull himself up as the deafening sounds of more powerful impacts echoed across the landscape. Each angel landed with an earth-shattering crash. They seemed endless, and the planet sustained permanent damage to its surface from the massive wounds they were inflicting. The collisions seemed to go on and on until Lucifer began to wonder just how many of his followers had remained defiant.

There were so many slamming into the ground that the sounds became muddled into one long, thunderous blow. Finally they started to slow until the last one had completed his damaging plummet into the planet's surface. Eventually an uneasy silence settled in. Nothing could be seen through the smoke, rock, and dust clouds, but the groans and clanking of armor could be heard unceasingly as Lucifer brought himself up from his newly formed crater.

He was proud not to be alone. The craters were countless, and the angels all worked their way up slowly from the depth of the craters to the damaged surface. Lucifer climbed to his feet, which had also changed. He could feel that they were slimmer underneath his ornate armor, more wiry like his hands. The armor covered all but the long toes and thick steam rose from it. The plates covering his feet were gleaming brightly, and the pliable steel seemed to be white hot.

The white canvas of metal that engulfed him was threaded with brilliant designs of intense golden highlights that sparkled against the beautiful metal, but as his armor began to cool quickly, he noticed something odd. It completely defied his understanding. The steam grew thicker and the luminescent finish started to dim. As he moved his foot forward, the armor made clacking sounds, and it became still cooler and turned to grey. The ornate gold charred and curled up like burning paper— starting from above his toe and moving up his foot and around his ankle.

The same was happening on the other foot, and his soft toes began to lose their pink hue and take on a chalky gray color. His silky skin dried up, becoming pale and ashen. As he reached a steady walk, his gray skin darkened to deep charcoal all over. It felt like the liquids in his body had dried up and half his mass was gone. He felt shrunken, twisted, and bone dry. Around him, the ground shook violently, and lava erupted from volcanoes and spilled down them to the ground. The planet was responding to its new inhabitants' unwelcome and destructive entrance.

Just behind him, an angel as gloriously bright as the heavens crawled up from a hole in the ground and spread her wings. He recognized Arrayah, but she was too bright for his eyes to take in. A small glimpse of her former glory was captivating even as her brilliant luster began to fade. Her beautiful, feminine face was perfectly smooth and fair as if silky cream had been perfectly poured into the shape of a face. Why was he noticing these things? Her lips were a subtle pink with a heart-shaped top that was hardly noticeable once she opened her hypnotic blue eyes. They were like crystal-clear waters inviting him to dive in. What was happening to him? All of a sudden, he felt an agonizing burning all over. The pain consumed him as he felt every inch of his body burn. He clenched his excruciating muscles and soaked in the punishment. He knew God was doing this to him, and he would not falter. Instead, he stared into Arrayah's eyes.

While her beauty was more undeniable to him than ever, so was the look in her eyes. They quivered as they blinked and welled up with tears. She looked haunted and deeply broken. It wasn't horror from watching him burn; it was pain. The emotional wound written on her face was without question. She felt a tormenting loss. As she stared ahead and the first tear fell, the blackness of her pupils grew and transformed the whites of her eyes as if ink had been splashed over them. Imperfections spread like wildfire across her glorious face. It was like watching a masterpiece slowly being overtaken by flames. Her enchanting body darkened all over.

Her soft skin began to turn ashen while her white feathers caught fire and burned from the tip to the root, beginning where the wings met on her back. The flames crept around the thick base of her wings twice as quickly, and the soft feathers burned even faster there. As the flames lit her wings, she turned with shock. She had no idea what was happening to her but quickly realized it was the same fate she had just seen Lucifer endure. The flames burned out to reveal the grotesque skeleton of her once-brilliant wings. She moaned and wept while her skin finished its grueling transformation. The silver necklace that read *Humilitas* broke away and dropped to the ground, shining in the dirt. Her wings were charred and smoking as she fell to her knees, head down on the ground. She sobbed uncontrollably. With trembling hands, she grasped what was left of her necklace, and Lucifer knew where her heart belonged.

Before a backdrop of smoke, ash, and lava, hundreds of thousands of figures crawled out of the craters. Just behind Arrayah was an enormous, ominous angel with six wings. It was Abbeus. He too looked more brilliant than ever. Before he could stretch them, his six wings caught fire. He jerked his head around to see what was happening and caught eyes with Lucifer. His face became hardened, and he no longer moved. Lucifer hadn't uttered one sound. He held onto the pain and realized its power, and he was proud of Abbeus for doing the same.

Out of respect, the six-winged angel stood tall and tried to hold in the groans as best he could as he stared at his leader. The flames engulfing his wings were even more vicious and relentless from the force of six burning wings. The creature closed his eyes and gritted his teeth as the fire consumed his feathers and moved on to his body and skin. He continued to stand tall although it looked like his knees were going to buckle. He knew Lucifer was watching. Lucifer was impressed.

Each and every one of these beautiful angels went through the process of losing his or her magnificence. They were fallen now. Wailing and groans filled the crater-pocked landscape, both from physical agony and the morbid terror of realizing what they had become in their separation from God. Lucifer, though, bathed in the power of it.

The number of dark creatures seemed endless, and the farther away they were, the more they seemed to race each other to catch up to Lucifer, the one who had landed first. They varied in size and form, and they scurried around him like his children. Perhaps they were now. The air grew colder, and darkness took over the dust and debris. Hours went by as Lucifer walked and the others followed. Some stopped along the way and fell to their knees sobbing, but they quickly jumped up and scrambled forward to follow again as if they were scared to leave the newly formed pack. A thick, heavy rain began to fall. It happened quickly, like Heaven suddenly started crying. He loved it, and his bitter hatred fueled even more pride in him. This would not stop him. Nothing would ever stop him.

The ground became soaked with rain and dusted with ash. Travel became harder, yet still not a word had been spoken by Lucifer. He looked down into a puddle and caught his own reflection lit by a blaze of lightning overhead. Deep thunder echoed around them. He knelt down to catch a closer look, and as he saw what was reflected in the water, he punched the image in a sudden fury. His face and skin had grayed to a pasty leather, and his hair had burned and curled up around his head. His famously beautiful eyes, always changing color, were now fixed permanently black. The air was rancid with the stench of rotting bodies and burning hair. He turned from the puddle in disgust. *God, do you think this is the end? It has only just begun.* The temperature dropped so rapidly that their breath began to steam out in clouds despite the driving rain. Thick pieces of ice began to fall from the Heavens and break themselves all over the fallen angels.

Lucifer had the largest and blackest wings of them all, like the unsearchable dark of a bottomless abyss. They had grown, and he could see them easily himself. The others' wings were a deep charcoal color while his were a sinister tar. Now featherless, they had twice the span of some of the smaller angels struggling behind him. Although the others were engaged in different degrees of wailing, he was the only one who never emitted a sound. Not even a grimace. He stood tall and walked with purpose. He felt proud. He would be a leader, and these newly formed dark creatures would follow him like one.

As Lucifer marched north, he started to hear angels talking behind him about God and being cast out of Heaven. He heard one say, "God is punishing us. Maybe we were wrong to oppose Him."

Lucifer whipped around and soared in the air above his dejected followers, flapping his massive wings to hover. From the looks on their deformed faces, many were horrified at his transformation. "We no longer serve anyone!" he declared at the top of his voice. His beauty might be gone, but his intelligence and passion were not. "I heard many of you weeping and some questioning what is going to happen. Make sure that is the last time I hear any of that! We have work to do, and those of you who rise to the challenge will be greatly rewarded with power and possession. Rankings will be earned here based on performance and who wants it the most!"

The fallen angels were still in shock. Some shouted cheers. Others remained silent. One loud voice cried out above the others. "I miss God! I shouldn't have been cast down! This was a mistake. A horrible mistake. Please help me! I want to go back to Heaven!"

Lucifer didn't even recognize him. It didn't matter. "Shut up now!" Lucifer snarled, and with a growl he flew down to the dark angel and hovered over him. The angel cowered, like prey.

"I don't deserve this! I need God!"

Lucifer began to fume. "Don't mention His name one more time, pathetic angel!"

"What has happened to me?" the angel wailed. He sunk to his knees and rocked back and forth. "Why would God do this to me?"

Lucifer dropped like a stone and trampled the dark angel into the dirt. He grabbed him by the throat and beat him with heavy blows. The angel tried to curl up, but Lucifer crushed him into the ground repeatedly. He would make an example of this angel. With black nails and the jagged edges of his wings, he scraped and pierced the angel's flesh. Then he ripped the creature's charred wings off and broke the bases of them over his knee. He turned to the crowd of angels who were watching and cast the pieces at them. Many had turned their faces away. Lucifer left the remains of the angel there, mangled and motionless.

Lucifer flew up to address his minions. They looked terrified. "Let that be a lesson! Never mention His name again, and never show me a pitiful display of weakness! You are no longer weak, subservient angels. You are my strong, merciless army, and each of you will be stronger from the lessons I teach! Now, does anyone else have something to say?"

Silence blanketed Terra. The angels stared back at him in wide-eyed disbelief. He noticed the creature that was once Arrayah in the crowd. She was upset but trying not to show it. In another time and place, Lucifer would have gone and comforted her, but now he did not. Perhaps that was the best kindness he could muster now, to ignore her weakness instead of making an example of it. Painfully, she stood up and collected herself. He knew she was strong. He would give her time, but he would show no mercy to others.

He saw potential in his new domain. He would be a ruthless leader here, and his convictions would quickly overcome any regrets he had. There was no time to feel sorry for what he lost from God; instead, he must focus on building his new empire. He had a plan, and while he felt pain and regret, he saw it as weakness to be buried deep in the depths of his soul. He would never allow any other angel to see weakness in him. He had what he wanted now, and his dark army looked to him for everything they needed. Some of his angels loved him and some didn't, but all would worship him as their new god. They had no choice.

From conversations he held with God long ago but never understood until now, Lucifer realized there would be new inhabitants on this world. It dawned on him that God had a plan for this planet long ago. No matter. He was its god now. He needed to build his army up to full strength to rule this world and to have his revenge. "Everyone search the land, for this is our new home. Whoever finds me the coldest place in the depths of Terra will be rewarded greatly. Now, go!"

Over the coming months, Lucifer established his hierarchy of dark angels, assigning leaders over each of the many antivirtues he had discovered through his rise and fall. God had called them "sins," and so be it. He gave them to his most loyal followers as gifts. They were to discover how deep and dark they could possibly reach in order to fully oppose the teachings of his enemy. He created envy, greed, pride, wrath, and sloth. Lucifer pointed out their power. He would never stop searching for more.

Abbeus, Delia, Saraquel, Arrayah, and many other high-ranking fallen angels played their parts in creating the powerful creatures of sin. They all had a hand in developing everything that was the opposite of God. They worked together to move beyond sin. They created true evil, and the first steps of Lucifer's plan were coming along better than he could have imagined.

Lucifer no longer called his army angels. As they transformed into darker and more evil creatures, he renamed them demons. He found he thrived on evil and destruction. He made a whole new world for his demons, and he grew more powerful with every passing day. Lucifer pried into the depths of every dark sin and was completely thrilled with his domain on Earth. This was just the beginning, he thought. Heaven had better be prepared. He was coming for everything.

CHAPTER

XXIX

The day after the war, many angels were distraught like Gabriel because they had also lost loved ones. They were deeply gratified that God had returned and Heaven was back to normal, but then again it wasn't. They were thankful for the restoration of peace, order, and grace, but the loss of so many left holes in many of the angels' hearts. Heaven once again smelled of fresh flowers, and the dark, hazy mist was no more, yet many mansions stood empty, and many posts had to be filled. It was a bittersweet time in Heaven.

Most angels believed that the fallen, as they were now calling the banished ones, had crossed the point of no return and could never get back. But Gabriel didn't feel that way. He held strong to the belief that God was a forgiving God and would one day bring Arrayah back into Heaven and back into his life. God did not say that it could be done, but He also did not say that it could not be done. Gabriel sought an audience with God and pleaded for her forgiveness, but God told him it was not for Gabriel to decide the fate of Arrayah. It never was. Gabriel still held onto the belief that nothing was impossible. He had to in order to move forward.

On the night of the war, when Gabriel, Michael, and Merithah finally got up and went home, Gabriel did not speak more than two words back to them. But the next day he was refreshed, confident, and happy. He knew he would never stop fighting for Arrayah. It was his mission, his hope. Michael and Merithah were the first ones to notice a drastic change in Gabriel, and they let him know about it.

In the days following "the Fall," as the angels called it, Gabriel began to voice his thoughts and feelings openly like never before. He was known throughout Heaven by now, and he wasn't afraid to speak his mind. Many remembered his role in the war and his speech that had saved so many. Many angels went to him for comfort and answers in the following days while others came to him to give thanks for his plea to God on their behalves. One day, in the inner city near Gabriel's house, an angel ran up and grabbed his shoulder. He had fought on God's side in the war.

"Hello, Teniel. I am glad to see you're here," said Gabriel.

The angel stood up tall. "It is only because of you. I was scared, and many of my best friends and my true love were followers of Lucifer when we fought that day."

"I am sorry to hear that."

"I was able to bring back two of my friends, but I have lost the one dearest to me. I can't stop thinking about her." There was pain in his eyes and a longing that Gabriel would say something the others had not.

"Many have lost those dear to them, including me. I will tell you what I am going to do. I am going to stay strong and believe that they can once again be saved. I believe that I will get to see my love again someday. When I do, I will be ready. Hold onto your hope, Teniel. In the meantime, find your passion and live for yourself now. Be happy and be strong. You will meet again."

A glimmer of a smile came across Teniel's face. "I will," he said. Teniel left with a bright outlook even in the darkest time Heaven had ever known. It was the feeling Gabriel lived for now—giving hope to others. He spoke to many angels throughout Heaven as the word spread of his message of hope for the fallen. It was a concept that no other angel thought possible. It was a small chance but still a chance, and many clung to it tightly along with their love for the lost if only to ease the pain. Gabriel believed if God were truly a forgiving God, then there was nothing to say he would never forgive the fallen and even Lucifer for that matter.

A few weeks later, Raphael walked up to Gabriel. His demeanor was different than it had always been. He wasn't as perfectly dressed, and his facial hair wasn't as trimmed as it used to be. He wasn't as joyful either. The betrayal of the fallen angels had affected him, and ever since Azrael's attack, he had never gained total forgiveness in his heart. It was difficult for him to understand how so much animosity had been built up on his account. He couldn't let it go. God had restored his wound and Raphael's wings were even larger and whiter than before, but Raphael still had to search for complete forgiveness, and that would take time.

"Why do you give angels false hope?" Raphael said. "They are gone."

"I believe they will have another chance."

"They had their chance. They are gone, as they should be."

"Where is Amitiel?"

Raphael looked away. "Never mind her. As I said, they are gone! Stop giving false hope!"

"There is no limit to God's mercy. Even faith as small as a mustard seed can move mountains. I will hold onto hope for the fallen." Gabriel had angels to forgive as well, and he saw what would happen to him if he didn't. He had only to look at Raphael.

Days turned into weeks, weeks into months, and months into years. Some others still held onto their hope as Gabriel did. He never faltered. Many generations passed since the Fall. Gabriel became a leader of the army of God and a staple among the wise leaders in the hierarchs. He provided understanding and stayed strong, spreading God's messages throughout Heaven.

Almost every angel who had lost someone believed what Gabriel said, which was that all could be forgiven through love and faith. For those with lost loved ones, the Fall actually strengthened their faith in the Creator. Gabriel tried to keep controversy away, but some angels, especially those who had not lost someone dear, felt the fallen were gone forever and would never be allowed back into Heaven. Gabriel did his best to avoid debates about it.

Not even Michael could believe the transformation that had taken place with Gabriel. He no longer sat around eating fruit and complaining. He now lived a life of moderation and purpose. He learned to do many things and indulged his artistic side, creating astonishing paintings, captivating writings, and even moving music. His creations were fueled by his love for God and Arrayah. Some reflected his joyful soul while others captured feelings of loss to comfort other angels in the knowledge that they were not alone. The Fall taught many lessons in Heaven, and it was agreed unanimously that it should never be forgotten. The upheaval of the Fall led to the most artistic time Heaven had ever seen, and its beauty was heightened as a result.

Gabriel truly was God's messenger. This role helped the mourners make the decision to see hope and forgiveness rather than become bitter and angry with God. At least that was how Gabriel saw it. Gabriel thus helped avert a second war by affirming the good and keeping angels on the right side during this difficult period.

Michael rose in stature until he was among the highest of God's leaders. He had proven himself to be one of the most loyal throughout the tribulation and war, and it didn't go unnoticed. Michael was among the most respected angels in all of Heaven. He could no longer be introverted even if he wanted to be, and it made Gabriel laugh every day. Angels looked up to him like they once looked up to Lucifer. Stories were often told by worker angels of the time that they had seen "the brothers," as Michael and Gabriel were now referred to, bringing all of the seraphim, cherubim, thrones, and virtues back to God from their hiding place in the White Woods. Every time the story was told, it proved over and over again that rank and class in Heaven did not define them as angels. If archangels could lead Heaven, then anything was possible. This image, of Michael and Gabriel leading the army of hierarchs, was carved into the gold of the ornate bridge right before the steps that led to the upper tiers. For all time, it would remind angels of their inner abilities and what they could become.

XXX

God had a new plan that Lucifer knew nothing about. He explained to Gabriel His plan of creating a being in His own image, one that would be called "Man" and would have free will to choose to worship Him or not. God needed Gabriel to go to Earth to deliver a special message to Satan. That was how all angels in Heaven now referred to Lucifer; God had changed his name. It meant "the accuser," for Lucifer had falsely accused God of being a liar.

Gabriel once again asked God about the possibility of forgiveness for the fallen, but God told him everything would happen according to His divine plan. He told Gabriel to be patient, so he would be. Gabriel hoped he would see Arrayah while on his mission.

God prepared Gabriel for what to expect. He told him of the growth of sin to pure evil and the transformation of dark angels to demons. He told him of Satan's extreme power, strength, and constant lies, but Gabriel wasn't worried. He reminded Gabriel of what a deceiver Satan was and therefore to be careful of the other liars and deceivers as well. He described to him what Earth would look like and how to deal with the demons. Most importantly, He promised to protect him every step of the way and not let any harm come to him whatsoever.

When fully prepared, Gabriel left Heaven behind and traveled down with God's message. He shot through the cosmos and headed toward Earth. Gabriel knew the planet had never truly been Terra because it had never been Lucifer's to name. He was still trying to shake out the water from his feathers when he entered Earth's atmosphere. Instantly dark demons confronted him. The one in front was tall and had charred to a grotesque caricature of his former glory, but his face was recognizable. Gabriel looked at the burned seraph and noticed his distinct features and mannerisms were still there. They were exactly the same as those of the once-beautiful Abbeus, and Gabriel immediately knew it was he.

He had no shirt, only a black robe with ash-streaked jewels on it and a hood over his head. He had six black, bony wings. Pieces of his wings were broken off, perhaps on purpose. Gabriel could sense the evil that flowed through this skeletal creature even in its youth as a demon. Abbeus was bitter and full of hate, and it oozed out of him like sweat.

"How dare you come here, archangel!" he hissed. Behind him were thirteen more hideous creatures similar to him who silently flapped their bony wings. The air around them smelled of mildew. They were all shirtless, charcoaled creatures with bodies so emaciated that their ribs and joints stuck out. They were hunchbacked and seemed to have shriveled to two-thirds of their original size.

"I am sorry to see you this way, Abbeus."

"My name is not Abbeus! I am so much more now. My name is Abbadon, Gabriel. I am a king now! Lucifer has granted me an antivirtue of my very own," he hissed.

"You are not a king."

"I am. I am the king of greed. It is the feeling you get when you want more. We all want more, Gabriel, and you will see that."

"No more angels will ever choose to follow you or Satan. I have a message for him from the living God."

"Who is this Satan? We know no Satan," said Abbadon. His eyes were angry and hollow.

"Yes, you do. Lucifer is Satan. God has renamed him according to his deeds. I have a message for Satan. God has a new creation."

"God has a new creation? How wonderful." He let out a sinister laugh. "You will be proud to see the wonderful new creations our master Lucifer has made. He has created something so beautiful with your perfect Arrayah."

Abbadon was baiting him, and it was working despite Gabriel's awareness of it. Gabriel wanted to slap the grin right off Abbadon's face, but he had been prepared by God and the other angels in Heaven to handle whatever lies Satan and his demons threw at him. Even so, listening to the creature that Abbeus had become made Gabriel cringe. He shuddered at the thought of Arrayah living with these filthy demons, and it pained him that she had had to go through that excruciating transformation. He wondered what she looked like, and part of him didn't want to know what she looked like.

"Your words are poison," he said.

"We are so proud to have what was once Arrayah among us. Humility has given birth to its sister, its antivirtue. It's called pride, and it's my master's favorite. After all, which is more fun? Being humble or bathing in the glory? I think you know the answer."

"I feel sorry for you."

"Even you know I'm right. My master's most-prized creation has taken it to a new level. The leviathan is its name, or should I say her name? It resides in the coldest cave we could find. It is no longer male or female to be honest, and it has delved so deep in its pride that its power is godlike. Actually, you had much to do with it. I cannot wait for you two to meet!" Again, Abbadon laughed, an empty, screeching sound.

"There is nothing godlike about that, and I know what you are trying to do. I know Arrayah would never turn into some prideful creature, some demon. I know that you are a liar, just like Satan. Now take me to the one you serve."

"As you wish, Gabriel."

With that, Abbadon spun with a whip of his robe, and his pack of demons followed close behind. They surrounded Gabriel in a demonic escort. The group flew south toward the cave controlled by the leviathan, whose lair served as the main hub and meeting point of the demons according to Abbadon.

When they entered the cold, icy climate at the southernmost tip, Gabriel saw hundreds of thousands of demons. The further south he went, the more the white landscape was infested with these charcoal creatures. He couldn't recognize any of them. They amassed near a severe, dark crack that appeared to go into a mountain cave. The entrance was around five hundred feet high but extremely thin. The creatures were going in and out at will.

The subfreezing temperature was uncomfortable, but Gabriel thought only of delivering his message and hopefully finding Arrayah before leaving. He had waited so many years that he could barely remember how beautiful or charming she was. He missed her face. He missed her laugh. He knew her beauty would be gone, and he wasn't sure what he would find when he actually saw her, but he didn't care. He could feel his anticipation mounting and realized he still loved her just the same.

Abbadon escorted Gabriel toward the front entrance of the cave as demons all around were taken aback by his glory. They had not seen it in a long time. They were furiously jealous, but they wouldn't approach him, and it made Gabriel even less comfortable. The wide-eyed looks on their faces showed how much they longed to be the angels they used to be. He saw all sorts of creatures roaming the area, coming and going near the opening. The majority were skinny, emaciated angels who looked like the worker angels of Heaven, but there were many variations of other creatures. Some were beasts made from combinations of angels' body parts and parts of mammals, amphibians, invertebrates, and reptiles. He wondered how that could even happen. There was an air of dark secrets to this place and an evil he never would have imagined.

"Wait here," screeched Abbadon. "I will tell our master you have arrived."

The thirteen creatures around Gabriel surrounded him in a loose circle. Abbadon walked into the cave while Gabriel waited. He waited for what felt like hours. He was the center of attention for every demon who entered or exited the cave. Most stared at him with hateful, envious eyes.

Eventually an immense gust of wind and a dark shadow came over him. Gabriel turned around, ready for battle. As the shadow passed, he looked up at the hindquarters of a black-winged horse twice his size flying toward the thin entrance. The demons around him laughed at his nervousness and made snide remarks. The demons at the opening made way for the creature, and it raised its wings to slow its descent and then landed with a twelve-foot slide. A band of smaller demons escorted the creature into the cave with their eyes lowered respectfully. It was apparently important. Gabriel heard them refer to the creature as Pegasus.

As Gabriel stood by watching, every dark angel in the vicinity entered the cave of the leviathan through its thin, icy entrance deep in the southern tip of Earth. The numbers were multiplying, and he felt his anxiety rise as the entrance got more and more crowded. After about forty-five minutes, Abbadon walked back out.

"Come, archangel, he is ready for you," said Abbadon.

Gabriel felt a chill go down his spine as he entered the ominous, icy entrance with his escorts. Adrenaline flowed through his body so powerfully that he felt he would burst out of his skin any minute. The smooth walls of the long entrance eventually opened up to a massive pool of frozen water that looked like a thin glass layer breathed over a murky pond. Then he saw the meeting.

On top of the frozen pond stood what seemed like millions of demons. Had they multiplied? Impossible. The smoothness was unique to the entrance as the cave inside was covered in jagged, dagger-like icicles. The daggers became more menacing closer to the opposite side where another much smaller, darker cave within the cave emptied into blackness. Gabriel saw smoke rising from the darkness of the second cave in the distance.

He was escorted closer and focused his attention on the smaller cave. Every few seconds, thick smoke escaped from its opening. A dark, heavily scaled tail was barely visible from the blackness of the cave, but it was part of something massive. Abbadon wasn't lying—the leviathan was real.

At the head of a rocky platform next to the cave elevated at two hundred feet was Satan. Below him spread a multitude of demons. Gabriel peered at the fallen angel high on his podium of rock and ice, and his heart dropped again. This army was much worse than he expected. The blackness of their condensed bodies made them blend together like a large shadow. He felt sick.

Satan turned his blazing eyes on Gabriel and smiled a wicked smile before addressing the sea of demons below. "Welcome, everyone! We have a glorious visitor! Please welcome Gabriel the archangel." As always, he spread his large, powerful wings for dramatic effect. An eruption of hisses, moans, and cheers filled the cave and vibrated off the icy walls.

The demons walked Gabriel past the entire crowd and up to the front of the icy ledge Satan stood upon. When they finally stopped, they left Gabriel alone in the front. He could now hear loud breaths from the nearby cave on his right.

"I have come to deliver a message to you," Gabriel called up to Satan.

"Please do, archangel."

"The creation of man is soon to come. Man will be a being created in God's image but will have free will. He will reside in the Garden of Eden here on Earth." Gabriel did not understand His plan, but God intended to place these naïve beings in the midst of all the demons on Earth. They would have free will to make decisions just as the angels did. Gabriel continued, "Man will rule over all the Earth. Man will rule over the fish of the sea, the birds of the sky, all the wild animals on the ground, and all the small creatures that creep on the ground."

Satan acted totally unsurprised. "And why do you think God would banish us to this place and then place His most vulnerable creations in our midst? Isn't God supposed to be merciful and benevolent? Seems pretty cruel to create something and then leave them among us, doesn't it?" All of the demons erupted in laughter.

Gabriel didn't know what to say. He had no answer to that question. He paused briefly. "I do not pretend to know God's plans. I am here as His messenger. God is just; therefore, I know He has his reasons."

"Of course, you do not know, archangel. God never reveals His reasons. He has His angels follow blindly, just as you do now coming into our domain. Are you even safe here, Gabriel? We will rule his new creations before it is over."

"No, they will be above you."

"That is what God tells you, but He already knows what will happen, right?" Satan's wicked smile surfaced again. "If He loved them the way you believe, He would keep his precious new creation somewhere far away from me. It is a game to Him, and He toys with you the same way He is going to toy with them."

"God would never toy with me or any of His creations. He gives us free will to make our own decisions. I choose to follow Him."

"Why did He send you here then? I already knew what He had planned, and He knows that."

Gabriel paused again and thought of Arrayah. "I do not know."

"I'll tell you why. To make you suffer. There is someone I want you to meet, Gabriel." Satan turned his attention to the cave below him, and Gabriel did the same. Gabriel concentrated on the thick smoke and deep breaths. The leviathan was real, and this was where it resided. It couldn't be her though. It couldn't be Arrayah.

Satan looked up. "There was once a beautiful virtue angel named Arrayah who helped me get to where I am now. That angel has become something so much more beautiful, so much more amazing."

Gabriel's vision swam, and he felt he could throw up. He knew where Satan was going with this.

Satan continued, "It is because of her I know exactly what we will do to win this war. I know exactly how to rip the heart and will out of God forever!" The demons cheered, and when they did, the leviathan roared so loudly the cave shook and icicles rained from the ceiling.

Gabriel dodged an icicle that landed right by him. It was impossible for someone so beautiful to transform into something so large and vile, he was sure. It had to be impossible for any angel for that matter. But where could the creature have come from? Gabriel knew God didn't make the leviathan. It occurred to him that pride was the antivirtue of humility, and humility was Arrayah's virtue in Heaven. How prideful did Arrayah become? It had to be a coincidence—they were opposites.

He bent over and tried to catch his breath, which came harsh and pained with the extreme cold. His head was light and his neck was heavy. "Please don't let it be her. Please God," he whispered.

"I think you and Arrayah knew each other a long time ago, Gabriel. Do you remember her?" asked Satan. He knew Gabriel remembered her. He knew exactly how Gabriel felt about her. Gabriel didn't answer him.

As the demons continued to cheer, Gabriel caught his breath, rose up, and slowly walked toward the leviathan's wicked tail. It swayed back and forth.

"There is one thing we will destroy, Gabriel, to defeat your God. The Liar calls it love. Love is weakness!" screamed Satan. "Love is the sickness that made us blind all those years! We followed the Liar in Heaven because we thought we loved Him. We will take that away from Him now. We will do it one by one if we have to."

Gabriel kept walking, and as he did, demons moved out of his way. He had to have hope she could be saved no matter what she had become. He had to have faith. Without it, what did he have left?

Satan kept talking. "Since God doesn't seem to think we are of any worry to Him, we'll have to prove Him wrong. I mean, what does He think we've been doing down here?" Satan spread his wings again with a loud snap. Gabriel glanced up and saw infected scabs running the length of those wings that had never healed from the burns. "If God wants to create a new being in His image, so be it. I've waited so long for these children of His to come. We will control them. They will never love Him the way we did. It is my time." Satan gestured toward the crowd. "It is our time. We must take our powers to the next level. Those of you who have been assigned to the seven antivirtues, it is time to delve deeper. Below me is the leviathan, proof of what can happen when you do your job! The leviathan has taken pride and created something incredible by running away from humility. The rest of you must learn from leaders like this one. Abbadon, Belial, Pegasus, and Asmodai are ready. It is our time!"

The ice cave reverberated with the horrific, screeching cheers of the demons. Shutting them out, Gabriel walked right up to the tail. It was covered with iron-like plates so close together that not even air could sneak through them. It looked impenetrable. Gabriel's heart thumped powerfully in his chest. He could no longer take it.

"Arrayah! Is that you in there?"

The uproar of the demons' cheers silenced.

Gabriel again addressed the beast that breathed heavy smoke from its cave in the wall. Its breaths seemed to be getting shorter and faster. "Arrayah, it's me, Gabriel. Is that you?"

A thick, wide plume of heavy smoke poured from the black cave.

"I've finally found you after all these years, and I want you to know I will never give up on you. I don't care who or what you have become! I know who you really are."

There was no verbal response from the creature, but it began to stir and swing its tail rapidly.

"I know you can hear me. I will never give up on you! I know God will one day give another chance to all of those who want it!"

An epic roar sounded from the cave, shaking the entire area. Out of the hole emerged the ferocious leviathan, and the demons scampered away, leaving Gabriel alone to face the monster. It was a giant, serpent-like creature with two segmented wings and four thick legs. Its black body was covered with scales, its charcoal underbelly thick with armored plates, and its hot-black eyes stared straight through Gabriel. It was like nothing he could have imagined. The leviathan blasted gray smoke right at him, and he was engulfed in its cloud.

Satan laughed from high above. "You are still a pitiful archangel, Gabriel. Your time is up. After all these years, she still wants nothing to do with you! Greet your love! Look at her now! Look at your ray of hope before she consumes you!" His laughter continued to echo through the cavern.

Gabriel stared through the cloud to see the leviathan stand up on its hind legs. It was massive. Its wings stretched so wide they slammed into a group of demons over a hundred feet away, knocking them down. The leviathan came down on its forelegs, pummeling the ice below and sending a crack rippling through the surface of the frozen pond. It landed with its neck lowered and its head close to Gabriel. Its pitch-black eyes met Gabriel's once again.

Gabriel didn't flinch as hot, noxious smoke erupted from its nostrils all over his face. Instead he reached inside the chest plate of his armor and pulled out a dried-up red rose. "I know who you are, and I didn't forget our plan. I have planted roses all over Heaven. I know you better than you know yourself. You don't belong here, Arrayah. Do what you want to me, for I forgave you a long time ago. I rose up once, and now it's your turn to do the same." Gabriel placed the rose carefully on the ground next to its feet. He stood there waiting. A few seconds passed, and the leviathan puffed up and inhaled deeply.

"Gabriel, wait!"

He still knew the voice after all this time. It was Arrayah. But her voice didn't come from the leviathan in front of him. He turned around to see a swarm of demons racing after a charred female. They were stumbling and staggering like they were wounded.

"I haven't forgotten either, Gabriel!" she yelled.

She broke free and ran toward him. It was undoubtedly Arrayah. Her beautiful eyes were gone, and her long, flowing hair had become ash, but the sound of her voice sent a tingling wave through his body. All his memories of her came rushing back so powerfully that he felt a surge of energy all over. He jumped up and with a mighty thrust of his wings headed for her. Calmness and joy overtook him and his surroundings became irrelevant. She was all right. She still had hope, and that was all he needed to keep pushing.

"Saraquel, no! Gabriel, watch out!" Arrayah shouted, pointing behind him.

Gabriel turned around as the monstrous beast let out a deafening screech and raised its head up toward the roof of the cave. The leviathan spewed white-hot flame from its mouth. Gabriel jumped behind a tall block of ice and the fireball turned it instantly into a pool of water.

He was shocked to hear the archangel's name, but the giant plates on the demon reminded Gabriel of Saraquel's scaly skin as he watched the beast move forward. Its jagged features confirmed that it was a hideous transformation of the archangel from long ago. He couldn't help remember beating him senselessly on the battlefield. All those years ago, Saraquel's armor had said *Ab uno disce omnes*—from one learn all. It wasn't a reference to God after all. How could Satan be so powerful, and what caused Saraquel to become this monster? What could be learned from an aberration like this? He had so many things in his head he couldn't keep them straight, but only one thing mattered now. He turned toward Arrayah. They had to get out of there.

Arrayah didn't get more than a few hundred feet before a demon from the crowd clutched at one of her deformed wings and yanked her backward. He restrained her and covered her mouth as the group chasing her caught up. Gabriel jumped back into the air as the leviathan drew another breath, and Satan dove off the platform above and bolted to meet him with a black sword drawn. Demons were closing in on him from every direction, and even if he reached Arrayah, they were surrounded on all sides. It was over. There was no escape. He flew forward, knowing he would be incinerated in a blast of flame or cut down by Satan's sword. *God, you said you would protect me. Now would be a good time.*

At that moment, a brilliant white angel came hurtling through the cave, weaving between jagged spires of ice with wings fully outstretched. Gabriel felt a rush of heat behind him as the fireball burst forth, and he saw Satan's upraised sword swinging down toward his wings as he passed. Then Michael crashed into him at top speed. The flame passed so close that it singed his armor, and he felt the razor edge of Satan's sword pass between the trailing tips of his feathers. He and Michael plummeted toward the base of the closest wall, smashed through spikes and columns of ice, and plowed through a crowd of demons in their path. They struck the wall and crashed to a stop. Gabriel barely regained his senses before he saw another burst of flame headed straight for them. He shoved Michael backward just hard enough for the flaming ball to sizzle past between them and into the wall of the cave, causing more spears of ice to plunge from the ceiling. The screech of demons filled the cavern as dagger-like ice pierced through six of them on the ground.

"Let's go, Gabriel!" shouted Michael.

"No! She is here, I'm getting her first!"

"We'll have to come back for her! Come on!"

Gabriel turned back toward Arrayah, but Michael grabbed hold of his wings as hundreds of demons swarmed at them. They jumped up and flew backward, kicking at the demons' wiry hands as they gained enough free space to separate them by a couple of feet. Satan was hovering over the crowd, skeletal wings beating, pointing at the archangels and shouting orders to the demons. They covered the floor and filled the air so thickly that Gabriel could no longer see Arrayah. There was no way to get to her. Gabriel screamed in frustration, kicking back one demon after another that clawed at them, and he still would have tried if Michael had not taken hold of his arm and physically dragged him toward the exit. He resisted a moment longer, trying to make her out in the sea of black, but she was gone once again. He turned away.

With a host of demons clutching at them in the air and more pounding after them below, they tore across the cave. They flew near the opening, and Gabriel saw it would be too narrow for them both to pass through, but there was no time to slow down. He retracted his wings for an instant, letting the momentum carry him forward, and rammed his shoulder into the ice as he and Michael passed through. A boulder of ice broke away, crushing several demons below them. He heard their bones crushing like kindling. He shot his wings back out and kept flying as thousands more swarmed out of the cave after them.

Directly behind the swarm was the giant leviathan, crashing through the opening and driving its way through the small demons. It was shooting enormous bursts of fire and lighting hundreds of them up in flames. Gabriel and Michael dodged the fire that streaked through the sky after them, flying at speeds the demons could not match. All of them, including the leviathan, pulled up as they reached the edge of Earth's atmosphere, and as Gabriel arrowed through it and into space, he knew that they, at least, were safe. He heard Lucifer's voice scream, "Have your God send his Son down here if He dares." He kept flying, with only sheer force of will preventing him from turning back around.

After putting hundreds of miles behind them, Michael apparently decided it was safe and slowed down. He turned to his brother.

"What were you thinking, Gabriel?" Michael yelled.

"I saw her, Michael! She's down there! She wants to be forgiven!"

"What were you going to do, Gabriel? Did you really think you could get her out of there all by yourself?

Did you think any of this through? God only sent you to deliver a message!"

"I want to help her! We can help all of them!"

"God won't allow her back in Heaven even if you did save her! None of them can come back. Do you want to stay down there forever?"

"Yes, if I have to!"

Michael looked at him with disappointment. "Don't become one of them, brother. God has a plan for us. Please keep your head and heart straight. His plan is bigger and better than ours will ever be."

Gabriel turned away, wordless. They soared for thousands of miles up through the cosmos without uttering another word. It was a time for Gabriel to calm himself and gather his thoughts. He needed it. So much had happened so fast. Finally Gabriel turned to face Michael with an unwavering, confident stare that Michael knew all too well.

"I will save her, Michael."

"You have to let her go."

"Never."

"She can't be forgiven. They don't even want to be forgiven, or they would have asked God to before they were cast down."

"She does."

"You don't know that, and it doesn't matter either way," Michael said.

"If God is a forgiving God, then who is to say He won't forgive the fallen?"

"They made their own choice, Gabriel. There is no hope for them. You must accept that."

"That is the difference between you and me. I believe God's forgiveness is limitless. I have hope for her. I have hope for all of them." He looked back to the beautiful blue world receding into the distance behind them. So much promise there. When he spoke again, it was with hard-earned wisdom. He could feel the truth of it. "Some see a hopeless end while others see an endless hope."

Acknowledgments

This manuscript has grown over the span of four years. During that time, I have accumulated many debts, made many friends I will cherish for a lifetime, and grown not only as a writer but also as a human being thanks to some very special people.

- **Travis McElroy** has been my brother, hero, and best friend for thirty-two years. Although he is harder to get ahold of than the president, I am forever grateful to have had such a perfect leader to make mistakes I could learn from. I want to thank him for all of his financial, emotional, and organizational support as a partner but, most of all, for always believing in his younger brother and never giving up on me. I thank him for giving me the idea to write a story about the fall of the angels and teaching me what being a man means. I simply could not have done much in life without him. I love him from the bottom of my soul.

- **Leah McElroy** has been my emotional and spiritual rock in life. She has loved me unconditionally, even though I have put her through more trouble than most mothers should ever experience. My entire base of religion that drove this book is thanks to her and her kindness, forgiveness, support, and love, unparalleled by any other.

- **Thomas McElroy** made me the fan I am today of epic stories and forced me to see the importance of hard work, dedication, determination, family values, and honesty—all by his example. He is a devoted husband, a kind father, and a humble master. Although he has experienced many struggles in life, they haven't gone unnoticed by his children, and I am forever grateful to have learned from him.

- **Tarran McElroy** is the coolest person I know and has grown to be a strong woman that I am truly proud to call my younger sister. Her interest in my life helped fuel my passion to keep going through the tough times of this process.

- **Kellie Foster** has been the most positive influence on my adult life and has helped me grow from an immature boy to a flawed but confident man. She has made me a better person and challenges me daily with sincerity and honest communication. When I look in her eyes, I see a future full of happiness, love, loyalty, respect, and passion.

- **Stephanie McElroy** has put up with me for over a decade now, constantly pulling at her husband for help. Her confidence during this process has been key to maintaining a positive relationship, and I thank her for her patience with me.

- **Tim Boswell** has been the single most influential person in my growth as a writer, and that is far more than I ever expected from an editor. He is a phenomenal writer in his own right, and with his help, guidance, criticism, and motivation, I can sit here truly proud to send this manuscript out to the world and call myself a writer. Enough cannot be said for what he brought to the guts of this novel.

- **Brian McCauley, Ryan Strawn, Todd Newsom,** and **Curtis Hale** have provided friendship and support. Brian has been a close friend for years, and I never expected the dedication he has given me, but I will forever be in his debt. Ryan Strawn has been a loyal friend and supporter who never asked for anything in return. I look up to him and thank him for his strength, intelligence, and loyalty. Todd Newsom started as my brother's best friend but became part of our family, and not only do we share the same birthday but also the same humor. He has always been there for me as a second brother. Curtis Hale has been an integral part in web design, conceptual art, and implementation. As a fellow fan of fictitious worlds, he shares a passion for the greats, so without him this novel wouldn't have been what it is today.

- A childhood friend of mine, **H. Kirk Childress**, passed this year after fighting cancer. He was a great writer and an even better friend. He was excited for this book, and he asked about it many times over the last couple years. In 2011, he wrote:

It is very strange adjusting to this recovery and diagnosis I have had. . . . It is a very lonely feeling to be fully aware with the knowledge that we all pass. Youth itself is somewhat eternal, but people never own it. I want to look at them with that bravado and ego, but I am now more defined by my scars. Very strange.

Little things . . . are joys of existing. I also think little stresses like work and relationship, money, etc., are joys. But I love listening to my friends and thinking about their lives.

I'll leave you with some things I read every day lately.

"Look at the swift approach of complete forgetfulness and the void of infinite time on this side of us and on that, and the empty echo of acclamation...All this visible world changes in a moment and will be no more; and continually bethink thee to the changes of how many things thou has been a witness."

—Marcus Aurelius

- I have been blessed with lifelong friends that have been with me through thick and thin, and I would like to thank them now for all of their support through this process: **Chris Knox, James Holacka, Rob Lowe, Taylor Russell, Drew Childress, Ben Waters, Will Walters, Tyler Sorenson, Josh Henderson, Josh Chapman, Mark Schultz, Clayton Carter, Peter Cavazos,** and **Kristen "Bear" Foster.**

- Throughout this journey I have met incredible artists, business leaders, coaches, and colleagues who have inspired my writing, influenced my actions, and served as people I aspire to emulate and think of as personal friends: **Howard Fine, Mark Hamilton, Janet Harris, Chris Fisher, Bret Roberts, Genevieve Van de Merghel, Natalie Shaw Revell, Randy Wilcox, Jim Fitzgibbons, Gene Sollows, Tony Miros, Reidland Tucker, Bastien Grivet, Nancy Chartier, Carl David Cedar, David Mauer, Alex Robles, Doug Adams, Nancy Campbell, Sharon Howell, Susan Karr, Darren Hayes, Travis Walden, Mike Rainier, Tommy Hernandez,** and **Eric Jayk.**

- I want to send a special thanks to the following for their support of *War of Wings* in its early stages: **Susan J. Anderson, Victoria B. Anderson, Dennis Hale, Joseph Harvey, Joyce Goss, Quintan**

Cockerell, Matthew D. Ketterman, Nick Mourton, Mike Mourton, Manuel M. Machado Jr., Junior Desinor, Georgia A. McLain, Leslie Kilgore Jones, Jay Randol Jones, Cathey Davis, Katelyn Elisabeth Jones, Jillian Grace Jones, and John Patton.

ABOUT THE AUTHOR

I n *War of Wings*, Tanner McElroy draws on his legacy of Christianity from his mother and a love of epic stories from his father. His novel is the culmination of a writing adventure that began early, bloomed as he played minor league baseball for the Texas Rangers, and flourished when he moved to California to study acting and writing. His passion for writing led him to create short stories, treatments, and screenplays in addition to *War of Wings,* his first novel.

Tanner excelled as a student and athlete. He attended Texas Tech University on an academic scholarship and graduated with a double major. In 2005, he was named

Male Student-Athlete of the Year and selected in the draft by the Texas Rangers. He is now a member of The Texas Writer's League and Romance Writers of America.